The WITCHES *of* EL PASO

ALSO BY LUIS JARAMILLO

The Doctor's Wife

The WITCHES *of* EL PASO

Luis Jaramillo

PRIMERO
SUEÑO PRESS

ATRIA

New York London Toronto Sydney New Delhi

An Imprint of Simon & Schuster, LLC
1230 Avenue of the Americas
New York, NY 10020

This book is a work of fiction. Any references to historical events, real people, or real places are used fictitiously. Other names, characters, places, and events are products of the author's imagination, and any resemblance to actual events or places or persons, living or dead, is entirely coincidental.

Copyright © 2024 by Luis Jaramillo

All rights reserved, including the right to reproduce this book or portions thereof in any form whatsoever. For information, address Atria Books Subsidiary Rights Department, 1230 Avenue of the Americas, New York, NY 10020.

First Primero Sueño Press hardcover edition October 2024

PRIMERO SUEÑO PRESS / **ATRIA** BOOKS and colophon are trademarks of Simon & Schuster, LLC

Simon & Schuster: Celebrating 100 Years of Publishing in 2024

For information about special discounts for bulk purchases, please contact Simon & Schuster Special Sales at 1-866-506-1949 or business@simonandschuster.com.

The Simon & Schuster Speakers Bureau can bring authors to your live event. For more information or to book an event, contact the Simon & Schuster Speakers Bureau at 1-866-248-3049 or visit our website at www.simonspeakers.com.

Interior design by Jill Putorti

Manufactured in the United States of America

1 3 5 7 9 10 8 6 4 2

Library of Congress Cataloging-in-Publication Data
Names: Jaramillo, Luis, author.
Title: The witches of El Paso / Luis Jaramillo.
Description: First Primero Sueño Press hardcover edition. | New York : Atria Books, 2024.
Identifiers: LCCN 2023055251 (print) | LCCN 2023055252 (ebook) | ISBN 9781668033210 (hardcover) | ISBN 9781668033227 (trade paperback) | ISBN 9781668033234 (ebook)
Subjects: LCGFT: Novels.
Classification: LCC PS3610.A737 W58 2024 (print) | LCC PS3610.A737 (ebook) | DDC 812/.6—dc23/eng/20231204
LC record available at https://lccn.loc.gov/2023055251
LC ebook record available at https://lccn.loc.gov/2023055252

ISBN 978-1-6680-3321-0
ISBN 978-1-6680-3323-4 (ebook)

For the Gonzalez sisters

The WITCHES *of* EL PASO

1

It's your fault," Sofia spits at Marta, sitting across the desk from her. "My husband left me. My children won't talk to me."

"Cases like this take a long time," Marta says, trying to be patient. Sofia is Marta's age, mid-forties. Marta and Sofia are speaking in Spanish. Marta takes a breath. "I know it's been hard for you."

"Your life is nothing like mine. You've got citizenship. Your husband's a doctor. You're a rich lawyer," Sofia says, hugging her purse to her chest.

Marta leans forward, the edges of the desk cutting into her forearms. Nobody could think Marta's getting rich from the work she does, that any of them in the firm are in it for the money.

"Why did you come to the office today?" Marta asks, trying to sound pleasant.

"I wish I'd never met you or Linda."

"Too late for that," Marta says. Easy, girl, easy.

"You're witches. You put the evil eye on me."

Marta's never been called a witch before by a client, never been told she's cursed anyone. And Linda Camacho, the community worker, is the most genuinely religious person Marta knows.

"All we've done is to try to help," Marta says, hating her martyrish tone. She feels a buzzing start up in her left ear, and she shakes her head.

Sofia stares at Marta, her already bulging eyes protruding further from her round face. "I'm going to tell the investigators I was wrong."

"Wrong about what?"

"About Soto. I'll tell them he never touched me."

Marta's whole body goes cold, and the buzzing grows louder. She rubs her temples. "If you change your testimony, you'll be admitting to perjury."

"I don't know what that is, and I don't care."

"Don't be stupid," Marta snaps.

Sofia recoils like she's been slapped, shrinking into the chair across from Marta. Marta could have put it in a nicer way, but she's not sorry she's spoken the truth. Sofia has no idea what she's doing, what work she's undoing.

Sofia jerks unsteadily to her feet, dropping her purse on the floor. It spills open, its contents scattering. Marta walks around the desk, squatting down to pick up a hairbrush, a compact, a tube of lip gloss, a little mirror, a pack of cinnamon gum, and a laminated prayer card with an image of Santa Muerte. She passes these things to Sofia, who stuffs them back in her purse. Marta spots a blue glass bead that's rolled by the leg of the desk. She picks the bead up, holding it in her palm. Sofia snatches the bead from Marta.

"I'm going to tell the other women how you've treated me. They're not happy with the case either," Sofia says on her way out the door.

Marta's glad to see her go. Sofia's always been a problem, even early on, when she raised a stink about the contingency fee, convinced that Marta was in line to receive a personal cut of the settlement funds, as if Marta were a partner in a corporate law firm instead of the deputy director of a legal aid nonprofit teetering on the edge of bankruptcy.

Marta turns to look out the windows at the craggy Franklin Mountains. Plumes of dust blow from the west, yellow against the blue sky. Below, cars slide through the streets of downtown El Paso. In San Jacinto Plaza, the paths glow from the light of the dipping sun.

When the firm brought the sexual harassment case against Soto Pecans and its owner, Marta warned her clients it would get ugly. During the discovery process, the women and everyone close to them have been subpoenaed and deposed, their secrets revealed. With the revelation of each new ugly detail, Soto's team has gone even harder against the plaintiffs. Meanwhile, with each new attack, Marta can feel a piece of herself splitting off.

Sometimes Marta wonders whether she's really helping at all, whether she wouldn't have been better off working to become a judge, like her grandma Olga and everyone else expected. On days like this, it seems like the Soto case has done more harm than good for the hardworking, strapped-for-time clients.

Clients like Sofia.

Marta feels a rush of prickly heat as regret settles in her jaw.

She hates losing her temper. No matter how glorious it feels in the moment, remorse follows shortly after. She can't afford to lose any clients in the Soto case. She knows it wouldn't take much for the case to fall apart. If Sofia can convince even a few other women to withdraw, then any hope of reaching a settlement, let alone winning at trial, will go out the window. Marta worries she's spread too thin to be the lawyer she once was.

The firm needs a big settlement to keep the doors open. Marta knows this all too well. She's in charge of the budget. The executive director, Jerome, nicknamed "El Tiburón" by his wife, Patricia, because of the myth that sharks must swim constantly to breathe, is almost eighty, still litigating cases. He's a very good lawyer, and a friend, Rafa's godfather, but Marta can't seem to get him concerned that there's only enough cash for a couple months of payroll. If the Soto case fails, Marta will be responsible, and the firm will be one step closer to shutting down. If that happens, who will Marta be?

A ladybug lands on her hand, walking across her thumb knuckle, tickling her skin. Marta wonders how the thing got in here. None of the windows in the building open. The insect's shell is like hard candy, a brilliant red. Marta's college roommate had a theory about this shade, that the biggest brands in the world used this red to appeal to young people because of its resemblance to blood. Marta had always thought she meant that youth is fixated on danger. But blood means other things. Blood is another word for family.

Blood is life, and Marta is at least halfway through hers. For the past twenty years, this firm has been Marta's life, Jerome and the other lawyers and staff her closest friends, her other family. But there's a secret part of Marta that longs for something different than the world she lives in. The secret part wants to take control, if only to lose it, to be outrageous, irresponsible, to blow it all open, to be free. If the secret part were in charge, Marta would have an affair, just to see what it was like. She would lose the Soto case, intentionally. She'd be so incompetent that she'd be fired and unable to ever work as a lawyer again. She'd start over, leaving the boys in El Paso with Alejandro while she traveled with her lover, a younger man, visiting the great swimming pools of the world and having wild sex in fancy hotel rooms.

The ladybug crawls to the center of Marta's palm. It digs into her skin, as if it has little claws at the end of its legs. Marta brushes the thing off her, disgusted.

She has to get a grip. This is just daydreaming.

What Marta needs is to focus, to win the Soto case in a major way. A settlement of a couple million dollars would keep the practice afloat and might even be enough to convince Jerome to retire, so that she can finally be in charge. She's tired of waiting. If Jerome needs a shove to make him leave, she'll give it.

For now, Marta pops two ibuprofen tablets and goes to the kitchen for a cup of burnt coffee, all their ancient drip machine knows how to make. She heads toward Jerome's office to tell him about Sofia. Jerome is still the boss, and Marta has always sought his advice, whether she follows it or not. The suite looks the same as the day she joined the practice, somehow feeling both under-furnished and cluttered at the same time. Dusty law books sit on sagging shelves, boxes of files stacked on top of dented filing cabinets. The humming fluorescent lights show the wear of the office, the brown institutional carpet threadbare, stained with spilled coffee. In the open area in front of Jerome's office, Linda is parked at the paralegal Cristina's desk.

Linda shakes her head, her hoop earrings moving back and forth as she laughs, a rich peal. Marta is struck by her love for these women. She's not going to allow them to lose their jobs through any fault of hers.

She raps forcefully on Jerome's open office door, startling him.

He throws down his pen and stands up.

"I screwed up with Sofia Hernandez from the Soto case," Marta says, taking a sip of her coffee. "I called her stupid."

"Not good, Marta, not good," Jerome says, shaking his head, but the corners of his mouth twitch. Marta doesn't think this is a laughing matter.

"We can't afford to lose this case. Have you looked at the quarterly profit-and-loss statement?"

"That's not good either," Jerome says. "That's why you're going to win the Soto case. You'll bring the chingona energy, and you'll get it done."

Marta doesn't like that word. A man is never said to be pushy.

"It's Nena on the phone," Cristina says from the door.

"I'll call her back," Marta replies. It's odd for her great-aunt to call in the middle of the day.

"She's had a fire at her house," Cristina says, as Marta rises, worried. "Don't freak out. She says the fire department came and everything's fine. But she wants you to come over."

"I'd better go check on her," Marta says to Jerome.

"She's your tía, the witch?" Jerome asks.

"Don't call her that."

2

For part of May and all of June, Nena had been hearing a hum, a noise that vibrated along the surface of her skin. Nena had been afraid to ask her sisters if they also heard it, knowing she'd be scolded for speaking again about things that no one else heard or saw, like the flickers in the corners of her vision, or the whispers of people long dead. It was 1943, and no one was supposed to talk about sustos and corazonadas anymore. But her sisters definitely saw the ladybugs that followed Nena around. Every time Nena went anywhere, from the kitchen to the bathroom, to the Obregons' grocery store, to the post office, las mariquitas came with her, a swarm of little red dots clinging onto her clothes, like living embroidery. When the ladybugs came too close to Olga, she brushed them away, saying, "Que bonita!" *how pretty*, in a high-pitched voice that meant the opposite. Luna squashed as many of them as she could reach.

Ever since their parents had died, Nena and her sisters had lived all together on West Overland Avenue, so close to the Rio Grande that from the street corner they could see Mexico. Olga was four years older than Nena, and Luna three. When Nena was growing up, she watched them, not sure if she would end up more like Olga or more like Luna.

One was smart, the other was beautiful. Olga polished her shoes without being told, she kept her pencils sharpened, she didn't chew her nails. She did her homework long before it was due, and she prayed every night, using the rosary Papá gave her for her first Communion. Olga was awarded a full scholarship to Southern Methodist University, and Nena had been very angry on her sister's behalf when she wasn't able to go, there not being enough money to pay for travel or books.

And then there was Luna. When she was six, she took a knife and chopped the heads off a half-dozen chicks. When Mamá asked her what she was doing, Luna said, "I'm playing butcher." In high school, Luna wanted to be a gangster's moll, and she dressed the part, wearing skirts that she hemmed very short. She was a cheerleader for Bowie High School, and she was so famously beautiful that young men from other high schools asked her to dances.

Now that Nena was no longer a child, she understood she would never be like either of her sisters, and that was fine with her. In the spring, she'd fallen in love with the movie *For Whom the Bell Tolls*. Señor Obregon's daughter Fina worked at the Palace Theatre ticket booth, and Fina had always said that Nena could come as much as she wanted for free. After her ninth viewing, Fina's boss said Nena couldn't come to the theater anymore.

It didn't matter, because by that time, Nena had memorized all of the dialogue in the movie. She'd never seen anyone as beautiful as Ingrid Bergman, who played Maria, an orphan and a fighter with short-cropped hair and too-big trousers, neither of which stopped her from having a grand romance. But who most fascinated Nena was the character Pilar, a fierce commander of anti-fascist partisans who could ride a horse and shoot a gun better than any of her men. And like Nena, Pilar saw things other people couldn't.

Pilar was also very ugly, her face and clothes grimy, the opposite of Ingrid Bergman, who glowed. Nena had curly hair, and she thought if she cut it short, she could make it look like Ingrid Bergman's in the movie, yes, black instead of blond, but with the same kind of fluffy glamour. Nena used Olga's sewing scissors, carefully snipping, evening out the sides, one and then the other, as she looked in the mirror, cutting and then cutting again until there was hardly anything left.

When Luna saw Nena's hair, she crossed herself in an exagerada way. "You tonta, don't you know why Maria's hair is cut short in the movie?" Luna asked Nena, but of course Nena knew. Pilar tells the hero Robert Jordan that Maria "had the worst time a woman can have, if you know what I mean." Nena could guess what Pilar meant, what men could do to women.

Using all of her savings, Nena bought herself trousers from The Popular, justifying the purchase by wearing them every day. This drove Olga and Luna crazy, neither of them thinking it proper for a lady to wear pants, even though many women did now that there was a war on.

Anyhow, Nena didn't care what her sisters said; she was preparing for the trouble to come. There were rumors that the Germans and Japanese would come through Mexico to invade the United States, and when they did, Nena would be ready for them. In the desert, almost every plant protects itself with sharp thorns, and Nena was a child of the desert. She didn't know how to fire a rifle yet, but she'd learn quick. She already knew she had the courage to do what was necessary. One morning, Olga found a rattlesnake curled up on the back step. She ran out into the street to find a man, and Luna threw her hands up, screaming like she was being murdered. But Nena didn't waste time; she found a shovel and cut the head off the snake.

Luna worked as a waitress at the officers' club at Fort Bliss, and Olga operated the switchboard at the Hotel Cortéz, a tall building overlooking San Jacinto Plaza, where the alligators lived in their pond. Luna's and Olga's husbands were away at war, Olga's in Europe and Luna's, Beto, in the South Pacific. Nena stayed home and took care of the babies, Olga's daughter and Luna's son, both nine months old, biding her time until the Germans attacked.

She sang to the babies, played with them, jiggled them on her hips, one on each side. She washed diapers and did the household laundry, keeping pots of water boiling on the stove. She cooked all the meals except breakfast, she swept and mopped the floors, she dusted, and she tended to the chickens. But even though she was up at five and worked all day, the house never stayed tidy, the laundry never got completely done, and the babies were rarely clean, full, or happy at the same time.

One day, the babies fussed all morning, refusing to nap all afternoon, and then they had a competition to see who could cry louder and harder, far into the evening. By the time Olga got home, Nena felt like she'd been awake for three days straight, her skin greasy, her eyes dried out by the heat of the summer.

"Why do you insist on always leaving the dirty water in the laundry basin?" Olga asked. "Always" was a terrible word to use, and it wasn't even accurate. Nena only *sometimes* forgot to dump out the water. She knew better than to speak these thoughts out loud.

Late that night, Luna flung open the front door, kicking off her shoes in the corner and singing "The Battle Hymn of the Republic." She danced through the house, the sour scent of beer trailing after her as she picked up a sleeping Chuy from his crib. He woke up crying. This woke up Olga's daughter, Valentina, and then both babies cried and cried and cried some more. It took forever to put them down again.

Please, Nena prayed when she was finally able to go to bed. *Please end this war and bring back the men. Please let me have something of my own.*

When she was alive, Nena's mamá often told the girls that they could be whatever they wanted, except maids. But what was Nena other than a muchacha—a servant girl, nanny, and cook for her sisters? Nena couldn't stand the long days anymore, she couldn't take the humming noise or the ladybugs flying in their swarm, buzzing with messages that she couldn't understand, but that they seemed bent on delivering anyway. *Help me*, she prayed.

Nena was twelve the first time she had a serious vision, when they were still living in the old house. For Nena's whole life, her papá was only able to speak in a raspy whisper, his lungs so tattered from being gassed in France during the First World War that he couldn't work with his brothers at the family trucking company.

Nena's mamá worked as a cook in a restaurant. She didn't make enough money to support the family with that job, so on Sundays she sold pozole in the little park across from the church. During the week, the Montoya girls made the soup, soaking the hominy in lye to better slip the skins off the kernels, wringing the chickens' necks and plucking them, making the broth, and then on Sundays, Nena and her sisters helped their mamá carry the heavy pot wrapped in blankets, along with sawhorses and planks to form a table.

The soup was hot and spicy, warm in the winter, and in the summer, it felt nice to eat something even hotter than the air. All afternoon on Sundays, Nena ran back and forth to their house, cleaning the clay bowls and bringing back refills of the condiments—the chopped-up onion, the chiles, the cilantro. People milled about in their Sunday finest, talking and gossiping and flirting. In the middle of the park, a pack of dogs nibbled at their fleas, scratching themselves. There were always lines to buy the soup. When someone couldn't afford a bowl, Nena's mamá gave it away for free.

Weekday mornings, Nena's mamá helped her papá out of his bed, letting him lean on her as they slowly made their way through the house and onto the little piece of concrete that he called his patio, a corner of the small, dusty yard. When he was having a strong day, he pulled Nena up onto his lap and told her stories from his childhood in New Mexico.

The family house had been built low and close to the ground, adobe covered with stucco, four rooms with a woodstove, clay tiles on both floor and roof. The house was dark in the morning where it sat on the western side of the Tularosa Mountains, high on a mesa for protection from the Apaches when the place was first built. By the time he was born, only the house, the corral, and a patch of garden remained of the many acres that had been granted to the family in the eighteenth century. Centuries before this, the family had been at the side of the explorer Oñate when he claimed the land north of the Rio Grande for King Philip II of Spain, in what Nena's papá called La Toma, The Taking.

"Who did they take the land from?" Nena once asked, and her papá had laughed, explaining, "From your cousins the Indios, of course."

One night, a pack of dogs dug their way into the chicken coop, devouring all the chickens. In an instant, there were no eggs for the family to eat, no meat or bones to make the broth for the pozole, and no extra money to make up the rent shortfall.

At the end of the month, Señor Echeverria, the landlord, came by the house, as he did every month, to collect rent. Nena's mamá explained that she would have it for him soon. Señor Echeverria grunted at the kitchen table, dunking his pan dulce in the chocolate Nena's mamá had made for him, squishing the pastry in his mouth with ugly slurping sounds. When he was done, he wiped his hands on his pants instead of on the napkin that had been placed in front of him.

He got up fast, pushing his chair away, backing Nena's mamá up against the counter, pressing his body then his lips against hers. Her hands flew up to his chest to shove him away, but he was too big, his belly pinning her. He pulled open the front of her dress, the buttons flying off, tapping on the floor. He reached into her dress with one hand, touching her breasts, using his other hand to muffle the sound of her yelling. Nena's papá was in the bedroom, too weak to help even if he heard the commotion. Nena knew she was the only one who could come to her mamá's aid. The big knife for butchering the chickens was right there in the drawer. She would pull it out and stab Señor Echeverria in the space between his ribs.

Before Nena could reach the drawer, a buzzing started in her ears, the room wobbled, and then she found herself on a crowded street. Nena was inside Señor Echeverria's chest, and something was wrong, broken, and then she was at a funeral mass. When Nena's mind returned to the kitchen, she was splayed out on the floor, her head in her mamá's lap. Señor Echeverria was staring down at them.

Nena sat up, meeting his hard eyes. "You have three weeks to live," she told him.

Her vision would prove to be correct, but it wouldn't do Nena or the rest of the Montoya family any good. Señor Echeverria evicted them before he died, and in the years after that, Nena made things even worse by using her ability to try to fix their situation.

Help me, Nena prayed in her hot little room. *Please let me be something other than what I am now. Please, God, let me be brave and have adventures.*

The three sisters shared one fan, and it was Luna's night to use it. Nena had set a bowl of tap water next to her cot so that she could dunk a washcloth in the water and lay it across her forehead, but the washcloth grew hot so fast it was hardly worth the effort. Nena kicked the sheet off herself and spread her legs, hanging one off the side of the cot, pulling her nightgown up and flapping the hem to make a breeze.

Moonlight shined into her room. The hum buzzed in Nena's ears, louder than ever now, in an awful harmony with the noise of the cicadas outside. She watched the hands of the clock, the second hand tick ticking, every moment bringing her closer to the morning, when she would once again wake and rise to work like a dog. At four o'clock, she heard a baby start to fuss, making a sharp cry, whimpering, and then going quiet.

Nena touched her damp forehead, pushing back her limp hair. She worried about the long workday ahead, not the first she had tackled with as little sleep.

"Elena," a woman whispered.

No one called her by her name. Everyone called her Nena, baby.

Another whisper. "Elena Eduviges Montoya."

Nena got out of bed and opened the door to the backyard. No breeze greeted her, only hot, dry, dead air. The cicadas crawled thick on the ground under the bright moonlight.

"Elena."

Nena looked around the yard. She couldn't see anyone, but the voice was so clear, the person calling her had to be very close. Maybe on the other side of the pecan tree. The cicadas crunched under Nena's bare feet. She rested her hands on the tree's trunk, feeling the smooth bark under her fingers.

"Elena," she heard again, closer this time.

Nena turned to see a woman approaching. The lady wore a dark dress, black under the light of the moon. On her head was a tall peineta, covered by a black lace mantilla that fell over her face. The fabric of her dress hissed as the lady moved. The closer she came, the louder the cicadas buzzed. The frogs in the irrigation ditch cruá cruáed, and the owls uu uued.

The woman stopped in front of Nena and lifted her veil. She had a long, oval face, and pale skin, dark eyes, her eyebrows plucked into two high, thin arcs. Lace creeped up from the top of her dress, covering her neck. A cameo held the collar closed at her throat. A black rebozo hugged her shoulders, and even in this heat, she was shivering, pulling the shawl around herself.

"Your name is Elena Eduviges Montoya?"

"Yes."

"I've come to bring you home."

"This is where I live," Nena said, waving at the little house behind her.

"Madre Inocenta sent me to escort you to the convent."

"Who?"

"Our abbess. The head of the aquelarre."

A coven? But this woman had also said that this Madre Inocenta was the head of a convent. Which was it? One word had to do with God, the other word brought with it the darkness Nena knew and feared, a darkness she couldn't seem to escape. Rushing blood throbbed in her ears, the noise that usually signaled the arrival of a vision, except that the vision seemed to be not in Nena's head, but in her yard. Nena had always hoped that there were other people like her in the world, others who heard the hum, who understood the language of the ladybugs. She'd prayed for help. For all she knew, this help may have arrived in the form of this lady.

"How can nuns be brujas?"

"Tcht. Brujas. That's not a word we use. We are servants of God."

Now this was starting to sound heretical. Nena crossed herself. Was this woman La Llorona, the spirit who stole children away in the night? In the stories, La Llorona dressed in white, but that didn't mean she couldn't disguise herself, or that this costumed woman didn't wish Nena harm. She shivered in fear.

"Why would Madre Inocenta want me?" Nena asked.

"If you're like us, your visions will grow stronger. You won't just faint, you'll have fits, episodes that last for days. No doctor or priest will be able to alleviate your suffering. It's lucky for you that we found you. With our help, you can learn to control La Vista instead of allowing it to destroy you."

Nena's eyes fixed on the beadwork on the woman's dress, black and glittering in the pale light of the rising sun.

"Why aren't you dressed like a nun?" Nena asked, suspicious.

"We are a cloistered sisterhood. To leave the convent, I had to dress like a lady of the world."

"You haven't told me your name."

"You may call me Sister Benedicta de la Cruz."

Nena bowed, she wasn't sure why, although this was a rather grand name and seemed to suit this lady.

"Well, what are you waiting for, child? Come with me to the river," Sister Benedicta said. It was an order, not a request. She did not dare defy the sister. And did she even want to?

Nena considered going into the house to get some shoes, to put on her trousers, but she might wake up her sisters, who would then scold Nena and prevent her from seeing what this woman wished to show her. The river was so close, Nena reasoned. She would be home long before anyone noticed she was gone.

The neighborhood was at its quietest, the time of night when the lights were out even at the big brick Mansion House, where the prostitutes lived and worked. She noticed then that all the streetlights were out. How strange.

Nena followed Sister Benedicta through the yard, and where there should have been a fence, there wasn't anything but sandy soil and the plants of the desert. The sun was rising, the strengthening dawn light painting halos around the peaks of the mountains, the air cold. In the summer, temperatures dropped overnight, but it never grew this frigid. Odder still, Nena saw that all around her now was desert, the humps of creosote bushes and sotol stretching all the way to the Franklin Mountains. The houses and stores and cars of El Paso had disappeared. The railroad, the smelter, Fort Bliss, were all gone, the fences and border checkpoints gone. No barbed wire, just scrubby bushes and stands of cottonwood between plots of farmland, dug with little canals. The land now felt endless, open in a way Nena had never experienced before.

Nena's curiosity kept her on the razor edge of fear. But she was a soldier at heart, and she knew how to be brave. When they reached the river, Nena encountered another surprise. The Rio Grande ran fast and full and loud. Nena had never seen the river like this before, and she should have been afraid, but the roar of the river soothed her. Whatever force existed that could bring water down from New Mexico so fast was something to be respected. Nena had asked for something to take her away from her life, and now it had.

She shivered in her nightgown, hugging her arms around herself. She really should have taken the time to change into proper clothes. Her nightgown was ruined, dark with grime. Olga and Luna would be so angry at her. They'd already used up their ration books for work clothes and baby dresses.

"We can't have you going into town dressed like that. If anyone sees you, they'll take you for a puta. Here," Sister Benedicta said as she unwrapped the black rebozo from her shoulders and handed it to Nena. "Pull it over your head and hide your face."

Nena wrapped the shawl tight, and they stood on the riverbank, watching a man on a ferry pole himself across the wide, rushing river toward them. While they waited, Nena had the sudden disappointing thought that she was dreaming, though she had never had such a vivid dream. There was no other way to explain what was happening. Usually thinking while dreaming made Nena wake up, but nothing happened, and Nena stayed in this strange place, awake.

Sister Benedicta handed the ferryman a coin, and he took them across, helping them up the muddy bank on the other side. Walking up a dirt road, they arrived at a pueblito, its narrow streets dotted with brown adobes. Some streets had cobblestones, but they were buried in layers of horse caca, broken shards of clay, the ends of carrots, and rotten onions. The stench of sewage hit Nena like someone had thrown a bag of it at her. She wrapped her rebozo tighter around her mouth and nose.

They had left in the night, but Nena saw that this town was now opening its eyes to the day. Servants bustled through the streets, carrying bread from the bakery, vegetables from the market. Nena followed

Benedicta past the huts of the poor. These dwellings, made of woven sticks with thatched roofs, were even more humble than the house they lived in after Nena lost her family's money at the horse races.

Sister Benedicta walked fast, her head high, her veil pulled down over her face. She didn't seem bothered that her dress was sweeping up the dirt and everything else. The hem was caked with mud and straw and hair, like it had been sweeping the earth forever. An unwashed odor wafted off Sister Benedicta, a mix of mustiness and woodsmoke and old wool, manure, and worse. A horse and buggy pulled past them. There were no cars anywhere, no bicycles.

"Where are we?" Nena asked.

"El Paso del Norte."

"When are we? I mean what's the year?" Nena asked.

"The year of our Lord 1792," Sister Benedicta said. "Why are you asking such foolish things?"

"I'm sorry, Sister," Nena said, at a loss for words. She pinched herself, but she still did not wake up. 1792. If that was true, Nena was in New Spain, not modern Mexico. Nena knew now that she had done something impossible—she was no longer in her time, but deep in the past. Sister Benedicta was from this other time, and she hadn't yet noticed that Nena had come from the future. When had Nena made the jump? When she'd walked to the pecan tree? Nena suspected that if she'd turned around for a last look, her house would have been gone like the rest of her El Paso.

Nena and Sister Benedicta passed the whitewashed adobe church, Nuestra Guadalupe del Paso, the same church Nena recognized from the Juárez of her own time. They crossed the square, with an outdoor market on one side and a row of little stores on the other. At the far edge of the square, they turned onto a narrow street with high adobe walls, and wooden gates shaded by graceful cottonwood trees.

A man on horseback approached, the horse glossy, so black it was almost blue. The man wore a linen shirt with a brown suede jacket, tight pants with gold buttons, a red sash around his waist. He had a thick mustache and dark eyes. Sister Benedicta stiffened, adjusting her veil to conceal her face. She pulled Nena to the side of the road and against a wall. Nena looked up at the man, but he didn't meet her eyes. He raised his whip, clicking with his tongue, and the big horse danced and snorted, trotting into the distance.

"Who was that?" Nena asked.

"Don Emiliano. My brother. He would have been confounded to discover me outside the convent."

At the end of the street, Sister Benedicta pulled on a rope hanging from a wall, clanging a bell. A huge wooden door swung open. A small, dark older woman in a simple homespun dress and a long braid bowed to Sister Benedicta. Nena followed Sister Benedicta into a room cut in two by a grate that reached to the ceiling. Sister Benedicta swept through the turnstile in the grate, whirling around on the other side to glare with impatience at Nena, who held back.

In Nena's El Paso, there was no one to talk to about a world only she saw and heard and smelled. Sister Benedicta had promised that Nena could learn how to keep from fainting when her visions came to her. And if it was possible to so easily jump one direction in time, then it should be just as simple to jump back. Nena would return home soon enough. Olga and Luna could take care of their own babies for one day. Maybe they ought to see what it was like without Nena around. Maybe then her sisters would appreciate her more when she returned. Nena pushed through the turnstile.

Nena and Sister Benedicta walked down a short, dark hallway and entered a courtyard of hard-packed dirt. To their right was a vegetable garden, empty but for a few bolted cabbages, their stalks long and spindly. To the left stood a small building with a smoking chimney and a chicken coop. In the wall across the yard was a door. Walking through it,

Nena was greeted by the chants of the nuns in a chapel. She detected the odor of tallow candles, which had made greasy streaks on the wall. At the end of the passage, Sister Benedicta unlocked a door with a key from a big iron ring she kept under her dress.

"Stay here," she said, guiding Nena by the shoulder into a small room. Sister Benedicta turned around, left the room, and closed the door behind herself. Nena heard the cell door lock.

3

At Nena's house, the air reeks of charred food and melted plastic. Black soot coats the wall behind the stove. The pot that caught fire sits in the sink, its handle twisted into a bubbled clump. A big box fan blows burnt hot air around the kitchen. Marta looks out at the dry backyard, at the line of yuccas against the back fence. She sets her bag down on the chipped Formica table, slides off her suit jacket, and drapes it on the back of the vinyl chair. Her headache has only gotten worse since she left the office, the buzzing now impossible to ignore.

"I left the rice on for too long and the pot caught fire," Nena says. She's wearing bright red lipstick. Jeans bought from the Walmart boys' department. Fluorescent running shoes. Her eyes are brown, bright, like she's excited. Even now, as frustrated and worried as Marta is, she can't help but feel a rush of affection for Nena.

"Nena, you could have burned the house down," Marta says, not meaning to scold, but Nena's cheerful expression worries her. Nena doesn't seem aware of the danger she's put herself in.

"I know it looks bad. There was a lot of smoke, but the fire was out by the time the firemen came. Not that I minded having them here. So handsome."

"Where's your bucket?" Marta asks.

"Under the sink. Don't bother with cleaning up. I can still climb a step stool and use a sponge. I'm not like those other viejitas who put on an organ recital every chance they get."

"Organ recital?" Marta asks.

"You know, blah blah my bladder, ay chihuahua my heart. The medication I have to take, dios mío, it makes me pee at night, my hips, my colon and my caca, my eyes, my liver. That's the worst thing about old people, you know, the complaining?"

Nena isn't a complainer. Ninety-something and still living on her own. No children, no grandchildren. Friends, dead. Olga and Luna, her sisters, both gone.

When Olga was on her deathbed, she made Marta promise to take care of Nena. Marta agreed immediately, not wanting Olga to be anxious about Nena in her last moments, but a promise wasn't necessary. Marta and Nena are the only two family members left in El Paso, great-aunt and grandniece, a funny connection that for most people means very little, but for Marta it matters a lot. Nena is like no one else in Marta's family—in fact, like no one else she knows. Nena has never been afraid to be outrageous, and Marta loves her for it.

Marta fills the plastic bucket with warm water, then squirts in dish soap. She rolls up her sleeves and carries the bucket closer to the wall, then uses the rough green side of a sponge to scrub the soot off the yellow wall. Underneath the soot, a crack runs from the ceiling to the floor. The house is in terrible shape, the linoleum in the kitchen peeling, the front yard overgrown. It's been clear for a long time that Nena shouldn't be living alone, and Marta regrets not forcing a decision earlier, though Nena hasn't made it easy, refusing to talk about health aides or retirement homes. Nena will stay with Marta for the time being, and then they'll find her a decent place to live, like Los Piñones, where Luna spent her last years.

"I'm going to make you una tisana. Chamomile?" Nena asks, turning on the tap to fill the teakettle.

"You can't use the stove. The firemen shut off the gas," Marta says. "Anyway, it's too hot for tea."

Marta doesn't have time to sit and chat, as much as she'd like to. Nena's always good for an interesting conversation, but Marta's on a schedule. She needs to finish cleaning up the mess, and then get Nena packed. The boys have to be picked up from science camp, and after that, Marta will swing by the grocery store, fix dinner, and get the boys ready for bed. Once they're asleep, she'll put in a couple more hours of work. Soto hasn't yet sat for a deposition, his lawyers throwing up every roadblock possible, and Marta is preparing another filing this week to make him talk.

"Luna really liked living in Los Piñones," Marta says. "She made her casita so cute."

"Do you remember when you used to help me with my clients?" Nena asks.

"Didn't you sometimes go to the line dancing class with Luna?"

"You were always such a good assistant."

"There was no *always*, Nena, it was once, only once that I helped you," Marta says, scrubbing the wall. She recalls what actually happened, even if Nena can't, or won't.

One summer when Marta was eight and visiting Grandma Olga in El Paso, Nena asked her if she wanted to help with a reading. Marta said yes, long, delicious shivers of excitement running up and down her arms. She and her brother Juan had just been dropped off at Nena's for the afternoon. Marta knew without being told that Grandma Olga wasn't to know about the reading.

At the office, Marta corrected Jerome's use of the word "witch" because Nena has always been particular about what she calls herself. She doesn't use any of the usual Spanish words either, not bruja, not curandera, not hechicera, not claravidente. Instead, she says she's a guía, a guide, and she believes she can help the living speak to the dead. When Marta was eight, she believed it, too.

Before the client came, Nena showed Marta how to melt piedra blanca on the comal, the white crystals of the rock spreading to the edges of the round pan. Sliding her glasses on, Nena pointed at the melted salt, tracing in the air what she called dibujos, drawings that Marta couldn't see herself.

Nena said that the pictures told a story about Marta's future: when she grew up, she would live in El Paso, in a house with a pool, she would be a lawyer, her husband would be a doctor, and she would have three children. Back then, Marta found Nena's prediction peculiar, not least because Marta intended to be a doctor, like her parents, in California, where she lived. But when Nena's prediction mostly came true, down to the pool, Marta quietly wondered whether Nena wasn't as crazy as her sisters made her seem.

When Señora Hurtado arrived, she sat down on the couch in Nena's tiny living room, clutching her purse and looking around, twitching her nose like she smelled something bad. The room looked pretty much as it does now, cluttered, with piles of old newspapers in a corner, mismatched garage-sale dishes stacked in the glass-fronted cabinets. Bundles of herbs hung from the rungs of an old ladder propped against the wall. A giant brass bowl on the floor held fist-sized chunks of piedra blanca.

Señora Hurtado wore a navy skirt suit and a white blouse with a bow at the throat. Her maroon hair had been blown into a fluff so wispy that Marta could see through to her scalp. Señora Hurtado said she needed to reach her husband.

Nena eased herself down on a pillow on the floor, closing her eyes. She muttered and swayed, and then she started to hum, the sound rising from deep within her body. In those days, she had dyed black hair and a powdered face, one dark mole on her left cheek, right in the center, sprouting a short hair that Marta had the urge to pluck with tweezers. Marta's job once Nena went into her trance was to hold a shallow bowl under her mouth, catching any saliva that dripped down. Because he was so young, Juan's assignment was to stay in the kitchen and arrange cookies on a plate.

Nena's humming grew louder, accompanied by a terrifying whistling sound from her nose. Her eyelids cracked open, showing the whites of her eyes, her irises flicking up and down. Marta positioned the bowl under Nena's chin. Nena exhaled three breaths out, like hoo hoo hoo, but loud, and then she called out in a language that wasn't English or Spanish. Something crashed in the kitchen.

"Felipe!" Señora Hurtado screamed. "Please forgive me!"

Nena's eyes flew open, and she scrambled up off the pillow, fast for someone so old. Marta and Señora Hurtado followed her into the kitchen. Juan was on his hands and knees on the floor next to the stove, shoving an Oreo in his mouth with one hand while trying to pick up the yellow shards of a broken plate with the other. He was crying so hard he couldn't quite get a breath, fat teardrops flying out of the corners of his eyes. Marta considered giving him a slap to calm him down, but Nena scooped him up, helping him to his feet. Marta looked over at Mrs. Hurtado, wondering why she had asked her husband for forgiveness, but the terror on her face had faded, and now she had the same sour expression she'd come in with.

"Aren't you going to finish my reading?" Señora Hurtado asked.

"There's a child crying. Right in front of you."

"And?"

"You can leave us now," Nena said quietly, kissing the top of Juan's head. Señora Hurtado glared at Nena, huffing her way out of the kitchen, slamming the front door, shaking the house. Nena blended a disk of Ibarra with scalded milk, making the hot chocolate frothy and richer than anyone else made it. She served it in little teacups from one of the glass-fronted cabinets, with saucers, like Marta was a grown-up. Juan soon forgot that he was upset, and he started to show off for Nena, pulling up the hems of his shorts to show her the mosquito bites on his thighs. Disgusted, Marta discreetly scratched her own bites, mad that Juan had ruined her chance to see a ghost. For months after she returned to California, Marta said hoo hoo hoo, trying to make a ghost appear, but none ever did.

That time with Señora Hurtado was the only occasion Marta saw firsthand what Nena was up to in her work. The adult Marta understands that the only ghost around that day was Juan. But Marta gets why Nena would gravitate toward witchy stuff. The same reason that Sofia believes in it. Magic, or the idea of it, is a way for the powerless to imagine they can become powerful.

Marta knows where real power lives in this world, in money and blood. That's what the law concerns itself with. The system of law is arranged like a kind of game with high stakes that can be won, and Marta likes to win, forcing the other side to do her will. This is true power. She just wishes she were winning right now.

"You'll come home with me tonight and stay at the house for as long as you'd like. But we really do need to decide where you want to be longer term," Marta says.

"Cecilia Fonseca told me that at Los Piñones they put extra wax on the floor. When you fall and break your hip, they move you to the building with twenty-four-hour care, where they tie you to a wheelchair, and you can't do anything for yourself."

"That doesn't sound fun. What can we do to make sure you're safe and happy?"

"Safe?" Nena asks. "There is no such thing as safe. And sometimes I'm happy, sometimes I'm not. I'm always free inside my head. I could live in a jail cell if I had to," Nena says, her voice rising louder and higher pitched.

"Nobody's sending you to jail," Marta says, surprised at the intensity of Nena's response.

"No, if you're in prison at least you can get parole."

This is morbidly funny, and Nena has a point. Once she goes into a place like Los Piñones, she won't come out until she's dead.

Poor Nena. *Ay, pobrecita Nena*, Luna and Olga were always saying.

Marta remembers being a kid, sitting in Luna's restaurant, La Sirena, after the lunch rush, reading a library book, sipping from a glass of Coke kept full by the waitress, Luna and Olga talking about Nena's latest antics in tones alternately worried, amused, judgmental. Marta was taught to feel sorry for Nena, taught to think that what Nena spent her life doing was reckless and without value, that Nena's spirituality wasn't the right kind of seeking, but something self-indulgent, private, shameful. But the judgment of Nena's older sisters made Marta pay attention to Nena more, curious about how she'd gottten to be who she was.

Nena reeked of patchouli oil, she laughed too loud, she was insistent on peering into Marta's eyes and asking her questions like if she'd had her period yet, or, when Marta was older, if Alejandro was the kind of man who knew how to pleasure a woman with his mouth. *Leave her alone*, Olga would beg Nena. Not that it helped. *It must be hard to be so tall*, Nena would say when Marta was young, as if Marta didn't already know that about herself. *The rest of us in the family are such chiquititos.* By the time she was ten, Marta was taller than Nena, taller than anyone in her class, and she kept growing. She didn't like having Nena call attention to her height, but she appreciated that Nena always saw her as a real person, worthy of being asked provocative questions and of discussing things that mattered, even things that hurt. Nena's right about happiness, how it comes and goes. But safety is something else. You can put your finger on it sometimes, like now. It's not safe for Nena to live in this house.

Insects whir and click out in the yard. Marta's done cleaning the wall, though a lot of good it's done. Even with all the scrubbing, the wall still looks dirty. No, that's not quite right. The soot is there, as black and furry as though she didn't clean at all.

And then, in the next moment, it's gone, the scrubbed wall exposed.

Marta closes her eyes, sure that she's imagining things. But when she opens her eyes again, the wall continues to blink, soot there, soot gone. With her fingertip, Marta pushes the black stuff around, making a path through it. She lifts her finger off the wall, examining its tip. There's nothing there. The air thickens, raising the volume of the hum in her ears, the buzzing deep inside her brain. Marta feels dizzy, weak. A flutter of nausea starts in her belly. She tastes salt in her mouth. Marta runs to the bathroom, making it just in time.

Heave, dry heave, heave, her forehead blazes. She spits and flushes the toilet, hoping she's done. There's nothing like throwing up to make you aware that all you are is a body.

Marta eases herself onto the edge of the tub, the porcelain cool against the backs of her legs. She breathes in the bracing smell of Comet. This is a very clean bathroom, even if the house is falling apart. The bathroom is pink—pink tiles, the toilet and sink pink. The room gives Marta the feeling like she's inside someone else's stomach. Another wave of nausea washes over her, but there's nothing left to get out.

Marta turns on the tap and splashes cold water on her face. She's not sure what she saw happening with the wall. She imagined it. Or maybe she's having little strokes. Those can make you nauseated.

Nena knocks on the door to the bathroom, pushing her way in before Marta has a chance to say anything.

"Pobrecita," Nena says, pulling a package out of the medicine cabinet and handing it to Marta. "Fresh toothbrush."

Marta rips the package open, squeezes toothpaste on the brush, scours her teeth and tongue. She examines herself in the mirror. When she was a kid, she spent so much time in the sun, she was always a nice reddish brown, several shades darker than she is now. She has lines around her mouth that weren't there two years before, and there is a certain sagging to the flesh under her jaw. Her hair is cut into a bob, meant to be easy to deal with. Today it's wild, flying in every direction around her face, except for a few wet strands plastered to her cheeks. Marta picks these off her skin, tucking them behind her ear.

"Let's get you packed up," she says to Nena.

"You saw it, didn't you?" Nena asks. "The door?"

"What door, Nena? Where's your suitcase?"

"Under my bed. The door in the wall, I mean. You saw something you didn't expect to see, didn't you?"

"I saw soot that was there from the fire," Marta says.

"Yes, but you were seeing it with La Vista. Everyone in the world is born with a little bit of it, but some of us have more, a lot more, and in the right circumstances it can be awakened into something that changes how you live in the world. I've lost a lot of what I once had. I use what's left to help my clients."

"Hoo hoo hoo," Marta says, mostly to herself.

"You do remember," Nena says, and Marta does. She remembers wishing she could be a person who saw things that no one else could, but to what end? Marta doesn't need to be special in that way anymore. She hasn't for a long time. Marta's life and work are in the world that can be seen, where she has a to-do list a mile long.

"Can we please go home?" Marta asks.

"Yes, bonita. We'll talk again tomorrow. The changes have begun, and you may have some questions for me."

4

In the locked cell, Nena shivered, and not only because it was so cold she could see her breath. She'd made a mistake, and now she was trapped in this room, in this time. Nena had prayed to be taken away from her life of toil, but not like this. That smelly old nun had tricked her. That was what had happened. But that wasn't the whole truth. Luna and Olga were always saying that Nena did things without thinking, that she was too headstrong. Nena had to admit that, in this case, they had a point.

Pobre winter sunlight shone through the one tiny window, falling on the tiled floor covered with wool jergas, a table with an earthenware jug and a basin, a carved wooden bed, and a darkly varnished armoire. Nena walked over to the bed and ran her hand over the mattress, or the place where the mattress should have been. The bed was nothing more than boards covered with blankets. Nena heard the movement of a key in the door again. The woman who'd let Nena and Sister Benedicta into the convent entered, carrying a tray. She set the tray on the bed and hurried out.

The tray held a taza of chocolate and a small basket of sweet rolls. Nena shoved an entire roll in her mouth, and she gulped the chocolate.

The woman returned with a gray dress draped over her arm and pair of boots held between her fingers.

"Como se llama?" Nena asked.

"María," the woman said.

Nena picked up another roll from the basket and tore it in half, offering it to the woman. Once you break bread you are under an obligation to your guests. Nena's papá had been very clear about this when she was growing up.

María took the roll, chewing it fast.

"Sister Benedicta said I have to help you clean yourself. Turn around," María said.

She pulled Nena's nightgown over her head, then helped her out of her underwear. Nena heard María mutter as she took a rag and wet it in a basin, running it over Nena's face, down her neck. María dressed Nena in the shapeless gray wool dress, much like a nun's habit but without a veil. María knelt in front of Nena, guiding her feet into boots that she laced up with a tool that looked like a crochet hook. It was strange to be undressed and dressed like she was a child again, and Nena didn't mind being cared for in this way.

Right as María was finishing pinning Nena's hair back with a small wooden comb, Sister Benedicta entered the room. She had changed out of her black dress and into a habit with a black veil. The cloth of Sister Benedicta's habit was a beautiful, rich-looking serge. It would have cost a lot of money back home, if that kind of fabric could even be found these days. Sister Benedicta ran her eyes up and down Nena's body, like she was looking for flaws.

"Madre Inocenta is ready to see you," Sister Benedicta said.

"There's been a mistake," Nena said. "I have to go home."

"You called for us, and Madre Inocenta sent me to get you."

"But I'm not from this time. I live in 1943, and you said that this is the year 1792."

"It is not possible to move in time," Sister Benedicta said, her tone firm.

"Yet here I am."

"You're confused. It's good I found you when I did, so we can guide you out of your delusions. Come with me," Sister Benedicta said, hurrying Nena out the door and through the convent.

Sister Benedicta opened a door to a big room with a long, heavy wood table in the center. At the back of the room, behind a delicate desk, sat a middle-aged woman who Nena took to be Madre Inocenta. On the wall above her head, a huge painting loomed, a dark oil of a bejeweled nun, an escudo on her chest and a crown of flowers on her head. Unlike the nun in the portrait, Madre Inocenta was dressed simply, in a habit made of much rougher stuff than Sister Benedicta's. She wore a plain wooden cross.

Nena could feel Madre Inocenta's eyes on her, but she gave off none of Sister Benedicta's high-handed impatience. Nena was hopeful that Madre Inocenta was someone who could be reasoned with.

"I need to return home. My sisters will be worried about me if I'm not back before the babies wake up," Nena said, though she was surely already too late for that.

"Sit," Madre Inocenta said, nodding at the two backless chairs in front of her desk. Nena eased herself down on one, and Sister Benedicta perched on the other, keeping her eyes fixed on Nena, as if she were afraid that Nena would run out the door. But where could Nena go?

"I tried to tell Sister Benedicta that I must have traveled through time, but she—"

"Nonsense," Sister Benedicta said.

Madre Inocenta leaned forward, squinting at Nena. "How, pray tell, do you know you traveled through time?"

"I just do," Nena said, and then because Madre Inocenta was staring at Nena in a way that made her want to be a good student, Nena said, "This time smells different."

"Come here," Madre Inocenta said, and Nena walked to the desk. "Give me your hand."

Madre Inocenta took Nena's right hand in her own, lowering her face until her breath tickled Nena's palm. Nena fought the urge to snatch her hand back. Madre Inocenta straightened up, and she smiled at Nena.

"Yes, I see what you mean. Or I smell what you mean, rather."

"What? How?" Sister Benedicta said, apparently angry at Nena, as if it was Nena's fault time had been altered.

"We've never had to travel so far for a niña who was calling for help. I thought I was sending Sister Benedicta to an estancia across the river, not centuries into the future. How were you able to open the door from your time to ours?"

"I didn't do anything," Nena said, remembering her prayer in bed. "I mean, I didn't intend to. It just happened."

"I believe we have been given a gift from God," Madre Inocenta said to Sister Benedicta.

"This is no gift. This is the work of the devil. We must send her back with haste," Sister Benedicta said.

"We don't know how," Madre Inocenta said.

"Then she shall find her own way. She doesn't belong here. She has broken a rule of nature, and there will be consequences. You know that as well as I do."

"The difference between us, Sister Benedicta, is that you believe that the consequences are inevitably bad. The manner in which young Elena traveled here and the reason why is a mystery that shall be revealed to us by God alone," Madre Inocenta said, turning to Nena. "Sister Benedicta and I may disagree on some matters, but we're of one mind about the purpose of this convent. We have, each and every one of us here, been afflicted by visions and other unwelcome gifts thanks to La Vista. This is why we meet, to put all of our energy into La Vista in a controlled way, to expend it in a healthy manner without bringing ourselves harm."

"How do you do that?" Nena asked.

"We begin our meetings by singing the song of the aquelarre. The encanto lulls the rest of the nuns to sleep and it calls La Vista into the room. During our sessions we let La Vista work its way through us so that we're not taken unaware by it the rest of the week. At the session's end, the song of the aquelarre sends La Vista away."

"What's La Vista?" Nena asked.

"Another word for God," Madre Inocenta said. "When you have your visions, La Vista is in you, and you are one with the spirit."

"What Madre Inocenta means to say is that La Vista is one aspect of God," Sister Benedicta said. "La Vista is chaos and nature, and if we don't work to control it, to channel it, we'll be destroyed by it. La Vista is to be feared, not venerated. That's why we have rules here, and that's why if you've already broken the rules, you don't belong." She was looking at Nena, although Nena got the sense that the message was intended for Madre Inocenta.

"As I said, Sister Benedicta and I disagree at times. We brought you here to take care of you and that's what we'll do, even if you arrived from farther away than we imagined. What a journey! And for it to be worth such effort, you must have brought us something very special."

Sister Benedicta's expression all but made a hiss. One thing had become clear from this conversation—Madre Inocenta was in charge, in name and in reality, and it didn't really matter what Sister Benedicta thought of Nena. And Madre Inocenta considered Nena special, which pleased her.

"You said you can you make La Vista go away? How?" Nena asked. That didn't seem possible. All of Nena's previous efforts had failed. La Vista—if that was what it was—came for her at the worst possible times, squeezing her in its grip until it was done with her.

"We'll teach you how to calm La Vista later," Madre Inocenta said, standing. "We have other work to do first. Once the others are here, we'll begin the meeting of the aquelarre, and we'll call La Vista to us."

The door opened and three women entered; two wore black veils, and the one in a white veil wore her wimple tight around her chubby face. She was closer to Nena's age than the other two, and she smiled at Nena in a friendly way.

"I present to you Sister Francisca, Sister Paloma, and our novice, Sister Carmela," Madre Inocenta said. Sisters Francisca and Paloma trained their eyes on the floor. Timid women, Nena thought, taking note of how close they stood to Sister Benedicta. Carmela positioned herself right next to Nena, still smiling. As the other nuns began to hum, Carmela tugged at Nena's elbow, a signal for her to join them.

The nuns sang a long note, ahh, a short one, hmm, and then the order of the notes changed, the women singing loud, long vowel sounds that jumped up and down the scale, eh, eh, ah, ah, ooh, ooh, ya, the sounds not forming words exactly, but still seeming to have a precise meaning. Nena sang along with Carmela, surprised at how she knew what to sing next, but then she realized that the melody of the song was a familiar one: it had been hidden in the hum she'd been hearing all summer.

As Nena sang, a buzz grew in the bones behind her ears, and the hairs on her arms stood up, the electricity of the song flowing through her, jumping from Carmela to Nena to Sister Paloma, and so on, moving through the circle of women in a counterclockwise motion. Nena was dizzy and scared, not from fear of passing out, but from an excitement that threatened to shiver her out of her skin.

Madre Inocenta held up her hand, and the nuns stopped singing.

"La Vista is with us now," Madre Inocenta said to Nena. "Do you feel its power in the air? Close your eyes, and La Vista will sing through you. We'll see what encantos live within you."

Nena considered the word "encanto." It contained the word "cantar," to sing. She must have just sung a spell, but it was the only spell she had ever chanted. She didn't think she had any others inside her.

Carmela again put a hand on Nena's elbow, whispering, "You can do it."

Nervous, Nena shut her eyelids, and was surprised when she discovered that she could still see the room, not with human eyes, but with La Vista. The brujas, she could see now, were collections of energy, colorful knots of waves. Carmela and Madre Inocenta glowed in front of her, bright indigo with flickering edges. Sister Benedicta was maroon, and both Paloma and Francisca were pink. Nena squinted with La Vista, picking up something else running through the room, another wave.

She lifted her hand and saw, or rather, recognized, the thing she was supposed to catch, a wild spell, like yeast in the air. When she held her hand higher, the wave entered her through her fingers, running up her arm, into her lungs. A wild song emerged from her mouth, the notes bubbling out, and the room filled with the scent of roses.

"Perfecto!" Carmela said, laughing, as Nena opened her eyes.

"A child's trick," Sister Benedicta said.

Eighteen-year-old Nena didn't enjoy being called a child by Sister Benedicta. She had opened a doorway through time. Could Sister Benedicta do that? No. Sister Benedicta was so stupid, she'd been unaware that Nena had pulled her to her future. Sister Benedicta was a blind, jealous, and not very nice nun. Nena was already tired of dealing with her. If she had been envious of Nena's gifts before, wait until Nena really showed her. Nena was determined to find a more impressive spell in the room.

She kept her eyes open, using La Vista to distinguish between the layers of energy in the air. The candles flickered as a draft wound through the room. She knew what an odor spell looked like now. She needed something stronger, and though she didn't know how to recognize it or call it to her, Nena had a hunch that if she opened herself to it, the encanto would find her.

And she was right. Nena spotted a shadow snaking along the floor, darting up to the ceiling, shooting across a beam. She called it to her, and it dove down into her mouth. Nena started to gag, the thing sticking in her throat. She coughed, hacking so hard she bent over, falling to her knees. The familiar buzzing filled her ears, and the dark curtain of La Vista draped over her.

Nena came to, finding herself on the hard ground, the nuns peering down at her. She had fainted, like almost every other time La Vista had entered her body. Angry and embarrassed, she struggled to her feet, irritated at herself for losing control in front of Sister Benedicta. Nena coughed again, and then felt something on her tongue.

She reached into her mouth and pulled out a tooth, not one of hers, but the tooth of an animal, long and sharp.

"A coyote's fang," Madre Inocenta said with wonder, her eyes glittering.

Sister Benedicta glared at Nena. The other three nuns had backed away from Nena, even Carmela, who wouldn't meet her eyes.

"A coyote?" Nena asked, scared and angry at herself for wanting to show off.

"I suspect the rest of the coyote will be with us soon," Madre Inocenta said, sounding pleased instead of afraid.

"Am I going to turn into a coyote?" Nena asked.

"Unlikely. Allow me to reflect on what this means, and what we should do with the tooth. At our next meeting we'll see if we can purge the rest of the coyote from you so that it doesn't engage in any mischief."

Nena didn't like the sound of that. "Why do we have to wait? I don't want a coyote in me. When does the aquelarre meet next?"

"Patience. You've gone through enough tonight. You must rest. We need you ready for the regular meeting of the aquelarre on Saturday night."

Nena couldn't wait that long. By then Luna and Olga would have gone to the police. They'd already lost their parents. How would they feel if they lost their sister? And how would they be able to keep their jobs if Nena wasn't there to take care of the babies?

"I did what you wanted, but now I have to go home," Nena said.

"You'll go home when La Vista is done with you," Madre Inocenta said.

"I refuse to wait."

"I'm afraid you have no other choice. Do you know how you moved yourself through time?"

"No."

"Before you came to us, did you experience anything unusual?"

"I saw ladybugs. I heard a hum."

"And do you hear the hum now?"

"No," Nena said. "Now I know that the hum was the song of the aquelarre."

"I see. You must have followed the sound of our aquelarre to us, in the convent. But there's nothing for you to follow back. One could say that a once-open door is closed, and you must wait for it to open again," Madre Inocenta said.

"So what do I do?"

"You've arrived with a magic in you that we haven't seen before, and, for your sake and the safety of the aquelarre, it's our duty to understand what this magic is. Once we know what we're dealing with, we will help you find your way back to your time. Until then, the convent will be your home."

"I have to be a nun?"

"A niña. We will explain to the other sisters that you're a new niña."

Nena knew all too well what the word meant. Girl. Servant. "You want me to be your maid?"

"No, no. You'll be a student. My student," Madre Inocenta said.

"You'll keep the uniform you're wearing. Sister Benedicta is the vicaria. She is in charge of the schedule and of discipline. She'll explain the schedule to you. Our days begin with early-morning prayers."

Madre Inocenta may have said that she would be Nena's teacher, but it was Sister Benedicta who moved toward the door and motioned for Nena to follow.

5

The next morning, as Marta's making the bed, the glass door to the backyard slides open, and a tall older man, handsome, his hair shot through with silver, walks in like he owns the place. Which he does. It's Alejandro, his face skinny, stripped of the last bits of youth. It's weird that she didn't recognize him for a second. Weird and kind of hot.

"You missed a great run!" Alejandro says. He pulls his shirt off over his head, wiping his sweaty face with it as he goes into the bathroom, turning on the tap.

A hot stranger is in her shower.

Marta takes off her sweats and T-shirt. She opens the door to the shower and walks in, pushing Alejandro down on the tiled bench, kissing him on the mouth. He kisses back, pulling her to him. The tiles are slick with steam, the bench hard under Marta's butt. Alejandro puts his mouth on her. She braces herself with her foot so she doesn't slip. Marta looks down at Alejandro, and he's still a stranger if she squints her eyes. The stranger kisses her and licks her like she wants him to. Wordlessly, she moves him into the positions she needs him to be in.

"What's the plan for her?" Alejandro asks, after they've dressed and are in the kitchen making breakfast. He's asking about Nena. This is not sexy, and Marta doesn't want to talk about it right now. It's been maybe a couple of months since they had sex, and the last time wasn't anything like what they just did. She's not sure what's gotten into her. She's going to have a bruise on her knee.

Marta walks over to Alejandro, pinning him against the counter, tugging at his dress shirt, running her hand up his chest.

"Hey, hey," he says, but he kisses her back. He pulls away. "Seriously, what's the plan?"

She pulls away, resigned to the conversation at hand. "Los Piñones, I suppose."

"Do you have any idea how much those places cost? Who's going to pay for that?"

Marta gives him a look. Who does he think?

"We can put her house on the market," Marta says.

"Great, that'll cover a year. Maybe."

"Do you have a better idea?"

"All I know is, you've got enough going on without having to take care of her crap, too," Alejandro says, though she's pretty sure it's not her well-being he's worried about. He's thinking that he doesn't like being inconvenienced. Not that anything will change for him. He'll still leave for the hospital early and come home late. The glow from the shower is fading fast, and Marta wonders how she can make it come back.

It doesn't help to watch Alejandro assemble the makings of his morning smoothie. He lines up a banana, a bottle of cod liver oil, sliced poached chicken, raw broccoli, cooked sweet potato, and a glass jar of ground flaxseed. He drops the ingredients in the pitcher, splashes in oat milk, then claps on the lid. It's impossible to speak over the noise of the Vitamix, and Marta watches as the ingredients puree into a greenish-gray mush. Alejandro pours the mush into a glass.

Nena walks into the kitchen, dressed in her uniform of jeans and running shoes, freshly showered. She makes a beeline for the counter, and Marta watches as she uses her hip to nudge Alejandro aside, taking the blender container off the base. Nena gives it a whiff, her mouth forming into a horrified O.

"I guess you're not someone who likes to chew," Nena says, carrying the container over to the sink and filling it with water. "My motto is use it or lose it. If your knee hurts and you stop moving around, you can forget about ever walking again. If you don't use your teeth, they fall out," Nena says.

"This is the most efficient breakfast I can eat. I consume the right combination of protein, carbohydrates, and micronutrients," Alejandro says, in the cold voice that means he's as angry as he gets. Marta's embarrassed for him, hearing him as someone from the outside. This is not the sexy stranger, this is her logical husband. But what they did in the shower was out of character for both of them in a way that makes Marta hopeful that they can both change. She's buzzing with energy, even though she hasn't had any coffee. She's excited to go to work, to win the case, to put her plan to become the executive director of the firm in motion.

"I'll make you chilaquiles for breakfast tomorrow," Nena says to Alejandro.

He takes a sip of his smoothie, grimacing. He and Marta lock eyes, and she shakes her head at him.

"Chilaquiles would be very nice," Alejandro says in a false tone, but at least he's making an effort. He takes the glass with him to their bedroom.

Nena beckons Marta to her. She turns her palm up, revealing a ladybug.

"See? Here's another one," Nena says.

Marta watches the insect crawl up Nena's finger and dance on her fingertip.

"I keep seeing them everywhere. On my pillowcase. On the bus. A few weeks ago, I saw one walking out of Ruth Uranga's purse and it flew into my hair. Then, yesterday, right before the fire, I found one on the kitchen counter. The pobrecita was lying on its back. I thought it was dead, but then when I went to pick it up, its legs moved, and it flew out the window. That's when Sister Benedicta showed up, wearing her ugly black dress, holding Rosa's hand. They were so close I could smell them." Nena says this quietly, telling a secret, Marta leaning in to hear.

"Who are you talking about?" Marta asks, deciding to humor her.

"When you were little, I wanted you to help me with my readings because I didn't want you to be scared by what you saw, or to think that there was something shameful in La Vista."

"But, Nena, really, it was only once that I did that with you, and we didn't see anything that day," Marta says.

"After the reading, Señora Hurtado called Olga, furious. Olga made me promise that I wouldn't involve you again. Olga wanted to protect you from what was wrong with me, like it was catching. But she had it wrong, she never understood about La Vista. You either see the other world, or you don't. And you do. Yesterday you saw it."

"Did I?" Marta asks cautiously. She's not sure what happened with the wall. And she doesn't think Nena's explanations are going to clear anything up. But in spite of herself, she's curious what Nena will say. "What did I see?"

"The crossing to the other side has opened up again, and Sister Benedicta and Rosa were trying to come through."

"These are people you know from Juárez?" Marta asks, though she knows that this isn't what Nena is claiming.

Nena chuckles softly. "You've been trained as a lawyer. You like facts, and you put these facts into an order, you tell a story you want the judge and jury to believe."

"I'm not telling any sort of story. You're the one telling it," Marta says.

"When I came back from El Paso del Norte, I told Luna and Olga about my time in the past, about Rosa. They thought I was a loca. They made me go to a hospital. The El Paso Home for the Insane."

"I never knew that," Marta breathes, disturbed at this information, shocked that Olga and Luna would have done something like that. This could explain a lot, like Nena's ideas about magic, like Nena's distaste for institutions, even for a place as benign as Los Piñones. "That must have been awful for you."

"I'm trusting you to not think I'm crazy," Nena says. "I'm telling you these things because I need your help."

"What do you want me to do?" Marta hears herself say.

"Rosa couldn't make it across, but I think she'll try again."

"Who's Rosa?"

"My daughter."

Marta has never heard that Nena had a kid, and this alarms her. This Rosa could very easily be a confabulation, a sign of dementia, even if Nena seems sharp.

"You had a child?" she ventures.

"I did. I do," Nena says.

"You said she wants to cross over. Where is she coming from?" Marta asks, examining Nena's face for signs of confusion.

"Rosa was coming from the other side."

"As in she's dead?"

"No. I left her."

"Left her where?"

Nena doesn't answer, but she's trembling, pale, like it's cost her a lot to say these things to Marta. But what is it she's claiming? The "other side" has a metaphysical sound to it, a stand-in for the unknown, but Marta's not one of Nena's clients. Marta doesn't think that there's a way to pass to this world from wherever the dead go.

It's possible Nena lost a child. Marta can even see the baby, like she's right in front of her: dark hair, wide eyes, reaching to be picked up. What if when Nena was in the mental institution, the child was taken away from her? It would be hard to bear a truth like this, so difficult that Nena might have to make up an alternative story.

"Maybe there's something I could do to help you find her," she says, her work brain starting in on the problem. There are ways to find lost children. Private investigators who can track people down. Old birth records exist, even adoption records, if you know where to look.

"If you want to help me, we need to catch an encanto," Nena says.

Marta has to think about what the word means. "A spell?"

"I've never been able to do that kind of magic in this El Paso. It seems that power has been draining out of our world for many years. I need your help to bring it back to me."

"I don't know any magic spells," Marta says.

"You're sure about that? How do you feel today?"

"Fine," Marta says. "Great, actually."

"La Vista can make you hungry."

"I had some yogurt."

"Not like that. Like for making love," Nena says.

Marta wonders, embarrassed, if Nena heard her and Alejandro having sex. Surely, she can't be asking about that.

The boys run into the kitchen, Rafa yanking open the pantry to pull out cereal boxes, Pablo retrieving milk from the refrigerator. They scrape stools across the floor, fling dishes and cutlery on the counter, and eat like they've never seen food, rattling their spoons in their bowls.

"Did you have sweet dreams?" Marta asks.

"We don't dream. We tell you every morning, and you never remember," Rafa says. "Can we get a dog?"

"Your father's allergic," Marta says automatically, which isn't strictly true; he just doesn't like dogs, their mess, or when they lick him.

Pablo puts his mouth against Rafa's ear, making pss pss pss noises. The boys giggle in a way that usually indicates a bathroom joke, but

Marta has a creeping suspicion that they're laughing at her. She closes the tops of two cereal boxes, wipes up a puddle of milk on the counter, disposes of a banana peel draped on the back of a chair.

Nena loads the dishwasher, and Marta's surprised she's not chatting with the boys. She seems like she might be upset, her mouth a line.

Marta starts to make lunch for Rafa and Pablo, pulling out a loaf of bread, the jar of mayonnaise, a bottle of yellow mustard, salami and cheddar cheese, lettuce. The smell of the salami hits her, salty and foul. She holds her breath as she makes the sandwiches, cutting one diagonally for Pablo, the other straight across for Rafa. She puts an apple in each paper bag, hoping against hope that the fruit won't be thrown away. Cookies in Ziplocs, paper napkins, initials on each bag. Marta smooths the front of her skirt. She spies at the end of her sleeve a bright yellow squirt of mustard.

"Dammit," she says out loud.

"Dammit. Dammit!" the boys echo, laughing, and now she's sure they're laughing at her. This is only going to get worse, the ridicule, the older they get. Pablo is six, small, with long limbs for his short frame. Rafa, eight, has an oversized head and a big beak of a nose. Marta remembers how when she was their age, her parents had seemed like creatures of another species, with bad memories and no sense of what was important, like television, candy, and swimming. Well, Marta is an adult now, and she knows what it takes to keep the machines of work and life humming. How she spends her time probably does look ridiculous to the boys. It often seems ridiculous to her, the tasks never-ending and mostly pointless.

"Where does this go?" Nena asks, holding up a whisk.

Does it matter? Anywhere. Nowhere. Marta doesn't want to have nothing conversations about kitchen tools with Nena. They don't have enough time left together to waste any of it.

What happened to Nena's daughter must have some logical explanation, a traumatic sequence of events that have made Nena's memory of her daughter confused. There's a mystery here, and one that Marta wants to uncover as much for her own sake as for Nena's. Marta's curious about the baby girl with the dark hair that she can picture so clearly.

Marta thought she knew all the family stories, though whatever happened with Rosa must be more of a family secret. Family stories teach us how to live. Family secrets teach us to kill parts of ourselves. Marta wants to know what this secret has passed down to her, what she was taught to kill.

"Nena, I'll do whatever I can to help you find Rosa," Marta promises.

She's surprised and annoyed when Nena shakes her head sharply no.

6

The memory of the coyote's tooth still rested on Nena's tongue as she followed Sister Benedicta through the convent, struggling to pay attention to what the nun was telling her—instructions of some sort, rules, a schedule.

"You'll spend most of your day in chapel, prayers, or in silent meditation. During the hours reserved for work, you'll embroider for an hour, and then you'll help in the kitchen." Sister Benedicta opened a door that led into a small chapel.

A mass was already underway. Behind the altar, streaks of soot ran down the face of the statue of the Virgin. The walls may have once been whitewashed, but they were now dark from the smoke of countless candles. Nena shivered from the cold, even in her wool habit. She wished she'd brought Sister Benedicta's rebozo with her.

Nena ached with exhaustion after her meeting with the aquelarre, suffering from the dull pain behind her eyes that followed a vision, hoping she could go back to the cell to lie down on the narrow bed, if only for a few minutes. She eased herself onto a bench, grateful to sit.

The priest had a Spanish lisp, and his voice traveled up and down the scale as he said Holy Ghost in Latin, "spiritus," very high, and "sanctus," very low. If Nena had been with Luna, they would have erupted into giggles at this. Nena could imagine Olga sending them disappointed looks out of the sides of her eyes, but Nena wasn't about to laugh now. She was too scared and alone and worn out to be silly. If time was progressing as usual, then Olga had already left home for work, and Luna would be dealing with the two babies, furious, wondering where Nena was. But what could Nena do?

She'd come here using her own mysterious magic, making Madre Inocenta curious and Sister Benedicta mad. The tooth had scared the other nuns, even Carmela. Nena had only been here for a few hours, and she was already afraid about how she would be treated from now on.

The way the priest prayed the mass was almost exactly the same as the priests at home. Nena kneeled, stood, crossed herself, sat back down, and this familiar ritual made her feel a bit more like herself. She inspected the other women in the chapel, noticing that there were three types: nuns in black veils, nuns in white veils, and girls in the same gray uniform that Nena wore. The women all wore crosses, some of wood, some of gold, and one girl, a gray-clad niña of all people, wore a gold cross with big jewels stuck in it. A few nuns wore habits made of material as rich as that of Sister Benedicta's.

Nena thought about the circumstances of these women, where they'd come from, if they'd grown up in El Paso del Norte, or if they'd been sent from elsewhere. Nena couldn't imagine desiring the life of a nun. That was the exact opposite of being a soldier. Even in normal life, mass was an obligation and a bore, and having to go to multiple services during the day, sitting and kneeling endlessly, seemed like a cruel punishment. Nena's favorite thing in life was to walk, strolling around the neighborhood, talking to the shopkeepers, visiting Señora Guilez and her parrot, and chatting with the ladies of the Mansion, who came out late in the afternoon, walking in pairs, pretty, their lips red.

Growing up across the street from the Mansion, Nena was made aware that there were two kinds of houses, two kinds of women. To be respectable, you either had to get married, or you had to be a nun. That was one reason Nena had loved *For Whom the Bell Tolls*. In that world, women could be soldiers. Nena imagined that in this time, this El Paso del Norte, it had to be even worse, with even fewer options for women. From what she had seen so far, the whole town was poor, and far away from the center of things, a provincial outpost in the far reaches of the Spanish Empire, not like the bustling, important city that she lived in.

Nena felt a ladybug crawling on her finger. She looked at it closely. This particular ladybug was a very deep shade of red. Nena studied its spots, its little black face, watched as its translucent wings folded down over its body, disappearing. The insect moved around on her finger, doing a little dance. And then it blinked out. It hadn't flown away, it had simply disappeared.

The ladybug blinked in again, this time landing on Carmela's hand. Carmela let out a strangled cough, like she was trying to keep from laughing. Nena was intrigued.

Once the service was over, Nena followed the other women out of the chapel and down the hall to a big room with a low ceiling and rows of long tables and benches. Big pewter jugs of water stood on the tables, along with baskets of rolls. Servants moved around the room, handing out bowls of a soup made with chicken and vegetables. Nena hardly ever had meat at home, even before the war, the family joke being that they had two meals, rice and beans or beans and rice. Nena was hungry, hardly able to wait until after the prayer to dip her spoon into her bowl.

During the meal, the nuns were silent, or nearly so, barely saying anything more than "Pass the water, sister." All through the meal, Sister Benedicta moved around the room, her hands folded in front of her. When she paused at Nena's table, Nena continued eating under Sister Benedicta's narrowed eyes. The nun sitting across from her rolled her bread into pills that she popped into her mouth, one after another, her lip quivering, nervous like a rabbit. Sister Benedicta leaned over Nena. Nena felt everyone turn to look at her with curiosity, and maybe with fear. Had she already done something wrong?

"When we're done with the meal, you'll go next door to work on needlepoint," Sister Benedicta whispered, as though this were top-secret information. Nena nodded, not sure if she was allowed to respond. Sister Benedicta straightened up, and everyone else in the room seemed to relax. What was it that they thought they were going to see?

After the meal, Nena and the other niñas moved into a room with small windows and hard wooden chairs, but here, at last, the women appeared to be allowed to talk.

"Sister Benedicta said that you didn't bring a work basket to the convent with you," Carmela said, waving her over, and Nena was relieved to see that Carmela wasn't afraid of her, even though she'd coughed up a tooth.

"No, I don't have any sewing things," Nena said. "And I don't know how to embroider."

"I have an extra hoop," Carmela said, handing Nena fabric and thread, along with the hoop, which Nena had no idea what to do with.

"Will you show me how to do it?" Nena asked.

Carmela took the hoop from Nena's hands, then expertly fit the fabric in the ring and handed it back to Nena. "I'm in charge of the kitchen, so during your work shift, you're going to be with me."

Nena was glad for this. She needed to be able to ask someone questions. Madre Inocenta might be the person ultimately in charge, but Nena didn't think she could wander into her office whenever she wanted, and she certainly wasn't a friend. From the little she'd seen of the convent, divisions were strictly upheld. The nuns in the black veils were more senior to the nuns in the white, and the niñas were students, below the nuns in terms of rank, but higher than the servants.

"The ladybug that was on me jumped to you, didn't it?" Nena asked.

"What do you mean?"

"I mean it didn't fly, it disappeared, and then somehow it appeared on you, right?"

Sister Carmela shifted so that only Nena could see her face. "The message you sent me about Father Iturbe's lisp made me laugh," she whispered.

"I sent a message?"

"You certainly did," Carmela said.

"I didn't mean to. How?"

"The ladybugs travel on the golden thread that connects everything."

"Could you show me how to send a message on purpose?"

"Yes, but don't let Sister Benedicta catch you. Magic is only allowed during the aquelarre."

"What would she do if she caught me?"

"One time she made a nun—an elderly lady at that—eat her supper off a plate on the floor, like she was a dog. But who knows. That punishment was for someone who wasn't one of us. And besides, she seems afraid of you, of what you can do."

"Really?"

"You didn't see how she looked at you? And that trick with the tooth was new. What you can do is more than any of us, even Madre Inocenta." Nena was surprised, thinking back to how Madre Inocenta's eyes had glittered during the aquelarre.

"But I don't want to do more than anyone. I want to go home."

"I pray you can. Maybe you could take me with you."

"You don't like it here?"

Carmela lowered her embroidery hoop. "I've never known anything else. When I was young, La Vista visited me too much, bringing great trouble, but here I've been safe. What happens to girls like us where you're from?" Carmela asked.

How to answer the question? Nena gripped the embroidery hoop, her limbs frozen. What happened at home was that girls like Nena were alternately feared and loved, asked for help on the sly, and then talked about in whispers.

Nena heard a loud scraping noise. She glanced up to see one of the niñas dragging a stool across the tiles and setting it down next to Nena. This was the girl whom Nena had noticed earlier, the one wearing the jeweled cross. Nena would have rather asked Carmela more questions, but she was going to have to wait.

"I'm Eugenia," the girl said, sitting down on the stool. "You're not from El Paso del Norte, are you?"

"No," Nena said, telling both a lie and the truth.

"What's your family name?"

"Montoya."

The girl wrinkled her nose. "Which branch of the Montoyas?"

Nena understood that this girl believed there were better and worse Montoyas, and that she would judge Nena on her answer, so Nena decided to answer a question that hadn't been asked. "My parents died, and my uncle wanted me to be educated, so he sent me here."

"Do you want to be a nun?"

"If I'm called to God, then yes," Nena said, not thinking for one moment that this would happen.

"I wouldn't be a nun for anything. I can't wait to get out of here."

"You're allowed to leave the convent?"

"Yes, of course I can."

"You mean we niñas can go out into the town when we want to?" Nena asked.

"Well, no, not exactly. What I mean is that I'm not sequestered here for the rest of my life. Unlike Sister Carmela," Eugenia said loudly, but Carmela appeared not to have heard. "My time here will be over soon. I'll leave when I marry Emiliano de Galvez next year."

"Who's that?"

"Sister Benedicta's brother. Half brother," she clarified.

"Hmm," Nena said, thinking back to the man on the big horse.

"I know what you're thinking, but you're wrong. He's not old or ugly, like her. Our marriage will bring together the most important families of El Paso. Emiliano's father is giving us a third of his vineyards."

Nena supposed Eugenia was pretty in a way, with even features and a small nose. But her eyes sat too close together, and her nails had been bitten down to nothing, her fingertips raw. Her bragging meant nothing to Nena, and it was absurd to harbor any sort of jealousy over Emiliano, so Nena pledged to try to be friends with this not very nice girl.

"You make such neat stitches," Nena said, which was true. Eugenia had embroidered a spray of red roses on a black background, using different colors to make the blossoms and leaves look almost alive.

"Any real lady knows how to do it," Eugenia said, looking down at Nena's blank hoop.

"Oh, Elena knows all about roses," Carmela said, laughing. "Come with me, Elena, and I'll show you how you'll help in the kitchen. Eugenia, it's time for you to start your shift, too."

7

At the office, Cristina is standing in the corner of the conference room, her hair pulled into a tight, long ponytail, her arms crossed in front of her, watching as Linda takes food out of a cooler: containers of beans and rice, tubs of salsa, an aluminum tray of enchiladas, pan dulce from the Bowie Bakery. The big percolator bubbles, sitting on the credenza in the conference room, filling the room with the smell of sweet coffee and cinnamon. Linda hands Marta a foil-wrapped package. Marta rips into it, pulling out one of Linda's homemade flour tortillas, tearing the soft stuff in two and cramming the folded tortilla into her mouth.

"How did you know I needed this?" Marta asks, the tortilla calming the shaky, queasy feeling she's had since she left home. She still doesn't understand why Nena turned so cold when she offered to help find Rosa. Marta will have to try another approach, lay out a plan for the ways they can search for records about Rosa.

"The food's not for you," Cristina says to Marta.

"Ay, don't pay attention to her. You eat as much as you want," Linda replies. "After you left yesterday, Jerome and I talked, and we hatched a plan to have the women from the Soto case come in to have some breakfast. It's always easier to talk if there's food. People need to feel taken care of. If everyone else is strong in their commitment to the case, then maybe they can convince Sofia to come back."

"Linda, you must have spent all night cooking," Marta says.

"I told Linda she should have asked you first before arranging the meeting," Cristina says.

"I didn't mind doing it, Mamá helped me cook," Linda replies serenely, setting out paper plates and cutlery in neat piles on either end of the credenza.

Cristina reaches for a tortilla. "Good thing today's a cheat day," she says. "I try not to eat things like that. Refined flour and all that lard."

"I don't use lard, I use Crisco," Linda retorts.

"Marta, I have to talk to you about something personal," Cristina says.

"Yes?" Marta asks, sure that nothing good can come of an opening like this.

Linda makes her way to the conference room exit, locking eyes with Marta, who shrugs back at her, like *I have no idea, honey*.

As soon as Linda is gone, Cristina turns to Marta, a hard expression on her face. "I think it's wrong to send Nena to Los Piñones. My mother-in-law lives with me. I have to listen to her talk about the news. Fox. And worse, online junk. And she criticizes. But that's what Hugo wants, he wants his mamá at home with family, not strangers, and it's the right thing to do, to let her live with us."

"Nena's at my house, not Los Piñones," Marta says, trying to be patient. "And nothing has been decided. Anyway, what's wrong with Los Piñones? She might like being with other people instead of being stuck at home by herself all day."

"That's what I'm saying, you can't just leave her alone. You've taken her away from the neighborhood she's lived in her whole life. She has friends there. She can't live up by the mountain, where there's nothing but rattlesnakes."

"We don't have rattlesnakes."

"Yes, you do. You just haven't seen them," Cristina says. Marta can't help but think that it isn't altruism driving Cristina to insist Nena stay in her own house. Years ago, Marta knew Cristina as the raggedy kid who lived next door to Nena. Cristina's mom treated Nena like a free babysitter, and she hopes Cristina hasn't been doing the same thing. Nena's far too old for that.

"Have you ever heard of Nena having a daughter?" Marta asks, and saying this, she sees the dark-haired baby again, her chubby weight in Marta's arms, smelling of soap and milk.

"She's never mentioned that," Cristina says, sounding intrigued.

"Right. Except this morning she told me she did."

"The old have lots of secrets," Cristina intones.

It's clear Cristina knows nothing, and whatever advice she has about Nena isn't helpful.

Linda ushers five women from the Soto case into the room. Two of the women are in their early twenties. They're small, young, wearing tight shirts, dark jeans, boots, dangly earrings. The remaining three are older, closer to Marta's age. They've put on makeup, dressed up like they're going to church, in scarves and pins and ironed dresses. Linda's handing paper plates to the women, pouring out horchata, chatting about the food, asking about kids, parents. Marta's grateful that Linda is there to maintain the flow.

"We don't agree with Sofia," Belén Florez says. "We think you're doing a good job."

Marta hears a "but" in this.

"We know she can be pesada. But it's been very hard on all of us."

"I've been visited by ICE agents. More than once," one of the older women says.

"Me too," says one of the younger ones, nodding her head so that her dangly earrings tinkle.

"And you think it's because of Soto? Do you have any proof?" Linda asks.

The women shake their heads no.

"Look, ICE knows that you're part of an important investigation. We've filed paperwork with them so that you can stay in the country legally while the investigation is being conducted."

"That's not what they said. They said that we could be deported. They showed us their badges and everything," the older woman says.

"Next time, get a card from the agent. If he says he doesn't have one, write down his name and badge number," Marta says.

"That's right, you always have to write everything down, even if you think it's not important, and even if you think you'll remember it without writing it down," Linda says. "I was a client here once, and that's why we won our case. Because we had so much evidence."

The women nod. She's told them this many times before.

Belén raises her hand like she wants to be called on in class. Marta nods at her.

"I was having a birthday party for my granddaughter at a park, and there was a man standing by a tree. He had a gun in a holster. He kept his hand on his gun, and he wouldn't stop looking at us. My husband went to tell him to go away, and the man said that he was in a public place, and that he could have a gun if he wanted, it was his right."

Texas, Marta thinks. El Paso may think it's different, but it's still part of this state.

"The same thing happened to me, but it was outside of church. I was leaving mass with my daughter and son, and there was a man right there, same thing, with his hand on the gun in his holster."

"What did he look like?" Belén asks.

"He was tall, with a cowboy hat."

"Mine was fat. Wearing a tracksuit."

"How about at work? Anything disturbing going on there?" Marta asks. The women are still all on the line at the Soto packing shed. "Any new harassment there, sexual or otherwise?"

The women shake their heads no. So, Soto's not that dumb. But sending out people to torment the women seems not just cruel, but desperate. Marta's going to find out who these men are, and she'll tie them to Soto. He's not the only one who can hire private investigators.

"If he's pulling this kind of stuff, then he's scared. We'll get him to settle within the year. Maybe even within six months," Marta says, and she feels the women relax in the room, their shoulders dropping. Marta kicks herself. She shouldn't have made that promise. The firm needs the money in that time, and the women need relief, but wanting it doesn't make it so. Still, Marta likes a deadline. Six months to nail that bastard and get her clients their money, tick tock, tick tock.

Marta's phone dings, and she looks down at it.

Alejandro:

didn't think you'd have time to
focus on the Nena situation

had a friend from the hospital
call over to Los Piñones.
there's a casita opening up at
the end of the month

take her tonight to see it

I'll watch the boys

Marta's heart thumps as she taps out a quick response.

I'll take Nena tonight,
but I demand payment.

Like what???

I want a date tomorrow morning.

Shower?

meet you there

Marta's ravenous, and she's glad there's plenty of Linda's food left.

8

After the dogs killed the chickens and there wasn't enough money to pay Señor Echeverria the rent, Nena had accompanied her mamá to the tíos' trucking business next to Union Station. The streets around the train station smelled of axel grease, coal smoke. Men and women in clothes not much better than rags waited in front of the entrances, selling small paper bags of pecans, single cigarettes, ugly pink roses.

At the Montoya Brothers warehouse, trucks idled at the loading dock. Nena walked with her mamá up the steps, through the warehouse, past a shiny new Ford, to the glassed-in offices at the back. After Tío Agripino listened to Nena's mamá request a loan, he opened the safe, took out a small stack of bills, and put them in a manila envelope. He made Nena's mamá sign a slip of paper saying how much he'd given her, $31, exactly what she owed, and then he added interest on top of that. Nena hated that the tíos were going to make them pay the money back. It was wrong to treat family like this, especially since her papá would have worked for the family business if he were able.

The loan was only enough to cover rent, with nothing left over to buy more chickens. Nena had to do something to help the family, and she had an idea where she could start. When Nena had her vision that Señor Echeverria would die, she'd been terrified, but she also sensed that the place she'd been taken then was full of possibilities.

She waited until she was alone later that week, and then she took the money from where her mamá had hidden it, a pot at the back of the cupboard. Holding the envelope, she opened her mind, asking for assistance from the other side. Nena heard a buzzing in her ears, and her vision flickered. She tasted dust, saw the hooves of horses trampling her, felt them land on her body. When she came back to herself, she was lying on the floor of the kitchen, staring up at the ceiling, the long crack that went from the light fixture to the door frame wobbling. Nena got up, rubbing the back of her head, a bump already forming, but that didn't bother her. She was pleased, sure that her gift had shown her a way to make a lot of money out of not enough.

From the age of ten, Nena's father rode with his brothers out into the hills around Tularosa every spring to round up wild horses to break and then sell. The three brothers slept outside and made campfires of mesquite, cooked tortillas on a comal, ate dried beef. Once they drove the mustangs home, her papá's job was to hold the gate open while Agripino and Hernán herded the horses into the corral. The horses kicked and bit, they bucked, and her papá had to learn quickly how horses behaved so that he wouldn't be hurt or killed. He said that he only started to love horses once he'd learned to respect them, and he often talked longingly about the racetrack in Juárez.

Nena understood what the vision had commanded her to do. If her papá could see the racehorses in person, he would know which one would come in first place. When their horse won, her papá would praise her for being a smart, good girl, and her mamá wouldn't need to pray the rosary for so long every night, the sound of the beads clicking through her fingers. They could pay their rent, settle the loan with the tíos, buy new chickens, and everything could go back to the way it was supposed to be.

Nena should have left it at that. But she wanted to make extra sure that their bet on the horse would work, and so she went to see Doña Hilaria.

There were two curanderas in the neighborhood, Doña Hilaria and Señora Beatríz. Señora Beatríz was the nice curandera. She wore white huipils with pretty stitching, and she had a long braid that she wound around her head. Señora Beatríz always kept hard candies in her bag, little peppermints she gave to Nena when she saw her on the street. She did most of her business in love charms. One time she gave Señor León a charm, a maroon bag on a string that he tied around his neck, tight, so that it looked like a tumor. The charm was supposed to make Daisy Camacho fall in love with him, but then Señor León died of a stroke. Daisy met his nephew Raimuldo at the velatorio, the wake, and the next month they were married. Another time, Juanita Espinosa wanted to have a baby, so she went to Señora Beatríz for a charm to use with her husband. She didn't get pregnant, but her cat, who she thought was a gato macho, soon gave birth to six kittens that she had to give away to the neighbors.

The other curandera, Doña Hilaria, didn't make mistakes like that. When she put the mal de ojo on people, they got very thin, or they lost all their hair, or their teeth fell out all at once. And if she was paid to get rid of a curse, she could make someone who had a terrible cough and blue fingertips look rosy within the week.

Doña Hilaria lived alone with five little dogs. Everyone in the neighborhood said the chihuahuas slept with her in her bed, and that she fed them raw chicken from her mouth like she was a mama bird. Nena didn't know what stories about Doña Hilaria were true, but they all scared her. It took all of Nena's courage to make herself go to Doña Hilaria's house, to walk up the dusty road and stop in front of her yard. Mesquite grew so close together that their branches were woven into a thorny thicket that hid the house. Nena walked through the gate, past the mess of mesquite, and up the steps to the front door. She knocked. The dogs yapped, scrabbling at the door. She knocked again.

"Ándale pues," Doña Hilaria yelled. That could either mean go away or come in. Nena reached for the handle and turned it, pushing the door open. The dogs barked louder, jumping up and snapping in the air. Nena could feel their little teeth on her hands, their spit wetting her skin. She tried to push them away with her feet. The house smelled like dog, along with the sour, yeasty smell of things fermenting. In the kitchen, Doña Hilaria was at a big pot, boiling up something that didn't smell edible. She was a tall woman, stooped, and very skinny, wearing a thin housedress, white printed with blue polka dots. Her feet were bare, her toenails dirty and long.

"Sientate," she said, though there was no place at the kitchen table to sit. The smell of dog now hit the back of Nena's throat. Doña Hilaria must have let them go to the bathroom inside, and there was hair everywhere, on the chair, clumps of it on the floor, even on the wall where they dragged their bodies. Nena tried to brush the hair off her dress, but that just matted it down. Doña Hilaria poured milk in a saucepan. From where Nena sat, she could smell that the milk had turned sour, and no wonder. It was the summer, and Doña Hilaria didn't have an icebox.

Doña Hilaria unwrapped a bit of chocolate from a piece of wax paper and used a paring knife to shave the chocolate into the milk. Her fingernails were as grimy as her toenails.

She started to stir the chocolate into the hot milk, spinning a wooden molinillo between her palms. She dribbled the chocolate into a little clay taza and cleared room on the table for it. Nena was afraid to offend her by not drinking the chocolate, so she took a sip, tasting sour milk and dog. Nausea roiled in her stomach, and she swallowed hard to push it down. Doña Hilaria poured the rest of the chocolate into a saucer that she set on the floor. The dogs licked up the hot chocolate, chasing the rattling plate under the table and snapping at each other.

"Speak," Doña Hilaria said.

Nena told Doña Hilaria what she wanted, the name of the winning horse, and Doña Hilaria nodded, naming her price. Nena counted out the bills from the stack, handing them to Doña Hilaria, who put them in a tin on her counter. She took herbs down from her rack and shook them next to Nena's right ear, nodding her head yes, or no, making two small piles. The dogs calmed down, lying in a tangle on an old blanket in the corner of the kitchen. Doña Hilaria banged around tins and jars, putting herbs into a molcajete, pounding them into a fine dust. She poured the powder onto a piece of paper that tipped through a funnel into a little bag that she tied with red thread from a spool, using her tiny sharp teeth like scissors.

Doña Hilaria stopped, turning her head, like someone was saying something to her. She grumbled a sentence Nena didn't understand, and then cleared her throat, collecting a big wad of mucus that she spat in the sink. She pulled a glass from a shelf and filled it with water from the tap, then banged it down on the table in front of Nena.

Doña Hilaria then handed Nena an egg, pretty and brown, with freckles, as perfect as the eggs from their best hens, now departed.

"Crack it into the glass," Doña Hilaria said.

Nena was disappointed that this was what she was spending her money on. Telling the future by looking at eggs was nothing special.

"What are you waiting for? I have other things to do today," Doña Hilaria said.

Nena held the egg, cupping it between her hands. She closed her eyes and said a silent prayer over it. *Please let us win at the horse races, please let us make enough money to pay the rent for this month and for many months to come.* She pictured a fast, muscular horse ridden by a jockey wearing blue and white, and she saw the cheering crowd, her papá holding a big wad of twenty-dollar bills. Nena prayed. *Dios nos bendiga. Amen.*

She opened her eyes, giving the egg a little shake for extra good luck. Doña Hilaria leaned in, watching her closely. The dogs got off their bed, clicking their little nails over the linoleum, pointing their noses up at Nena.

She held the egg in her fingers, then cracked it on the side of the glass, carefully opening it. The white and the yolk slipped out of the shell, but something else did, too. Blood filled the glass, bright red.

Doña Hilaria jumped at Nena, grabbing her chin in her hand. "What is this? What kind of trick are you playing on me?"

"I prayed to win. That's all."

"Liar. Mentirosa. Bruja. Get out, demon, and take your money with you. Don't come back here ever again," she said, retrieving the wad of cash from her tin, almost throwing it at Nena. Nena shook, dropping the bills on the floor. She bent to gather them away from the snapping teeth of the dogs. "Out!" screamed Doña Hilaria, like Nena wasn't just a girl, like she was something evil. When she shut the door with a bang behind her, Nena could hear the hum growing louder on the other side. She ran all the way home, not sure what she'd done.

Sitting in her cell in the cold convent after the last prayers of the night, Nena pondered why she hadn't taken the blood in the glass for the sign that it so clearly was. Stop, the blood meant. Danger ahead. Why had she persisted in taking her papá to the racetrack? She'd stupidly thought that the magic from La Vista was the solution to her problems. Instead, La Vista had brought more disaster. Here in the convent, she'd yet again called the awful power of La Vista to her, setting something in motion that she had no control over. Nena wished she'd refused to take part in the aquelarre, wished she'd walked right back out through the turnstile. She'd been careless, not having learned the lesson that magic always complicates.

But Nena was no longer that girl who went to see Doña Hilaria. She had to start acting like a responsible person. Step one was to focus on the most important thing: getting herself home. It may have been impossible to jump through time, but Nena had done it somehow. That meant there had to be a way to do it again.

And—exciting thought!—maybe she didn't have to look that hard for the solution. What about the ladybugs? In the chapel, she'd sent a ladybug through space to Carmela. That was how Nena had moved through time, fast, blinking from then to now, not even sensing that she'd made the jump. Learning how to send ladybugs might give Nena an understanding about how the movement worked. If she could transport a small body, maybe she could move a large one, her own.

Finding time alone with Carmela was harder than Nena could have imagined, and it wasn't until a couple of days later that she saw her chance. Carmela told Nena she was going to the portería to buy food, and Nena volunteered to come along.

The portería was the lobby to the convent, a space where the nuns could do business with the townspeople without having to leave the compound. When they reached the lobby, the majordomo was unlocking the big door to the outside.

"You said you'd teach me how to send ladybugs," Nena said as quietly as she could. She didn't have any time to waste, and that this was as close to private as a conversation was going to get in the convent.

Carmela scanned the room with her eyes. "First things first. To control the ladybugs, you have to be able to call La Vista to you without fainting."

"I was able to do it in the chapel."

"Yes, but you didn't have any idea what you were doing. And when you called La Vista to you in the aquelarre, you cracked your head on the floor. Here," Carmela said, lifting her little silver cross up over her head and placing it around Nena's neck. "My cross has spells sung into it that'll help balance you. Hold on to my arm so that you feel steady. La Vista uses your whole body. When you call the ladybugs to you, keep one foot on the riverbank—that's your body, this time and place—and one foot in the river—the river's La Vista—so that you're not swept away. Sí?"

"No," Nena said. "I'm not sure I understand."

"When you touch the cross, pray for God to help you control La Vista," Carmela said, but this felt wrong to Nena. Did God want things to be controlled? Nena thought not. From what she could tell, God liked chaos. She'd prayed plenty, and terrible things kept happening. "Are you paying attention? When you call to the ladybugs, you're going to allow La Vista to take over your mind, but at the same time, make sure all of your human body parts are working, your lungs especially. You have to breathe. That's what makes you faint, when you don't breathe."

"What if when I call the mariquitas, the coyote encanto comes for me instead?" Nena felt strange putting words to the image in her head, but she was truly scared. "I might grow fur or start to yip or howl. If the majordomo saw that, wouldn't he tell the priest?"

"If you grew fur, I would imagine so. We couldn't keep that a secret," Carmela said, laughing.

"It's not funny," Nena said, bristling. "What do they do to witches here if they're found out? Burn them alive?"

"What are you talking about? The Inquisition isn't interested in that kind of offense, they only care about heretics. Nobody believes in witches in the civilized world. And anyhow, that's not what we are. We live to glorify God. We don't make love spells, or help other people see the future, or put curses on people for money. Those are the sorts of things the Indios do, not educated ladies of God like ourselves. We practice using La Vista so that we can control it. Same thing with being a nun, an ordinary nun. We pray to help us get rid of our desires so that we can focus on God."

"What do you mean about the Indios?"

"What they do is not Christian."

"I'm part Indio," Nena said, shocked and hurt that her friend would say something like that. "On the side of my mamá."

Carmela put her finger to her lips. "You don't ever want to admit something like that here."

"My mamá was stronger and smarter than anyone I've ever known."

"That may be, but keep that to yourself. You couldn't stay here if anyone knew that you had Indio blood."

There were plenty of other women in the convent who were as dark as Nena, and not only the servants. But Nena stayed silent, not wanting to argue with Carmela.

The food sellers arranged their wares on the floor, unloading baskets and small wheelbarrows.

"I want you to try to call the ladybugs without letting any of these people see what's happening," Carmela whispered. "It'll be good practice for you. You wouldn't want to be caught doing magic and then get burned at the stake, would you?"

Nena wasn't ready to joke about any of this, and she didn't laugh at Carmela's teasing.

A woman with a shawl covering her head laid out a blanket on the floor, lining up bunches of dried oregano, thyme, bay leaves, cloves, cinnamon, chiles, epazote. She didn't look well, this woman. She kept coughing, pressing a handkerchief into her mouth, her body shaking with each hack.

Carmela pointed at the bundles she wanted. The herb woman bowed, and then the majordomo paid her a few coins, since the nuns weren't allowed to handle money.

Carmela pulled Nena down the line, stopping in front of a wheelbarrow with meat piled in it. The butcher was a stout man, a filthy once-white cloth wound around his neck. He smiled at Nena.

"Now? I should do it now?" Nena whispered.

"Yes. Tell me what kind of meat I should buy. Remember, one foot in the river, one foot on land."

Nena focused on the cross around her neck to hold her in the portería, while the waters of La Vista pulled at her. In this in-between place, she called a ladybug to her, part of her brain along for the ride as the ladybug shot through a tunnel of time and space, landing on her finger. She inserted a message in the ladybug's mind: "goat leg stew, with chile and cumin." She sent the ladybug back through the tunnel to Carmela, who nodded at Nena, a smile lighting up her face.

Nena smiled back, feeling love and appreciation for Carmela. This was the very first time she'd used La Vista on purpose and managed not to faint.

Carmela turned to the butcher, flashing fingers at him but not talking, and Nena discovered that this was how they bargained, with hand signals, so that the nuns never had to speak to anyone who didn't live at the convent.

The butcher bowed to Carmela, and the majordomo took care of the money. The leg was left for the servants to prepare.

"Go back to the kitchen and find yourself some food," Carmela said.

"I'm not hungry."

"It requires a lot of energy to use La Vista," Carmela said. "Your body needs to be replenished."

"I have one more question," Nena said, racking her brain for what she could do to prolong the conversation. She missed talking to other people, to her sisters. She landed on a topic that she was curious about anyway. "Is it true that Eugenia's marrying Sister Benedicta's brother?"

"Why do you ask?"

"She seemed so proud of it, I wondered if she was exaggerating."

"Sister Benedicta's family, the de Galvezes, own most of the vineyards along the Rio Bravo. Eugenia's father is as rich as the de Galvezes because he controls a lot of the trade that comes through El Paso del Norte, up to Santa Fe and down to Chihuahua along El Camino Real, but he started out as a mule driver, and everyone remembers where he came from, sleeping with the animals. He's trying to buy himself into a better class. The contract was made between the families when Eugenia was twelve. I'm sure they didn't expect that she'd turn out to be such a horror."

"Carmela!"

"Now, go and eat, or you'll faint, and Sister Benedicta will know what we've been doing."

Nena hurried back to the kitchen. One of the servants was frying empanadas, placing them on a tray next to the pot of bubbling oil. Nena picked one up and burned her lips as she bit through the crispy pastry, reaching the filling, meat and potatoes and raisins spiced with cumin and cinnamon. Nena devoured one after another. So much for not being hungry. And Carmela had been right, Nena felt much better once she had eaten.

She licked her fingers when she was done and tied an apron around her waist, ready to work. In the convent kitchen, there were always piles of pots to scrub. Of all the jobs around the house she shared with her sisters, Nena minded washing dishes least, enjoying the sensation of her hands in the warm water. She fell into the rhythm of the washing, reflecting on what she'd done in the portería. She was proud of herself, hopeful that with more practice she would be able to manage her gift without causing harm. She stretched her arms above her head. She felt free. Maybe she didn't need to get back to her time as quickly as she'd thought she did. Maybe there was more to learn here.

She wished she'd had someone like Carmela to teach her when she was younger. Maybe Nena would have been able to change what happened at the racetrack, saving her family so much pain.

Señor Obregon from the corner market went to the Jockey Club once a week, and when Nena had asked him for his help, he'd said he'd be happy to drive Nena and her papá to Juárez the next time he went.

In the grandstands, Nena smelled the tacos and hot dogs with sauerkraut for sale in the kiosk, and she longed to use ten cents of their money to buy herself a treat. But that would be a waste, and besides, she'd brought food for her and her papá to eat, tortillas wrapped tight around beans and chiles. She and her papá sat close to the part of the track where they could see the horses in the paddock. Her papá trembled, pale, with sweat beading up on his face. It didn't take La Vista to see how sick he was, but he was smiling, really smiling, and his brown eyes flashed, matching the dashing way he wore his hat. Nena felt proud of him.

Her papá examined the horses through Señor Obregon's field glasses, running his finger down the racing form. Nena could imagine him at her age, galloping across the mesa. Nena had a harder time imagining Papá's brothers riding, let alone whooping and chasing each other, pretending to be Apaches. She couldn't fit that in with how she knew them to be, wearing their suits and fedoras, smoking in their office, those greedy men with big noses, big floppy ears sprouting hair, and wild eyebrows that twirled into the air.

Her papá chose a horse named Potato Chip, whose jockey was dressed in blue and white, just like in Nena's vision, and, for the first time, she was glad she'd gone to Doña Hilaria's. Now she had a fix, a confirmation that this was the right horse. Nena's papá handed Señor Obregon all of their money.

"Just on the one horse?" Señor Obregon asked. The odds were twelve to one, Nena's papá explained when Señor Obregon left with the money, which meant that when they won, they'd have enough to pay rent for the year. This made sense to Nena, and it seemed like a good sign that the odds were so perfect.

It was a bright day, windy. The first race ended faster than Nena had expected, and then before the second started, the one their horse was in, the wind picked up. The horses spooked in the paddock, snorting and stomping. Papers fluttered. Nena looked to the east and saw a wall of dust approaching across the desert, fast.

The sandstorm hit all at once. Men clutched at their hats and ran for the shelter of the betting rooms. Nena's papá couldn't move fast enough to make it inside, but he put his body over hers to keep the sand from pelting her face. Nena heard thunder, but she didn't see any lightning. Pellets of hail fell down on them through the blowing sand as Nena buried her face in her papá's chest. This was not like any sandstorm Nena had ever experienced. It was wet, and the water turned the sand to a kind of mud that stuck to Nena's face and hands as a howling sound grew louder, roaring itself out in a big whoosh.

The wind died down as if a switch had been flipped, dust hanging in the air, far up, turning the sun into a big pumpkin. People slowly came back down to the grandstand, taking their seats. The announcer's voice echoed. The races would resume soon.

It took a while to get the horses calmed and ready, and then, at the pistol shot, the race started. Their horse sprinted fast out of the gate, leading the pack up until the first turn, running even faster around the bend. Papá stood, shaking, holding on to Nena's shoulder, shouting, "Córrele! Córrele! Run!" Their horse pulled ahead by half a length, hugging the inside rails, stretching out his long legs, his nose pointing toward the finish line.

And then he stopped.

The other horses streamed around him like he was a rock in a river. Potato Chip's jockey whipped the horse, but the act only made the animal turn around and start running the wrong way. Nena's papá dropped the betting slip. She watched it fall to the ground through the gaps in the grandstand. Her papá shook, pale. He held on to Nena as he sat down.

"Está bien, it's OK, mi hija," he said. But it hadn't been fine.

Nena was jolted from her memory by someone tugging on her sleeve.

"What are you doing?" Eugenia asked.

"What does it look like?" Nena said, pouring ash onto a rag and then attacking the bottom of a pot, using her weight to scrub. "Aren't you supposed to be working?"

"Plucking chickens. But it's too nasty. I told one of the kitchen maids to do it."

"You should work harder," Nena said, having spent the past few days watching Eugenia do as little as possible during her shifts in the kitchen. It was evil, not to mention lazy, to shirk one's duties.

"I don't know why they treat me like a slave. They should give me something else to do, a task I want to do and that I'm good at."

"Like what?"

"I don't mind sewing," Eugenia said.

Nena freed the last bit of crust from the bottom of the pot, satisfied with her efforts. She started in on the next pot.

Eugenia took off her apron, wadding it up and placing it on the table. "When Carmela comes back, I'm going to tell her that I will no longer work here."

Nena looked up from her pot. Behind Eugenia stood Sister Benedicta.

"Eugenia—" Nena said.

"What?" Eugenia said sharply. "I'm not afraid of that cow. I can't wait to tell her, to be honest."

Sister Benedicta placed a bony hand on Eugenia's shoulder.

A wave of surprise washed over Eugenia's face, quickly replaced by a tight, proud look. Eugenia spun around, tilting up her chin to look Sister Benedicta in the eye. Eugenia may have been stupid, but she was also brave.

"I refuse to work in this dirty kitchen anymore," Eugenia declared, as a challenge.

"Yes, you will. This is the task assigned to you," Sister Benedicta said.

"You can't make me do anything. I'm going to write to my father and tell him how I'm being treated."

"Put your apron back on and get back to work."

"No." Eugenia maintained eye contact with Sister Benedicta, her chin still jutted out.

Sister Benedicta didn't respond, instead taking slow steps to the cupboard and pulling out a jar of lard. She dipped a rag in the jar and brought it back to the table, where she dunked it in the ashes that Nena had been using to scrub the pot. The kitchen had gone silent, the nuns and the servants watching with wide eyes. Sister Benedicta grabbed Eugenia's upturned chin in her hand and proceeded to rub Eugenia's face with the cloth, smearing the black grease all over her skin.

Eugenia began to cry, softly, her tears slipping down the grease.

"Put your apron back on," Sister Benedicta said.

"Yes, Vicaria," Eugenia said, bowing, but her hands made tight fists at her sides.

9

If you hate it, we don't have to stay for long," Marta says to Nena. "But Alejandro was nice enough to set this visit up, and we don't want to disappoint him."

"We must never disappoint the great Dr. Torres," Nena says.

"No, we mustn't," Marta says, feeling disloyal even as she laughs with Nena. Marta is looking forward to her date with Alejandro in the morning.

At Los Piñones, Marta and Nena are greeted by the director, who hands them a key and a map with the path to the open casita traced in yellow highlighter. What deal did Alejandro make to get them this special treatment? Marta finds herself oddly turned on by his show of power and privilege—it was Alejandro's confidence that first attracted her to him—but she's also irritated on Nena's behalf by his presumption.

Alejandro certainly wouldn't want to live here. The hallways are too brightly lit, and the place smells like a hospital, with an odor of bleach and beef broth. A plastic Christmas wreath hangs in the hallway, either six months too late or too early. The art on the walls could be that of a primary school—painted paper plates, origami cranes strung on fishing line.

On the way to the casita, they walk past the rec room, where music is pumping, a disco ball swirling bubbles of light through the glass wall and out into the hallway. Nena stops, staring into the room. Women dance, wearing sparkly hats, a fedora glittering with rhinestones, a baseball cap bejeweled in electric-blue plastic crystals. A woman leaning on a walker sports a hat with cartoon cats outlined in glitter glue. A towering woman in a hip-length fur wears a cowboy hat decorated with the Texas flag.

"I wanted to talk to you about Rosa again," Marta says. Earlier, at the office, she'd called a friend in social services, who'd had some ideas about where to begin looking for old records. Marta's glad to be alone with Nena to broach the topic.

"Luna loved dancing so much," Nena says. "You've heard the story about the broken leg and the cast, haven't you?"

"Once or twice," Marta says. "What was Rosa's date of birth?"

"Let's go in. I want to dance."

"Did you hear me?" Marta asks, not understanding why Nena was so insistent on talking about Rosa but is now suddenly clamming up. It hurts Marta's feelings, and it makes her want to win Nena's confidence back.

"Luna sent us a sign from the other side," Nena says, gesturing at the dancers.

Marta hates talk of signs. "What's she telling us?" Marta asks.

"That we need to dance," Nena says, going into the room.

"You both need hats," the teacher says to Marta and Nena, hurrying over to a box on the table next to the punch, returning with a glittery red beret for Nena and a gold baseball cap for Marta. And then before Marta can get her bearings, the teacher has started the music again, "The Electric Slide" blaring through the speakers. Marta has trouble keeping up with the instructions, surprised that though the other women have at least twenty-five years on her, they can all do some version of the steps, and far more gracefully than she can.

They stay for the Hustle, the Macarena, the Chicken Dance, the Cupid Shuffle, and Marta's surprised to find that she's having fun. Nena, her face fixed with determination, wheels around, leans back, kicks out her leg a few inches off the floor. The class ends with a honky-tonk song accompanied by a routine that Marta suspects you'd do in a roadhouse. The woman in the fur whoops and smacks her butt.

"Punch and cookies on the table," the teacher says when the song is over.

"I got warm from the dancing," Nena says, fanning herself with her hand, glowing. Marta's hot, too. She's glad Nena suggested they go in. Luna would have been ecstatic to know that Marta was dancing; Luna used to always tell Marta that she didn't need to be so serious, like that was something Marta could change about herself. Anyhow, Marta could be serious *and* fun, couldn't she?

"If you lived here, I'd come to this class every week with you," Marta says. It seems that it's only since Olga and Luna have gone that she feels like she can really get to know Nena. She wonders if Nena has been holding back on sharing her witchy side with Marta again until her sisters were gone, and she was safe from the threat of being put back in an institution. Marta's not yet convinced that the sisters didn't have reason to hospitalize Nena.

The woman in the fur has appointed herself the server of the punch, and she hands Nena and Marta paper cups.

"I wear my coyote because it gets so cold in the refrigerated air," the woman says with a thick Southern accent, theatrically closing the front of her fur coat and shivering.

"And who are you, honey?" the woman asks Nena. "Did you just move in?"

"This is my great-aunt Nena. She's just visiting," Marta says.

"Well, we'd love to have y'all join us here. We keep ourselves real busy," the woman says, waving her hand at a bulletin board with an oversized calendar of the month's activities pinned to it. Tai chi. Cookie class. Daily prayer group, one Catholic and one Christian, which Marta considers an odd distinction. Bridge twice a week.

"I'll tell you what I would never do," Nena tells Marta. "The quilting circle."

"Why?"

"I *hate* sewing," Nena says quietly to Marta, in stronger tones than Marta would have expected. There's a story there. Nena has a million stories. But the one Marta's interested in most now has to do with her daughter.

"About Rosa—" Marta starts again.

"Let's go see the casita," Nena says. "So that we can say we did it."

Walking down the hallway, Nena grabs Marta's forearm, clamping on to it. As they progress, Nena eyes the floor like she's on the lookout for the wax. They leave the main building, heading down the pathway that leads to the casitas.

It's hot and very dry outside. Sconces on the walls and lights planted in the dirt shine brightly on the concrete path. Cactuses and creosote bushes in beds of rock line the walkway, straight lines only, no steps up or down into the houses, the doors wide enough for wheelchairs. Los Piñones is high enough up the mountain that the setting sun seems to be hovering directly across from where they are, painting everything in between a rosy red: western El Paso, the Rio Grande, the ramshackle houses of Juárez, and the Sierra Nevada of Chihuahua. It's a beautiful night, and when Nena squeezes Marta's arm, they don't have to say anything to understand each other.

The casita is less inspiring. The main room stinks of paint, the walls an off-white color Marta finds depressing, physically depressing, like there's a giant hand squashing her down. The Formica in the kitchenette is fake granite, plasticky and cheap. There's a two-burner cooktop, but no oven. A sink, a small refrigerator, and a narrow dishwasher round out the amenities in the kitchen. The most you'd want to attempt would be scrambled eggs. The tiny living room area isn't furnished, but you could fit in a petite love seat and a coffee table.

Nena walks past Marta and into the bathroom. Marta follows her. There's a walk-in shower with a safety bar on the wall. Next to the toilet is a bar, too. Nena flushes the toilet. She turns the lights on and off, runs the tap.

"I've always liked the smell of fresh paint," she says.

"Oh, Nena," Marta says, Nena's tone reminding her of Rafa on his first day of kindergarten, how he'd straightened his back and said, "It's OK, Mama, you can leave me now." Marta doesn't want Nena to have to be brave for her. Outside, she hears the yip yip of coyotes echoing in the hills, a lonely sound, the sound of hunger.

"Nena, why don't you want to talk about Rosa?"

"You aren't ready yet."

"What does that mean?"

"Why don't you let me help you for once?"

"With what?"

"Soto Pecans," Nena says.

"How do you know about the Soto case?"

"I looked at the papers on your desk."

"You really shouldn't do that, Nena, there are privacy issues. I could get sanctioned by the bar for something like that."

"How would anyone know? Olga won't tell."

"Olga?"

"You know she always knew everything about everybody, how they were related and all that stuff that I wasn't interested in. What's the matter? Why are you looking at me like that?"

Olga the ghost? Olga of Nena's memory? "You called her up on the phone?"

"You're making a joke, but you know that's not how I talk to my sisters."

Marta talks to them, too, but not in the way that Nena means. Marta imagines Luna walking into the kitchen now, in high heels and a tight red dress that slinks down her narrow hips, shaking a long cigarette out of her leather case and flicking open her gold lighter, bending into the flame. Marta sees Olga right behind her in a suit, a string of fake pearls, pantyhose. Marta imagines her shaking her head at Marta, *No, don't do it, don't encourage Nena.* The eight-year-old in Marta's brain pushes her way to the front.

"What did Olga say about Soto?" the girl asks.

"There's always been a connection between the families. Papá grew up with Sotos. Our families even knew each other way back when they settled the Doña Ana Bend land grant. Up by Mesilla."

"Settled?" That word! And Marta doesn't like to think about being connected to Soto by family or friendship. Nena's recitation of who's related to whom sounds much more like Olga than Nena, and Marta is again struck by a discordant trill in her body, her rational side bucking at the thought that this could be possible, the other part of her leaning in to hear what Nena has to say.

"A long time ago, when the tíos Agripino and Hernán finally died, the Sotos bought Montoya Brothers trucking. It became Soto Trucking. Your grandfather serviced the Soto trucks in his garage. A lot of his work was with Montoya Brothers trucking, both before and after it was sold."

Marta tries to remember her family history. When her grandfather came back from the war, Olga found him a job with her uncles' trucking company, which—and this is the new bit for Marta—was later bought by Benjamin Soto's father. Soto's money comes from this company, now called Soto Logistics, not from the pecans. Soto's trucks work in a pretty narrow niche, transporting industrial goods from the maquiladoras in Greater Juárez and then across the border, either to the train station or to other trucking companies that then move the cargo throughout the rest of the US. It's a big business, giving Soto the funds he needs to buy influence, to evade justice, to play whatever dirty tricks he wants to play.

"So, Grandpa worked for the Sotos? How bizarre is that?" Marta says.

"You know how things are in El Paso. Everyone is connected somehow."

"Right, everyone is connected," Marta says, imagining the lines drawn between Rosa and Soto.

"Your grandma was friends with Silvia Colón. They were classmates at Bowie High. Silvia married into the Soto family. The family eran conocidos, people knew who the Sotos were. They had a big house in Sunset Heights. It must have been a big change for Silvia, and lucky for her. If a family has money, then they can help their children, and their children can help their children even more, and it means that each next generation is richer, like your generation."

Nena's mention of Silvia Soto flips a switch in Marta's brain. She remembers stopping at a farm stand, a little wooden barn on the side of the road south of town on the way toward San Elizario. Marta remembers Señora Soto wore a skirt suit like Olga's. She perched behind the cash register, reigning over the simple room, making a show of throwing in a bonus with Olga's purchase, a bag of candied pecans that Marta and Juan shared on the car ride home. Somehow Marta hadn't made the connection.

"Did Olga have anything to say that could help my lawsuit?" Marta asks. "Or did she just want to chew the fat about old times?"

"You don't believe I talked to her," Nena says, her voice shaking with what sounds like anger. Marta shouldn't have said chewing the fat. She wasn't making fun of Nena. Now she's landed herself where she was before, with Nena not trusting her.

"It's not that I don't want to believe you, it's that I can't. It's not in my constitution."

"Like you have a contract with yourself?"

"I wasn't thinking that kind of constitution, but sure," Marta says, tickled. But she's also still offended that Nena won't talk about Rosa. "What did you mean when you said I wasn't ready?"

"Rosa can't be found in the way that you're talking about. If you really want to help, you have to admit that La Vista is in you now. You have to let La Vista show you the path."

"How would I do that?" Marta asks, surprised by the equal measures of fear and eagerness within her as she waits for Nena's answer. Marta wants to be the sort of person who is ready for everything. Hasn't she lived long enough and done enough that she is prepared to handle hard things? She wishes she hadn't said the thing about her constitution. It's more complicated than that. Marta is skeptical. And she's curious. Marta isn't naïve enough to think that she knows everything. But Marta sees clearer than ever what happens to people like Nena. They are disbelieved, institutionalized, made to live on the margins of society. Marta doesn't want any of these things for herself, no matter how strongly she feels drawn to Nena and her special way of living. Marta's warm, her skin buzzing.

"Do you remember when we had that talk at Luna's Christmas party?" Nena asks.

"There were lots of Christmas parties at Luna's."

"You're right. So many parties. That was her life. Do you remember the bonbons her maid used to make?"

"Now, those I remember," Marta says, along with all the other Christmas treats bought and made, the sopapillas and the little round almond tea cakes dusted in powdered sugar, the tamales of cheese and rajas, the gorditas made by the nuns at the Loretto convent and school. She remembers the tall silver foil Christmas tree and the luminarias that lined the granite walls of the neighborhood, glowing in the dark, meant to light the way for the magi to find Jesus, but what they really lit was a path to a family party, a house full of cousins and their cousins, a wealth of family that Marta didn't have in California. Marta remembers all that, but not any particular conversation with Nena.

"Think back to when you were thirteen."

"I'd rather not," Marta says, cringing.

"Please try," Nena says. "It snowed that night. Your brother Juan slipped and broke his wrist."

"Oh," Marta says, and then there she is, back in that magical time of year in El Paso, the huge star on the side of the Franklin Mountains lit up, the air chilly, scented with woodsmoke, Luna's house loud with music, the kitchen hazy from Luna's cigarettes, the women trading chisme, laughing, the men in the other room, drinking beer, the cousins and uncles of Marta's mother's generation acting like teenage boys, boasting about killing rattlesnakes in the irrigation ditch, sneaking over to Juárez to watch the bullfights, teasing Chuy about the time he lost control of his Impala and it ended up balanced on the low wall on Scenic Drive, miraculously not tumbling down the cliff, *how did you manage to do that, pendejo?* Marta had needed to pee, and the powder room and the bathroom off Luna's room were occupied. Marta found her way to the back of the house, to the guest room, where Nena sat on the edge of the bed.

Marta had the impression that Nena had been waiting for her.

"I sat next to you, and you took my hand. You held it like you were taking my pulse," Marta says, and she can feel the hum of her blood now, the slow and steady beating of her heart as she reaches back into the snowbank of memory. "Your eyes were closed, and when you opened them, you looked up at me and said, 'Yes.'"

"That's right. And then what happened?"

"I got scared. You weren't there. Behind your eyes, you were gone. I ran out of the room. What did you mean when you said yes?"

"I saw Rosa that night, too," Nena says slowly. "Not like the other day. It was just a flash that night. Right after I saw her, you came into the room. I held your hand to see if I could feel La Vista in you."

"And could you?" Marta's pulse is beating erratically now, like she's swimming at a meet. She doesn't know what she wants Nena's answer to be.

"The two times Rosa came to me, you were there, too. I know it in my heart that you are the one who will help me see Rosa again before I die. You're one of the Montoya women who has the gift. The curse. Whatever this is that makes us who we are."

Marta's breath catches, but she steadies herself. She has to be reasonable.

"I know who I am, Nena. Whatever it is that you have that takes you out of yourself and lets you see something different, I don't have it," Marta says, thinking whether she wants this thing that Nena claims she has. Not really. The vacant look Nena had that Christmas had scared her because it seemed like Nena was gone in a way that meant she wasn't coming back. This kind of look must have compelled Luna and Olga to put Nena in the hospital. Marta doesn't want this for herself. "This conversation makes me worried."

"I understand. I've been trying to get you to move too fast," Nena says. "But soon La Vista will make itself known in a way that you won't be able to ignore."

10

Nena had just taken the first sip of her afternoon chocolate when Sister Benedicta bustled into the dining room.

"Why aren't you at confession with the other niñas?" Sister Benedicta asked.

"Confession?" Nena asked.

"All niñas must confess on Fridays. You ought to learn the schedule if you wish to keep yourself out of trouble." Sister Benedicta chided her, and Nena pictured sooty grease being rubbed on her face.

"I'm sorry, Vicaria," Nena murmured, head down as she hurried toward the chapel. She slid onto the bench with the other niñas waiting their turns to admit to the silliest crimes imaginable, since there wasn't anything truly bad you could do in the convent except overeat or have hateful thoughts about the other girls. Nena now knew the niñas by name and sight—Leonor, Catalina, Margarita, and Luz—but that was pretty much all Nena had gathered about these girls. She wasn't interested in making friends with anyone who couldn't help her get home, like Carmela. Eugenia, however, seemed determined to sit next to her in chapel and in the dining room, talking when she wasn't supposed to.

Nena didn't see Eugenia in the line on the pew, which meant that she must be in the confessional.

Now that she knew she had to wait anyway, Nena wished she'd taken at least a sip of the chocolate before departing the dining room. The convent's chocolate was made with sweet cow's milk and cones of piloncillo, crumbled into the warm liquid and whisked with a molinillo. That the women of the convent drank hot chocolate every afternoon had been a pleasant surprise, chocolate being a luxury that Nena was hardly ever able to enjoy in her El Paso. Carmela had shared with her that for the Feast of the Three Kings, the nuns made the chocolate with ewe's milk, which had a flavor that was subtle and rich at the same time. Nena was curious about this version of the chocolate, but she planned to be long gone by the time Epiphany arrived.

The door to the confessional opened, and Eugenia emerged, her face flushed. She seemed not to notice Nena as she hurried down the side aisle and out the door. The rest of the niñas went into the confessional, one by one, until Nena was the only one left in the chapel. Nena let herself in, then latched the door behind her.

"Bless me, Father, for I have sinned," Nena said, making the sign of the cross.

"You're new in the convent, aren't you?" Father Iturbe asked.

"Yes, Padre. I arrived this week."

"What is the nature of your sin?"

Nena's mind raced through the options. She had to come up with something safe to confess.

She couldn't tell the priest of her dislike of Sister Benedicta, or that she'd abandoned her family, or that she was practicing witchcraft. She couldn't confess that at the meeting of an aquelarre in the convent, the tooth of a coyote had shown up in her mouth, and that tomorrow she was going to participate in a ceremony that was supposed to purge the rest of the coyote from her.

"Chocolate," Nena said.

"Pardon?"

"I confess to the sin of gluttony. I wish I could have extra cups of chocolate when we have our afternoon breaks."

Father Iturbe laughed. "And why shouldn't you? You're young and you need to keep the color in your cheeks. You have my permission to ask for another taza of chocolate from Sister Benedicta. I'm sure she'd be happy to give you one. But gluttony is a grave sin. Very grave. Say ten Hail Marys, then ask the Virgin to purify your thoughts."

In her haste Nena banged the door closed as she left the confessional. She passed through the chapel, dark in the corners and empty, echoing with the sound of the slammed door. Nena picked up the bottom of her habit, so that it wouldn't drag, and scurried to her job. As she walked into the kitchen, Eugenia grabbed her by the upper arm, pulling her close. Eugenia was pale, her lips chapped, worry lines around her eyes.

"Carmela told me to wash beans, but I don't know what that means," Eugenia whispered.

"You pick through them to look for rocks and other things," Nena said, dumping the big pot of dry beans onto a towel. She ran her fingers through the pile, pulling out sticks and tiny pebbles.

"Well, why didn't she just say that?" Eugenia said, poking at one bean with the tip of her index finger.

"Do you know what the priest said to me during confession?" Nena asked, feeling pity for Eugenia, and wanting to make her smile.

"What?"

"He told me to ask Sister Benedicta if I could have more chocolate."

"You'd better not do that," Eugenia said, pinching up a tiny rock and dropping it on the floor.

"I know! Can you imagine what Sister Benedicta would do if I asked for a second cup?"

"If you start drinking gallons of chocolate, you'll end up as fat as Carmela."

This was uncalled for, and now Nena regretted trying to cheer Eugenia up. "Carmela is beautiful, and she's my friend," Nena said.

"You only say that because she doesn't make you do any of the hard work."

"I do plenty," Nena said.

"I think there's something funny going on in this place, if you want to know the truth."

"You're just mad because Sister Benedicta punished you," Nena shot back.

"You'd be better off not being too friendly with these nuns." Nena wasn't sure what Eugenia was suggesting. "All I can say is, I can't wait to leave here and get married."

"Remind me again about your engagement," Nena said, still mad on behalf of Carmela, her only real friend in this place. "Who is it exactly you're marrying?"

"You know very well who my novio is, Emiliano de Galvez."

"Oh, right, Sister Benedicta's brother. I imagine she's very happy about that. It couldn't be why she smeared the grease on your face."

"She's an evil old witch. Emiliano is only her half brother, and he obviously got the good half."

"I'd be careful if I were you. You wouldn't want any reports to get back to the de Galvez family," Nena said, satisfied when she saw worry creep into Eugenia's face.

"What are you saying?"

"Would you be surprised if she stopped the marriage?" Nena asked.

"What? Why would you say that to me? You're being mean."

"There must be a reason she treats you the way she does. It's not just that you're lazy."

"Has she said anything to you about Emiliano?"

"No," Nena said, but she drew out the word, trying to make it sound like she knew something. Eugenia went even paler than before.

"You're right. She treats me worse than everyone else. I think she does hate me. What if she tries to keep me from marrying him?"

Nena took pity on her. Eugenia deserved punishment for being mean about Carmela, but Nena didn't want to be cruel. "Sister Benedicta is strict with everyone."

"Not you."

"You didn't see how mad she was at me when I wasn't at confession today."

"Did she rub dirty grease on your face? No. Why would she punish you, perfect Elena, who always does what she's told, Elena who is best friends with Carmela, a bossy, fat old cow who does secret things at night."

"What are you talking about?" Nena asked.

"What would you do if I told you a big secret? Would you tell Sister Benedicta?"

"No," Nena said quickly.

Eugenia waved Nena closer, whispering, "Carmela leaves her cell at night."

"Where does she go?" Nena asked.

"I don't know, but Sister Manuela, the portera on her hallway, told me that she's seen her sneak out of her room and not come back for hours and hours."

"If she witnessed something, she should have reported it to Sister Benedicta. This makes Sister Manuela just as much at fault as the person breaking the rules," Nena said.

"Sister Manuela can't say anything because Carmela put the mal de ojo on her. Last Saturday, Sister Manuela spotted Carmela leaving her room, and Sister Manuela tried to reprimand her, but she couldn't move her mouth to talk. And then the next day when she went to

Sister Benedicta to tell her what had happened, her tongue turned into a piece of silver."

"Absurd. What kind of fairy tales are you telling me?"

"She showed it to me."

"Her tongue?"

"Before it turned back to flesh, she was able to peel a piece of the silver off with her fingernail. She showed me the shaving."

"And you're saying Carmela did this to Sister Manuela?"

"Remember, you promised you wouldn't say anything to anyone," Eugenia said. The color had come back into her cheeks.

"What would I say? That a portera made up a story to cover up the fact that she fell asleep when she was supposed to be on duty?"

"Well, I believe Sister Manuela. And so does—" Eugenia made her lips into a line, like she was stopping herself from saying anything else, but like she also wanted Nena to try to guess what she was insinuating. Nena said nothing, sweeping the cleaned beans into the pot and carrying it over to the giant fireplace with its grates for grilling and spits that suspended bubbling kettles over the fire.

Nena was unsure what to do with this information. Part of her wanted to run and tell Madre Inocenta right away that some of the women were gossiping about the nuns of the aquelarre. But Nena didn't want to be the sort of person whose word couldn't be trusted. Nor did she want Eugenia or Sister Manuela to be punished for telling what was probably the truth. Besides, Nena had more important things to worry about, like what was going to happen at the next aquelarre, and how she was going to get herself home.

In Madre Inocenta's office that Saturday night, a copper pot hung on a stand over the mesquite fire, burned down to sweet-sour-smelling embers. The nuns of the aquelarre stood around the long table, singing the song of the coven. Even when the song was over, Nena heard the notes hanging in the air.

Madre Inocenta picked up a clay taza from the table in the center of the room. She dipped the cup in the pot and handed it to Nena.

"What is it?" Nena asked. This was same kind of cup the nuns used for chocolate, and Nena briefly worried that Father Iturbe had shared with Madre Inocenta her stupid confession. But no, whatever was in the cup wasn't chocolate. The liquid was clear and smelled strongly of plants.

Nena must have been making a face, because Madre Inocenta explained, "I ground up the tooth and boiled it with herbs."

"And you want me to drink it?" Nena asked, horrified.

"You'll do what she asks of you," Sister Benedicta ordered.

"No, she's right, Sister. She deserves an explanation," Madre Inocenta said. "The truth is we've experienced manifestations of La Vista with you that we've never seen with anyone else. You appear to have abilities that none of the rest of us do."

"I don't think so," Nena said, trying to be careful with her words. Sister Benedicta was noticeably angry at what Madre Inocenta was saying.

"I'm telling you it's true. You may have special powers, but you have no understanding of what you're doing or what you're capable of. Looking with La Vista, I'm able to determine that the tooth is but a part of the encanto. There's more of it deep inside you. If it doesn't come out, it may harm you. By drinking this tincture, you'll coax out the rest of the spell. You don't have to be afraid, child. We'll take care of you, no matter what happens. It's safe to use the encantos during the time of the aquelarre."

"What else is in the mixture?" Nena asked, stalling.

"Plants that open up the mind," Madre Inocenta said. For the first time, Nena detected a note of impatience in her voice, and Nena understood that Madre Inocenta was eager to see what was going to happen. Nena was curious, too, but she didn't appreciate being the guinea pig in this experiment. Unfortunately, Nena couldn't think of a way to refuse to drink the liquid, and Sister Benedicta was giving her a glare that said she was looking for an excuse to pinch Nena's nose and tip the brew down her throat.

Nena scanned the faces of the nuns. Sister Paloma and Sister Francisca seemed more afraid than curious. And when Nena looked at Carmela for help, Carmela raised her left eyebrow so high that it disappeared underneath her veil. Whether the gesture communicated that Nena should obey or keep resisting, she couldn't decide. Nena didn't want to be punished, and she surely didn't want Carmela to see it happen to her. That would be worse than the punishment, since everything became more real when experienced with a friend.

Nena tipped the taza into her mouth. It was hot, too hot, and it tasted like chalk but also sweet from the herbs that coated the back of Nena's throat. She tried to swallow the taste down with the liquid, but that only made it worse, like a hundred tiny teeth had lodged in the back of her throat, digging in. Nena coughed. The teeth moved down her gullet. She coughed again. The teeth marched down, and now she couldn't stop coughing, each hack jogging the teeth further down her throat.

Carmela patted her back, but that didn't help. The teeth continued down, chewing through the flesh of her throat, ending their march in her lungs. These teeth, this encanto, took control of her lungs. She drew in a painful, gnawed-up breath. She breathed out, ragged notes emerging from her mouth. She was singing. No. The encanto was singing her. The song was loud, and Nena's breath grew hot, burning her as it left her body. The smoldering mesquite under the copper pot flared up, the flames rising high.

Nena watched the song begin to rearrange the particles of the very air, drawing them into a path, a thread that shimmered under the light of the candles, leading into the pot. A mouse ran past Nena, and then five more. Nena recoiled as they leaped into the pot, squeaking out their deaths.

Something touched Nena's boot. She jumped back, pushing herself up against Carmela, who screamed. A cockroach. No, not one, a column of cockroaches. When they reached the pot, they climbed over the side, clacking their bodies against each other. Salamanders scrambled past, far too many of them, an oil slick on the ground.

Worms oozed up between the tiles, writhing on the floor, and then birds broke through the window, flocks, followed by impossible animals—where were they coming from and how had they climbed the wall?—a raccoon, a tiny deer, rabbits, a trio of javelinas, packrats by the dozen. Nena crouched down, the animals crawling over her, claws and toes and hooves trampling her to get to the pot, the room filling with the tangy odor of fresh meat, the musty stink of boiled fur. As awful as the procession was, there was nothing Nena could do to stop it. The encanto had her in its grip, even as she cowered on the ground, holding her hands up around her head.

As quickly as the encanto had emerged, it left Nena, flying from her throat. She stood up on shaky legs. The animals were gone. The only things left were droppings and the gamey smell of wildness. Madre Inocenta stared at Nena, and Nena feared that she had done something terribly wrong, once again bringing into the world a magic that hurt rather than helped.

The noise of breaking glass and the growls and cries and yips of the animals must have woken up the whole convent. How would they explain the dislodged tiles, pried up by the things of the earth crawling to the pot? How would they explain the paw prints and the smears from oily fur, the claw marks on the walls? What if the townspeople of El Paso del Norte caught wind of this? How could they allow what Nena had done with these witches to go unpunished? Eugenia would go straight to her father with the story, and Nena and all the rest of the aquelarre would be burned, no matter what Carmela had naively said about the church's enlightened new ways of thinking about witchcraft.

Sister Benedicta moved over to Madre Inocenta and placed her arm around her shoulders, though Madre Inocenta seemed not to notice. Sister Francisca and Sister Paloma walked over to the pot hanging over the fire, which had died down to a smolder. Carmela nodded her pale face at Nena in what Nena hoped was forgiveness for the destruction she'd caused, or if not forgiveness, then at least an acknowledgment that Nena had had no idea that the encanto would behave like this.

"I'm sorry," Nena said to Madre Inocenta. "How are we going to clean this up? And how will we explain it?"

"Our sisters have been lulled to a deep sleep by the encanto of the aquelarre. We don't need to worry about them. And as for the mess, well, the encanto isn't yet done. Don't you hear it singing in the pot?"

Nena stopped to listen. The cries of the animals were gone, and what remained was a low hum.

"We must now eat the brebaje you have made," Madre Inocenta said.

"Eat it? That?" Nena asked, sick at the thought of eating that stew of fluttering slithery jumping furry death.

"I understand if you'd rather not be the first to try it," Madre Inocenta said.

"The girl is right for once," Sister Benedicta said. "We should not eat that brebaje. We don't know what will happen. This is not what our aquelarre was meant to do. This is out of anyone's control. Look at the mess she has made."

"God has brought this young lady and this encanto to us," Madre Inocenta said briskly. She reached into the pot and plucked a piece of meat out with her fingers, then dropped it in her mouth, chewing fast. A faraway look came into her eyes.

"What is it? What's happening to you?" Sister Benedicta asked, holding Madre Inocenta by the shoulders.

Madre Inocenta nodded at the pot. "The rest of you may now have your portions." She was giving an order.

Nena watched as Sister Benedicta, Sister Paloma, and Sister Manuela picked out chunks of the awful meat. Once they swallowed, their eyes glazed over, same as Madre Inocenta. Carmela ate her share last, shrugging at Nena before she put it in her mouth, and then she was gone to wherever the others had traveled in their minds, or, more likely, into La Vista.

Nena had to admit that she was curious where they had gone, and at this point, what would it hurt to eat the stew? Nena was already damned, living in a kind of hell that she'd sent herself to. She inched closer to the pot. She was surprised at the aroma of the brebaje. The boiled fur smell was gone, replaced by the rich scent of cinnamon, cumin, oregano, bay leaf, garlic, and onions. In spite of herself, Nena's mouth watered. She stuck her fingers in the pot and pulled out a chunk of unidentifiable meat. Before she could ponder it too much, she closed her eyes and popped it in her mouth. The meat was buttery, the sauce as rich as any she'd ever tasted, better even than Mamá's chile colorado.

Nena let the flavors rest on her tongue. A buzzing started in her ears, an echoing hum that made her feel like she was inside a giant tin can. Nena knew all too well what was about to happen. Remembering what Carmela had taught her in the portería, Nena breathed, letting La Vista fill her. She kept one foot in the river, one foot on the riverbank. She felt herself get hot in her face. Her upper lip sweated, like when she ate very picante chiles. The spicy heat spread all through her body. La Vista had arrived, and she braced herself for the darkness to cover her like a black hood, to wake up dazed and sweaty on the ground, but she stayed standing, even as the buzzing took over, the vibrations making her burn hot, then hotter, until she was so hot she was the sun.

Nena flew out of the sun and into the sky. She saw the whole of the Chihuahuan Desert from above. She had wings and she was hungry, ravenous. She had the eyesight of an eagle. Better. She could spot the thorn on a mesquite branch, miles and miles away on the side of the mountain. Nena spied a mouse far below on the hard desert floor. She dove down, grabbing it with her talons, shoving the mouse down her throat, feeling the thing wiggle. She then became the mouse, overcome by the terror of struggle, and she had nowhere to go, but still she fought, not giving in to her fate. Then she was a flea sucking the blood of the mouse, and she was a creature even smaller that the flea, a flea's flea, and then she was smaller, a germ, no thoughts, just a feeling of life, of living, and then she was Nena sitting up in a chair in Madre Inocenta's office, alive, Nena, but more awake, with a new way to see and hear and smell.

On the edges of her vision, she saw magnetic fields, the paths to the poles. The encanto whispered to her that this was the way that foxes see the world. All the animals she'd eaten told her their secrets, and so did the earth itself, relaying the stories of rocks and rivers. Nena heard the lava in the center of the earth swirling in currents and eddies.

Looking around the room, she understood that light wasn't the opposite of darkness, it was energy in the form of waves—the waves of light like the waves in the ocean, making noise and letting off spray as they crashed into each other.

Nena had sat herself down on the floor. Sister Francisca sat with her back against the wall. She had one finger jammed in her ear, and a line of drool stretched from the corner of her mouth to the tiles. A laughing Carmela rolled back and forth on her back, hugging herself. Sister Paloma lay flat on the tiles, her arms stiff at her side, a crooked smile on her face, and Sister Benedicta was standing, barely, leaning against a table, her eyes white.

This stuff, whatever it was, made you look drunk.

Nena hated when Luna came home after a night of drinking, slamming into the house too loud, too happy. Nena, herself, hadn't tasted alcohol apart from the Communion wine, and that was supposed to be the blood of Christ. Nena hadn't ever been tempted to drink enough of that to make her feel funny, and what she was experiencing now scared her, even as she felt the power of La Vista surging in the smallest parts of her.

Time passed.

Maybe days.

Or years.

Minutes.

Maybe no time at all.

When Nena was finally able to move, she rose to her feet. A soft coolness entered her mouth, an encanto that soothed her throat as she sang, healing the scratches from the coyote's tooth. Nena made her way to Madre Inocenta's desk, floating across the room.

She gazed down to confirm what she already knew, and yes, her feet were indeed an inch off the floor, supported by the waves of light and sound underneath them, the song a kind of raft resting on the waves.

Nena was powerful, like Madre Inocenta had said. The tooth had shown up in her mouth; she'd sung the animals into the pot, and when she ate them, she hadn't fainted. She now knew things that she hadn't known could be known. Like how to fly.

Nena wondered if she could make the nuns fly. She started to sing the soft encanto again, weaving together the waves of sound and light to form another raft, sliding it underneath the brujas. She picked them up, making them hover above the tiles.

Madre Inocenta laughed, her face full of color.

Once she started, Nena couldn't stop singing, or rather the encanto couldn't stop singing through her, but this time the flow was much more pleasant, and Nena floated as she watched the tiles rattling across the floor, fixing themselves back into place. The broken glass from the windows rejoined in the air, melting into panes to refill the casements. The plaster of the walls churned, a thick slurry, swallowing the marks the animals had made with their paws and beaks.

This encanto was a true miracle, healing the destruction the first encanto had caused. Why? And how? Maybe it didn't matter. Nena was bursting with love for these nuns who had rescued her. Maybe God had brought Nena to this place after all.

"Put me down," Sister Benedicta said. "Put me down right now."

Nena lowered the nuns gently, one by one, setting Sister Benedicta down last, savoring the look of fury on her face. Nena would pay for this very temporary pleasure, but the feeling of the soft song was delicious, real power.

"Good girl," Madre Inocenta said when all the nuns were on their feet and together at the big table.

Sister Benedicta then scooped the stew out of the pot and into a clay jar, which she sealed with a layer of fat. Nena couldn't help but notice that Madre Inocenta's eyes glowed with something like greed as she gazed at the jar.

11

When Marta arrives home from the office the next day, she's surprised to find the house buzzing with activity. Jane, the UTEP student who sometimes babysits in the evenings, is sitting at the counter with the boys, who are eating cheese pizza. Alejandro's in a suit and wearing the kind of tie that makes him look like a Wall Street dude, a style that repels and fascinates Marta. In another life, the New York corporate law life, she could have ended up with someone who dressed like that all the time.

"Where have you been?" Alejandro asks.

"At work," Marta says.

"You forgot about the fundraiser, didn't you?"

"No," Marta says.

"Don't you know this is important to me? You always do this, Marta."

"This?" What exactly is she being accused of? Alejandro's anger is way out of proportion, especially since it was only this morning that he asked her the same question, nuzzling her neck as they lay on the cold stone floor of the bathroom together, "where have you been" meaning something completely different, his longing matching Marta's for how they'd once been with each other.

"Just give me a sec, OK?" she says.

In her closet, Marta slips on the dress she wears to these things, a black silk shift that's a little tired-looking, gone baggy in the middle. It's due to be replaced, but Marta hates to shop. "It's just that you're so athletic, cariña," Alejandro's mother said one terrible day when Marta and Alejandro were visiting Alejandro's parents in Miami. The boys were little, two and four. Marta and Dr. Kika Torres were shopping in Bal Harbour, but trying to find clothes that fit Marta at the stores that her mother-in-law favored was impossible. Marta's body, which had been ideal for swimming, strong and long, had softened. No, Marta didn't want to special order anything, she had to say to a mortified shopgirl. The day had ended at a jewelry store, a famous one Marta has since forgotten the name of, where Kika bought her a necklace, a heavy silver panther's head on a chain, diamonds wedged into the cat's squinted eyes. "Goes with everything," Kika said, which had mystified Marta, who was not able to think of a single thing she could wear the necklace with. When she got back to Alejandro's parents' place and closed the door of the guest room behind her, she'd cried in anger, telling Alejandro about her day. "I know what that necklace goes with," he said, kissing her all over her face, down her neck, taking off her clothes.

Now Marta digs through her bra drawer to retrieve the necklace. She pulls out a shawl, a pretty embroidered Mexican one, since the venue—wherever it is—is bound to be overly air-conditioned.

In the mirror above the dresser, Marta examines herself, surprised. Her color has returned, and in the pleasant light of the evening, her skin looks smooth, not like her lines have vanished, but like she's just come in from a swim, glowing. Marta applies a bright red lipstick, bold for her.

"You look nice," Alejandro says when she comes out from the bathroom. He walks over and kisses her on the lips, quick, dry. He cups her butt, giving it a squeeze, and Marta's glad his snippiness has gone. It'll be nice to have an adult evening out with Alejandro. The sex has been fun, but it's not the same as talking.

On the short drive over, Alejandro explains that the host of the evening is the new CEO of one of the big El Paso oil refining companies. The CEO's house is built up against the Franklin Mountains, much like Marta and Alejandro's, except that it's huge, the size of a hotel, each wing a block clad in a shiny white material. From inside, enormous glass windows frame a dizzying view of El Paso and Juárez. In the double-height living room hangs a chandelier of colored glass that looks like it was stolen from an airport. Towering vases hold waxy tropical flowers, violently red and orange. Marta understands that Alejandro has to do this for his job—fundraising is a new part of his appointment as associate dean of the medical school—but she doesn't like to hang out in places like this, owned by people like the CEO. This is who she sues.

Marta is introduced to the CEO, her cheeks are kissed, and then the hospital's fundraising director, Jacqui Silva, marches over. Jacqui's a very good-looking woman, but she's too skinny, and her boobs are obviously fake. She has dramatically long hair, extensions Marta guesses. Jacqui's encased in a taupe dress, the same shade as her nails.

Jacqui's hovering her hand over Alejandro's elbow. She coos, "I'm going to borrow these two for a minute," herding Alejandro and the CEO across the room and into a hallway, leaving Marta alone. She's disappointed that he's already been called to work. In the old days, they would have perched in the corner, and Alejandro would have told her the hospital gossip, pointing out the cardiologist having an affair with the pathologist, the hospital vice president who everyone knew stole Xanax from the ER.

Looking across the room, Marta is grateful to see Roger, the husband of Beth, one of Alejandro's colleagues in the hospital administration, another doctor. Roger's talking to a short, older man with a severely rounded back and iron-gray hair. Unlike every other man at the party, this guy's wearing a cardigan instead of a blazer or suit jacket.

Roger waves Marta over.

"Meet Marta, Dr. Torres's wife," Roger says, as the man turns around to face her, and Marta takes a step back, startled at who is standing in front of her. "You know Mincho? We were just talking about horses. Mincho keeps a string of them at Sunland Park. Races them."

"No, no, wrong. I sold off most of 'em. I'm left with three useless animals who like to give up right near the finish line. Quarter horses, not Arabian if you're thinking that."

Marta wasn't. What Marta's thinking is that Benjamin Soto is talking to her.

"You like horses? I can get you a good price."

"We shouldn't be having a conversation," Marta says.

"Why not?" Roger asks.

"I'm suing Mr. Soto," Marta says to Roger.

"Oh. I didn't recognize you," Soto says, but he's lying. He flits his eyes from her face down her body. Marta feels a surge of anger at his nerve.

"Mincho gives a nice amount of money to the hospital, from what I understand," Roger says.

Soto nods, like he's being modest. He's still looking at her like she's a piece of meat, but he's so little and hunched, she could squash him. She might do just that. "Roger, mind if I talk to Mincho alone?"

"I'll go get a refill," Roger says ambling over to the bar.

"Listen. Stop sending private investigators after my clients."

"What's it called when you talk outside of court, ex parte communication?"

"We're at a social event. No one can hear what I'm saying to you. Settle now, or you'll regret it."

"I'm not settling. Not ever."

"Shame on you. What would your mother say?"

"What?"

"Silvia. That was her name, right? Your mother, Silvia? Her maiden name was Colón?"

Soto takes a step back.

"I remember her working the cash register. She and my grandma Olga were friends from Bowie High School. You must have known Olga. Olga wouldn't have been friends with Silvia if she didn't think Silvia was an honorable person."

"Don't talk about my mother."

"Mincho!" Marta hears Jacqui say, returning to the room with Alejandro in tow.

"Sorry we had to rush away. It's been forever since you and I have caught up!" Jacqui says, though Marta and Jacqui have never spent a second alone together. Jacqui inches closer. Her perfume smells like cotton candy and tobacco. She leans in, looking at Marta's necklace. "Ooh, Cartier."

Soto laughs, nastily, like he's learned something important, which he hasn't. Marta wishes he'd get the hell away. She clutches the panther's head, hiding it in her fist, and she moves closer to Alejandro, pressing her body up against his. He smells of wine.

During dinner, Alejandro and Marta are seated at a table with Jacqui and the CEO and his wife. Soto is at another table. Marta still can't believe he's here. It shouldn't be possible that he can be at a place like this, free and rich and praised for his generosity. Soto's donations clean him up, make him seem legit, even if he's a cruel pervert. It's at parties like this where things get done in El Paso, where people meet and understand that they are of the same tribe. Marta's clients don't have access to this kind of power. All they can do is stick together, stay united in the face of indifference and worse. The law is designed to wear down the powerless until they give up.

"How was your tour of Los Piñones?" Jacqui asks.

"Fine. We joined a line dancing class," Marta says, curious how Jacqui knows about it. "Alejandro told you about us going?"

"Oh, he didn't mention it? That I set it up for you?" Jacqui says, her voice rising at the end of the sentence.

"Thank you for doing that," Marta says, puzzled.

"I'd do anything to make Alejandro's life easier. He has so much on his plate. He's so good at raising money, maybe I should be afraid that he'll take my job! Kidding! We're on a panel together at the hospital fundraising conference next month in San Diego."

"Yes, I'll be going to the conference with him," Marta says, feeling a stab of jealousy. She hadn't planned on going to San Diego until just this moment, but she doesn't like how Jacqui seems to be insinuating there's something between her and Alejandro. Anyhow, it's not a bad idea to go away with Alejandro. They could get up to all sorts of things in a hotel room.

"We'll have to get a drink together when we're there, just us girlies," Jacqui says.

"I'd like that," Marta says. Marta isn't a girlie. She's an adult who hates small talk and empty social arrangements, and she's annoyed that she's barely been able to exchange two words with Alejandro all night. "I don't know what all you know about Benjamin Soto, but I have a bit of advice for you. Don't take any money from him. He's a bad guy. Like really shitty. Harasses women. It's a bad look for the hospital to be involved with him."

"Oh, sweetie," Jacqui says, shaking her head. "You don't get to tell me how to do my job."

"Helpful hint is all," Marta says. "You don't want the bad publicity."

"No, we definitely don't want that," Jacqui says, her eyes narrowed.

At home, when they're in the bedroom undressing, Alejandro is gentle as he reaches behind her neck, unhooking her necklace.

"You hardly ever wear this."

"I don't really go to places fancy enough that it makes sense."

"I should take you out more."

"Yes, that would be nice," Marta says, turning around. "Can I talk to you about work for a second?"

"Now?" Alejandro asks. He leans in and kisses her with more force than usual. Marta pulls away, keeping hold of his arms.

"I think I annoyed Jacqui by telling her that you shouldn't accept any donations from Benjamin Soto."

"How do you know him?"

"I'm suing him. Soto Pecans."

"Right, right. Jacqui seems to think she can land him."

"What I'm saying is don't take the money. It's dirty. He's dirty."

"Any dirtier than oil money?"

"Different dirty," Marta says. "Just tell me you won't take it."

"Look, it's not up to me. I'm a fundraiser in training, but if I want to run the hospital, that'll be a big part of my job. There are numbers I'll have to hit every year, and if the money coming in isn't completely clean, who cares? It'll be doing more good with us than where it is. You know the population the hospital serves."

"What you're saying is you'll do what you need to do to move up the ranks."

"That's not fair."

"I just don't want him to clean himself up with donations. This is going to turn into a fight in the press, and it won't be helpful for him to look like an upstanding guy. This case is going badly as it is. The firm is in terrible shape, and we really need some wins. I know you care about your job, but so do I. It's my life."

"Look, if it means that much to you—"

"It does."

"—I'll talk to the fundraising committee about it, OK?"

"OK."

"Is the firm in that much trouble?"

"It is."

"Can I help?"

"Jacqui seemed to think that you're some kind of fundraising savant. You have any ideas how we can quickly bring in a couple million dollars?" Up until now, the fundraising has been Jerome's thing. But that's not where most of their money comes from. Their supporters buy $50 tickets for the tardeada, a few give five hundred bucks each. Marta lies down on the bed, and Alejandro drops down next to her, tucking his face into her neck.

"So, you want me to ask Benjamin Soto for money for you? Jacqui says he has bags of it."

"Not funny," Marta says, but she's glad that she's convinced Alejandro to tell the hospital to say no to Soto's donation. "I feel like there's so much for us to catch up on. I haven't even told you about my plan to get Jerome to retire."

"Does it involve poison? That guy is a workaholic if I've ever seen one."

"Pot and kettle."

"Guilty as charged," Alejandro says. "But you, too, you know? Being the boss wouldn't make you less busy."

"It's time for me to be the director. I don't have to explain to you why. You understand."

"You want to keep moving. It's boring if the job doesn't become bigger."

"Right."

"We'll hire Jane for more hours if you need help with the boys," Alejandro says, and then, done with the conversation, he folds himself into a tight Z against Marta's body. Within seconds, he's asleep, breathing evenly, a little whistling sound coming out of his nose as he exhales.

Marta's awake, disturbed by Alejandro's attitude. He's supportive to a point, but not in a way that he's going to change his life to help her. This isn't a new thought, that he's self-centered when it has to do with his career. He's always known exactly what he wanted to do, and he hasn't really changed, except that his running has gotten a lot more extreme, his hours longer. Marta sometimes wishes she could feel even a sliver of the certainty Alejandro does.

Marta met Alejandro when he was in his first year of med school, she in her second year of law school, and they've been together ever since, half her life. Her entire adult life. At this point, Alejandro is like a part of her. They've always been people who studied hard. They weren't out partying. Marta liked cramming stuff into her brain, getting good grades. If she could have, she'd have stayed in school for the rest of her life, taking tests until old age, but that wasn't possible, so she applied for jobs, the same positions her classmates applied for, and with the same kind of ambition, to land the shiniest thing.

Marta had called Olga excited and proud to tell her she'd been offered a position at Skadden, Arps in New York. Instead of congratulating her, Olga stayed silent. Finally, she asked, "Is that the best way for you to help other people?" No, clearly it wasn't, but Olga had approved of Marta's other option, and the one she took, clerking for a judge of the First Circuit. "You could end up on the Supreme Court," Olga had said to Marta, pride evident in her voice, and Olga wasn't being completely delusional. Only last month, one of Marta's friends from the *Harvard Law Review*, Kendra Cooper, was nominated for DC Circuit Court of Appeals, one rung below the Supremes.

But Marta's path was disrupted when Alejandro needed to move to El Paso for his residency. The University Medical Center was the only US teaching hospital where the doctors were required to speak Spanish, and it was the only decent hospital on either side of the border for hundreds of miles, many of the patients indigent. Olga was thrilled when Marta moved to El Paso, had approved of Marta's choice to work for legal aid, but over the years she told Marta that she should aim for more, should try to be a federal judge in El Paso. Even when she was in her eighties, Olga could have helped with this. She had spent decades volunteering for the Democratic Party in El Paso. She knew all the people who decided who should run for what office, who should be appointed to what commission or judgeship. Marta put Olga off.

At first, Marta was too young, just learning how to be a real lawyer, learning that though she liked being on the side of the little guy, what she really loved was working her ass off on cases and then winning. That was fun in its way, and not scary in the way that politics seemed. The path to a federal judgeship was not made for women, especially not for Latinas, and as fierce as Marta could be for her clients, she didn't have the same kind of competitiveness for herself. She wasn't that kind of chingona. Anyway, in her late thirties, she was too busy to think about a judgeship, as she tried to balance work and starting a family, going through rounds of IVF for both boys, then being a working mother with a toddler and a baby. By the time she emerged from that dark tunnel only a few years ago, Olga had withdrawn from her political work, and Marta didn't have the energy to pursue a nomination for a federal judgeship. Not that it's too late to try. Marta might be just the right age now.

What an idea, Marta being at the right place, at the right time, not too old, not too young. If she started now, it would take a few years to make this happen, enough time to put the firm on solid ground. Federal judgeship by fifty.

Excited, Marta slips out of bed, pulling on sweatpants and a soft, threadbare shirt. The air-conditioning hisses from the vents as she walks into the kitchen, the floor cold against her feet. Marta pours herself a glass of water. The kitchen is spotless, and she knows it's Nena's doing. Jane never even tidies when she babysits. On the stove sits a pot, still warm to the touch. Marta lifts the lid. Red sauce, made with roasted chiles, ready to use for the chilaquiles Nena said she'd make for Alejandro. Marta dips a spoon in the sauce and slips it into her mouth, the flavor taking her back to the kitchen of Luna's restaurant, La Sirena.

Luna was never interested in the natural, except when it came to the food at the restaurant. Everything had to be made from scratch, originally out of economy, but also because she believed that doing anything else would bring ruin, dishonoring her mother's memory. The recipes Mommie had used when she was a cook were written in the pin-narrow hand of the Victorian era, in a faded blue ink on grayish-yellowed paper. Copies of these recipes were used to teach each new cook. At her house, Luna had the originals framed, hanging in the hall between the altar and the powder room. These are the only family heirlooms to speak of.

Luna was much younger than Marta is now when she had to reinvent herself after her first husband, Beto, was killed in the war. Luna had used the death benefit from the army to open La Sirena. Right after the war, it was hard to find space to rent, but it had been especially hard for Luna, not only because she was a woman, but because she was also a woman who'd never owned a business before. Olga arranged for Luna to meet with an elderly man who lived in the Hotel Cortez. This man owned a significant part of downtown, including a vacant storefront right around the corner from the courthouse and San Jacinto Square, narrow and long, boarded up, and needing a lot of work.

Marta imagines Luna showing up at their meeting wearing a black suit with white gloves, a hat with a veil, surprising the landlord, who hadn't thought that a widow could crack jokes and look so elegant, be so young. Luna paints a picture for him, showing him a busy place where deals would be made at lunchtime over big plates of stewed beef in a rich red sauce, sopped up with soft flour tortillas. Luna hates to cook, but she tells the landlord that she'll make chiles rellenos with the lightest batter, flautas so crisp you could hear them crunch across the room. At the end of their meeting, this older man gives her a lease.

The name, La Sirena, The Mermaid, had to do with one of Luna's favorite jokes—that in El Paso there's plenty of beach, but no ocean. The mural on the back wall was sketched and painted by Luna herself, a mermaid lounging on a rock, a conquistador in a helmet standing at the bow of a longboat, staring at her like he had been enchanted. Marta loved this picture, loved that the mermaid looked like Luna herself, though when Marta asked her if it was her, she said no, no, she painted someone who visited her dreams.

You could talk to Luna in the restaurant, but she was never giving you her whole attention. It made everyone want to be near her, Marta included. One summer during college, Marta worked for a tutoring program during the day and as a waitress at La Sirena at night.

Luna kept one eye on the waitstaff, on the level of beverages in glasses. She noticed if picked-over food sat on a table too long. She didn't like paid checks to linger. Change or the credit card receipt had to be returned as quickly as possible, a few Chiclets placed on the little plastic tray.

La Sirena was never a fancy restaurant, but the waitresses wore black skirts and white shirts, and the waiters wore bow ties. On weekend nights, Fridays and Saturdays, mariachis played. As a waitress, Marta served tables of first dates, often overhearing the couples ask each other where they went to high school, a question often asked in El Paso, the answer communicating information about class and social status in ways that Marta still doesn't understand. She's heard Cristina say that Linda piensa mucho of herself because she went to El Paso High, though they both come from humble backgrounds, and if anything, it's Cristina who looks down on Linda, who until recently was a farmworker.

At La Sirena, Marta remembers serving young moms out with their kids, drinking wine out of thick, old-fashioned short-stemmed glasses, not really paying attention to the baby gnawing on a tortilla, the toddler picking gum off the bottom of the table, making a pile of it on a chair. Luna seated politicians and lawyers in the back room, a cave lined with leather booths. This group tended to tip well, but the good tips barely outweighed the lewd looks, the times men beckoned Marta close. "Hey, little señorita, want to come back to my place?" Or worse, "I bet you like to be in charge, nice strong girl like you." The junkyard dog came in handy with men like this, Marta growling, letting the men know that Luna was her great-aunt. That shut them up.

At the end of Marta's shift, Luna would sometimes pour her a tequila, light a cigarette, and tell stories that Marta was hungry for, stories about the Montoya sisters' childhood, about the chickens, about the Spanish Speaking Club versus the Speak English Only Club, or about the time in high school when Luna wanted to go to a dance even though she had a broken leg. She'd been asked by a guapo boy from a conocido family, and not wanting a broken leg to get in her way, she sawed off her cast. The boy drove her to the country club in Juárez, the dance starting at ten and lasting until dawn, when breakfast was served—coffee, chocolate, scrambled eggs, and pan dulce—eaten quickly before everyone went to five a.m. mass at the cathedral. The next day, Luna went to the hospital and had a new cast put on, having convinced the doctor that the thing had fallen off on its own. Marta suspects the doctor didn't buy Luna's story for a second. He just wanted to be around her for as long as he could.

Men loved Luna, and this was in part why La Sirena became popular. Luna flirted, she cajoled, she spun away when she felt someone getting too close. Luna told Marta cautionary tales, like how when she'd first opened the restaurant, she'd had to be extra careful. There were plenty of nights when she'd had a hand on her bottom, and one time a man had slipped his hand up under her skirt, leaving a note in her panties, his name and telephone number. Luna had made sure that she was never the last one to lock up, that there was always a trustworthy man from the kitchen to walk her to the streetcar. Luna told all of this to Marta laughing, always laughing, like danger could be banished if you only had enough fun.

It isn't more fun that Marta wants, but more hunger satisfied. More of the power she feels from taking what she wants.

"Hoo hoo hoo," Marta says out loud.

She fits the top back on the pot, carries it to the refrigerator, and then moves things around on the second shelf to make room.

A sound comes from the yard, the soft call of an animal.

Marta makes her way toward the sliding glass doors, and she's startled by her own reflection. She hears the sound again, a whine.

She squints, looking through the glass beyond her reflection, her eyes focusing on a figure in the backyard.

A coyote is staring at her, holding something in its mouth. The coyote drops the object, a white bundle, then lopes around the pool and clears the fence in one leap.

Marta slides open the door and steps onto the patio, looking down to see a balled-up sock. She picks it up. It's warm, still wet from the coyote's mouth. Inside the fabric is something hard. Marta pulls it out into the light, and the thing shines white. A tooth.

12

It had been a week since Nena was taken from her home. Her skin crackled with La Vista, frightening her. Though she was glad for her deeper connection to La Vista and her newfound friends, she wished she could send her sisters a message that she was being fed and taken care of, that she hadn't been hurt or killed, and most importantly, that she hadn't intentionally run away. What she wouldn't tell them, even if she could, was that she was now a real bruja, inducted into dark ways. When she ate the brebaje, she'd brimmed with the energy of destruction, drunk on death. The healing song, in turn, had made Nena able to fly, or at least to hover, and it had made her feel wonderful, but there had to be a cost for that.

The thing Nena most feared was that by participating in the ceremony she had bound herself even more firmly to this time. If Nena could leave the convent, there were probably adventures to be had in this time, but figuring out how to leave seemed almost as impossible as getting back to her own time. In this El Paso, she knew no one. She had no money. Sister Benedicta would hunt her down. Nena hated the vicaria for luring her away. Hated her for every cruel thing she'd done since. If Sister Benedicta died tomorrow, Nena would thank God for his kindness.

When Nena went to confession that week, she had many things to admit to, but none for a priest's ears.

"Did you ask Sister Benedicta for more chocolate like I suggested?" Father Iturbe asked.

"No, Father."

"Why not?"

"I'm sorry, Father. I forgot," Nena lied.

"Something's happened. Has Sister Benedicta disciplined you too harshly? I've heard reports from other nuns about how far she goes."

"She hasn't done anything to me," Nena said, dead certain that if she complained, it would get back to Sister Benedicta.

"Strange stories have been shared with me about happenings in the convent. I was hoping you might tell me what you've seen."

"Nothing, Father."

"Some sisters have confided in me that they find it difficult to wake up in the morning, like they've been put under a spell."

"Well, that hasn't happened to me."

"Sister Manuela told me she found a hole cut into her habit. A week later, strings of rotted embroidery thread came out of her when she passed water. And Sister Manuela swore that there was blood on the threshold of the chapel."

"Padre, no, I have no idea where the blood would have come from," Nena said, though she knew of one way. She pictured the animals fighting each other to fit themselves in the pot.

"Women often make up stories, and I don't believe everything I'm told," Father Iturbe said.

"Yes, Father," Nena said, believing it best to agree, even though she started to grow hot, angry, at what he was suggesting.

"The stories may be preposterous, but the sisters are complaining for a real reason. The nun in charge is failing in her duty to keep the sisters in line."

"You mean Sister Benedicta? She's the vicaria. It's her job to be strict."

"Don't disagree with me."

"I'm sorry, Padre," Nena said, making her voice small.

"There, there. Don't cry," he said, even though Nena wasn't crying. She never cried. "I'll take care of her, don't you worry."

"Yes, Father." What was he planning on doing?

"Will you do one thing for me?"

"Yes, Padre?"

"Put your fingers through the grill."

"Pardon?"

"Let me see the tips of your fingers."

Nena did as she was asked, feeling the smooth wooden slats of the grill slide against her fingers. A wetness spread on her fingertips, and at first Nena thought the priest was anointing her with oil, like for a blessing. Then she heard a sucking sound, and felt the nibble of his teeth on the end of her index finger. She snatched her hand back, wiping it on her habit as she jumped back, banging against the wall. She fumbled with the handle of the confessional, wrenching it open, then stumbled out of the box and ran out of the chapel, through the courtyard, and into the kitchen.

The kitchen was loud with the sounds of chopping, the crackling of the fire, the clang of pots in the washbasins, sand scouring copper. Nena felt like her brain was trying to detach its strings from her body.

What had she done to make Father Iturbe act that way? She hadn't meant to do anything. Eugenia was in the corner, peeling potatoes. With each swipe of the knife, she carved off huge chunks of white potato flesh along with the skin. Nena tied on her apron and tried to steady her hands as she started peeling alongside Eugenia.

"Eugenia," Nena whispered urgently. "I have to talk to you about something."

"Please don't tell me I'm peeling the potatoes wrong," Eugenia said, frowning at the pile of mutilated potatoes. "Carmela already scolded me, and I'm doing the best that I can."

"That's not it." Nena lowered her voice. "Has Father Iturbe ever done anything strange to you?"

"What do you mean?" Eugenia asked.

"Has he ever, I don't know, made you do something you didn't think was right for a lady to do?"

Eugenia threw her knife down on the table. "How dare you accuse me of that."

"But I didn't—"

"I knew your family was no good, that you had bad morals. Even thinking a thought like that. Disgusting," Eugenia said, her face red.

"So, he never—"

"No! The only thing Father Iturbe has done is listen to me. I told him that we're so burdened by all the extra chores we don't have time to pray. I shouldn't be treated like a servant. Nor should I have been humiliated like that by Sister Benedicta. She had no right."

"But—" Nena said.

"And I considered what you said before. It's true. She's been punishing me because she doesn't want me to marry Emiliano. I'd like to see her try to stop me. She'll regret treating me this way. Father Iturbe promised me that he would talk to the bishop about how this place is being run."

Nena had never had a friend like Eugenia, a rich girl. Eugenia was smugly certain that she would always get what she wanted. She'd clearly never been told no until she walked into the convent.

Eugenia picked up her knife and resumed peeling. Two bright raspberries of color pulsed on her cheekbones. Maybe it wasn't that she was mad at Nena's suggestion of impropriety, but instead that she was embarrassed.

Other than Father Iturbe, the only men around were the majordomo, a very old man with a wattle, and the market sellers who came to the portería. Father Iturbe was a small man, with tiny hands, nicely formed, greenish hazel eyes. His skin was pale, but the healthy kind of pale, rather than the sallow complexion of the diseased or hungry. His lips were a bit too full, and his head somewhat large for his body. Most people would probably call him handsome, though now the thought of him made Nena sick.

It could be possible that Eugenia liked the priest. He could have done more than lick her fingertips. Eugenia was bored and lonely in the convent, but Nena couldn't bring herself to believe that anyone would be attracted to a worm like Father Iturbe. If Nena's suspicions were correct, Eugenia had to be using Father Iturbe to get back at Sister Benedicta.

Nena had to warn someone that Eugenia was in trouble. Madre Inocenta, unlike Sister Benedicta, wouldn't immediately punish Eugenia. Madre Inocenta would see that the true culprit was Father Iturbe, and that the true danger to the convent came from him.

"I'll bring the abbess's chocolate to her today," Nena said to Carmela, who usually took the tray to Madre Inocenta's office. Carmela nodded her head.

"Want to tell me what's going on?"

"I'll tell you when I come back," Nena said.

In her office, Madre Inocenta was kneeling on the tiles at the foot of the small shrine next to the fireplace. She turned around at the sound of Nena setting the tray down on the desk and gave Nena a look of great warmth. Nena released all of her remaining trepidation. Madre Inocenta rose to her feet, taking the cup from the tray and folding her hands around it.

"Thank you, mija. Would you build up the fire for me?"

Nena set gnarled sticks of mesquite onto the grate above the embers. The fire crackled as the water hissed out of the mesquite. Nena looked for the words to tell Madre Inocenta about Eugenia and the bishop, without revealing what Father Iturbe had done to her. Before she could begin, Madre Inocenta spoke.

"I am beginning to believe that there might be a way to remain in La Vista for longer periods of time."

"Why would you want to do that?" Nena asked.

"Could you sing the flying encanto again?" Madre Inocenta asked.

Nena didn't think that was a good idea.

"You want me to sing it now?" Nena asked.

"Yes."

"Don't we require our sisters for a meeting of the aquelarre?" Nena said.

"Do it, child."

"If I sing the flying song for you, will you help me find the way home?" Nena asked. This was a trade she would make.

Madre Inocenta's eyes went cold. "You've made the brebaje once, and you can do it again. Now, sing the encanto, enough with your stalling."

Madre Inocenta was scaring Nena. Nena touched the silver cross, praying for access to the encanto. She opened her mouth in the hopes that the encanto would fill it with sound.

"What's going on here?" Sister Benedicta asked as she walked into the room.

"I've come to tell Madre Inocenta about Father Iturbe," Nena said, never happier to see Sister Benedicta. Maybe Nena had been wrong about the order of things, and it was Madre Inocenta she really had to fear.

"What about him?"

"He's discovered that we're doing things here, magical things."

"I very much doubt that," Sister Benedicta said.

"Father Iturbe told me that blood had been found on the threshold to the chapel. And Eugenia said that she heard that nuns have been leaving their cells at night. I suspect she told Father Iturbe."

"Why would she do that?"

"I'm afraid they've formed a friendship."

"Friendship? A priest and a niña can't be friends. Say what you mean or say nothing."

Nena blushed. "I think they may have become close."

"I see," Sister Benedicta said.

"She's complained to him about you, Sister Benedicta, and he told her that he was going to see the bishop."

"Did you hear that from Father Iturbe?"

"No, Eugenia did. But you shouldn't punish her, she doesn't know what she's saying, what she's getting involved in—"

Madre Inocenta cut her off with laughter, which confused Nena. What did they know that she didn't?

"Thank you for telling us," Madre Inocenta said to Nena. "Inform Carmela that you will be bringing me my chocolate tomorrow, too."

The instruction earned Nena a poisonous look from Sister Benedicta, but she remained silent. Nena couldn't trust either of these nuns. She was more afraid now than ever.

13

"And you're saying she looked you in the eyes," Nena states, not quite a question.

The sock sits on the kitchen island between them, the tooth next to it, shiny, yellowish.

"She? Yes, the coyote, it looked right at me," Marta says. She's shaking from a mix of anxiety and excitement. She hasn't slept. This morning, she had Alejandro drive the boys to science camp, and now finally she's alone with Nena. She called in sick to work, something she's never done.

"That isn't a coyote's tooth," Nena says.

"What kind of tooth is it?"

"A person's."

"Oh, Nena, that is so gross. Why in the hell would a coyote deliver a human tooth to me in the middle of the night?"

"A long time ago, before any of us were born, I coughed up a coyote's tooth in the convent."

"What?"

"Madre Inocenta mixed it with herbs. When I drank it, I received the encanto we needed to make the brebaje."

"What convent are you talking about?"

"Do you know why women went into convents?" Nena asks.

"No," Marta says, not sure where this conversation is heading. She's not sure about anything, not able to get her head around what happened last night. She's achy and sick-feeling from lack of sleep, but her brain is feverish, alive, trying to make connections.

"Women from poor families couldn't become nuns."

"Sure," Marta says, not wanting to talk about nuns. What she's interested in is how she said *hoo hoo hoo* to herself and then the coyote arrived. She knows the sequence of events, but she can't quite get herself to believe that she was the cause. If she made this happen, what else might she be capable of? Even the question makes her afraid. She doesn't want to call any more wild animals to her. She has her family to keep safe. But she can't help but feel a little excited by the possibilities.

"Families had to pay a dowry so that their daughters could enter a convent. Some convents grew very rich from these dowries, and they invested in ranches and vineyards. The really wealthy ones owned mines. Silver. Tin. Inside the walls of the convent, the women were in charge, but their power came at a high price. Once the women took their vows, they were completely cut off from their families. They lived in the convents the rest of their lives. The only time they left was when their coffins were taken to the graveyard."

"Don't nuns take care of the poor? Teach in parochial schools, that sort of thing?"

"You're right. Today the nuns live completely different lives. I'm talking about the convents from the last part of the Spanish Empire. 1792 to be exact."

"And how would you know about this?"

"I was in a convent in 1792."

"I see," Marta says. She doesn't. "Nena, that's not possible."

"Just because something seems impossible doesn't mean it can't happen."

"That's the exact definition of impossible."

"I was a girl. I was suffering. I called for help, and the witches came. If I hadn't done that, I wouldn't have had Rosa, but I also wouldn't have lost her. Everything that happened was because of my call."

Marta has to be the rational one here. For the world to function, we have to agree on certain things, one being that time works in a certain way. It moves forward, never backward; it passes at a constant speed, even if an hour at the school play is much longer than an hour in the courtroom. But it's not possible to move backward in time. Of this, anyway, Marta is sure.

"What you're describing is magical thinking, believing that what you imagine is manifested in the real world," Marta says.

"Yes, that's what I'm talking about, magical thinking."

"I mean it's a logical fallacy."

"Not true at all," Nena says. "Before I was taken back to that time, I'd been hearing a hum for months. Only when I arrived in the past did I understand that the hum was the singing of the aquelarre, and that the song had been passing through the open door."

"Sorry, I don't know that word. Aquelarre?"

"It's from the Basque language originally. When I got home from El Paso del Norte, I looked it up in the Spanish-English dictionary. It means the witches' sabbath. The aquelarre was the field where the women met with the black goat. The word in English is coven. I joined a coven."

"In 1792," Marta says.

"That's right."

"But if you were in a convent, how in the world were you able to have a baby?"

"I got pregnant outside the convent."

"Did you have Rosa when you were in the mental hospital?" Marta asks.

Nena shakes her head.

"You had her in the eighteenth century? That's what you're telling me?" Marta asks. It's too hard to believe, even if the thing with the coyote and the tooth had happened, which it did.

"Luna and Olga didn't understand either. They were ashamed of me. To them it didn't matter how I became pregnant, only that I was unwed."

"That can't be why they put you in the hospital."

"It wasn't because I was pregnant, but because I told them the truth. I shouldn't have told them anything. Even when I was young, they didn't know what to do with me. They didn't believe that La Vista sent me information. They didn't like that I saw things that no one else did, and they didn't understand that trying not to see or hear took a lot of energy. I wasn't smart in school. I wasn't a cheerleader or on the speech team or in choir because it took all I had to stay where I was, to not be taken away in my mind by La Vista's messages. I had to try to push it all away so I could be like everyone else. But sometimes the voices came through anyway, and I told people what I heard. So when I said I'd had a baby in another time, Luna and Olga saw that as proof of what they'd always suspected, that I was a real loca.

"In the hospital, they gave me injections. I slept all the time. When I woke, they gave me more shots. I wore my nightgown every day because I wasn't allowed to have any other clothes. I was in that hospital so long that nightgown wore itself down to rags, and then it fell off me. When it was gone, I was naked. For weeks. Maybe more. I ate my dinner off a metal tray they put on the floor. I remember it all.

"I know where and when I was when I had Rosa. A mother remembers such things. And I left her there," Nena says, the pride and guilt and hurt in her eyes a challenge to Marta.

Marta takes this all in, and it changes how she sees Nena. As a young person, Nena went through terrible trials. It's cost Nena a great deal to tell Marta this. But even though Nena may be convinced she's telling the truth, that doesn't mean everything she's said is grounded in reality.

Marta has to figure out how Nena's past explains her present, and what this has to do with the tooth, with her.

"What else can you tell me about Rosa? Do you have any documents for her?"

"There's no birth certificate, or anything like that, if that's what you're asking for. I don't know how many times I have to tell you."

"What happened after you gave birth?"

"Sister Benedicta sent me away, and she kept Rosa for herself. She always hated me. She finally had her revenge."

"Benedicta was one of the nuns? That's who you saw with Rosa after the fire?"

"Yes, and Sister Benedicta is why Rosa couldn't come through the wall, she was holding her back. That's why I need your help. The only way to pull her through is to get the encanto for the brebaje. Even then it won't be easy to go through the door. It's nearly impossible to move a body through time and space."

"I would think so," Marta says. "Even if matter and energy are the same thing."

"Where did you hear that?"

"The theory of relativity. Einstein."

"Hmm. He must have been a brujo."

"I don't know about that." Einstein being a witch is a funny thought. "What's brebaje?"

"When I sang the encanto for the brebaje the first time, the animals heard me. They came to their deaths willingly. We ate them and then we possessed their power."

"What did you do with the power?"

"Do? We *were* the power. I understand that now. That's why Madre Inocenta was addicted to eating it. There are no doors when you and La Vista are the same thing, and when there are no doors, you can be everywhere and everything at the same time."

"If you know the secret to bringing Rosa here, why haven't you made the stuff?"

"Because I can't. Not anymore. Not since I was in El Paso del Norte. When you're young, you're blind to what you're capable of. It's only when you're older that you can look back and see how you could have used what you had to make the impossible happen."

"I hear you, Nena, I truly do."

"No, you don't. You still believe in your own limits. Remember, the coyote brought the tooth to you, not me." Nena looks around the kitchen, then back at Marta. She stands up, quick, clapping her hands together. "Let's go to Juárez."

"What? Now?"

"The Cuauhtémoc Market was built on the site of the convent. The encantos of the aquelarre still vibrate underneath it. We'll take the tooth with us, and we'll pray for La Vista to come and show us the path," Nena says. She slips the tooth into a Ziploc snack bag and thrusts it at Marta.

On the bridge to Juárez, Marta peers down at the Rio Grande trickling along its concrete ditch. The air is heavy with diesel exhaust. People walk across the bridge carrying bright blue and red plastic bags, pushing granny carts toward El Paso.

Marta thinks back to when she was a girl, and women from Juárez would knock on Olga's door, looking for work. The women crossed the railway bridges, or they waded through the water of the river, finding a hole in the fence, walking across the highway. They went door to door, asking to do the ironing, to scrub the kitchen floor, to wash the windows. Olga never denied them, and the women would leave the house with food, with bills pressed into their hands as she whispered a quick prayer, dios la bendiga.

The clinic Marta's parents ran in California served migrant workers, people who picked fruits and vegetables, moved irrigation pipes, drove tractors. For them the crossing was way harder, the cost enormous, the journey brutal. It wasn't something to be done often or easily.

In El Paso, the situation was different. It was almost like the border wasn't there, como que no existe, people used to say. Nobody thought anything about driving to Juárez for lunch and back. Marta remembers arriving at the US border on the way back from lunch at the old market. Luna would say "American citizen" to the guards, and they'd wave her through, without even glancing at her driver's license. Things have changed, especially after 9/11, when the checkpoints were fortified, the lines of cars and people grew longer, and passports were scanned by computers only to be scrutinized again by unsmiling ICE agents. It was the drive back home that made the journey to Juárez not worth it for Marta most of the time, though more recently, it's been fear. It hasn't seemed safe or smart to go, even if many other people do it every day.

Today, Marta's calculations have changed. "There is no such thing as safe," Nena said to Marta on the day of the fire. Marta understands better why Nena would think that. She was orphaned as a child, she lost her daughter and then she lost her freedom.

Marta's taking Nena to Juárez because she has the overwhelming sense that if she doesn't, something bad will happen to her own family. What this bad thing is, she doesn't know, but the fear is real, bitter in her mouth. There's no way to use reason to take that fear away. Logic died when the coyote brought the tooth. Marta doesn't know the rules of this new world she's entered. She's not sure Nena does either, but Nena's all she's got by way of a guide.

At the end of the bridge, Marta turns toward the old plaza, making her way to Avenida Benito Juárez, a clean street lined with quartz-embedded sidewalks that glitter under the bright summer sun. The buildings are low, none over two stories tall, almost all of them painted a blinding white, so that the whole street appears lit from the inside. They drive past the old casinos, the jewelry stores, the pharmacies, the Kentucky Bar, where the margarita was supposedly invented, where Marilyn Monroe once bought a round of drinks to celebrate her divorce from Arthur Miller, and where Marta threw up on her shoes one night, when she and her friends from the tutoring program went out.

Even in the heat, people are walking in and out of the stores, making the center of Juárez busy and social in a way that El Paso hardly ever seems to be. It's odd to think that people have been kidnapped right here, shot in the street. At the city's lowest point, those with the money moved north of the border, as far away from the violence of the cartels as possible. Not that violence is the beginning and end of the story of Ciudad Juárez and El Paso. Cristina's family lives on both sides of the border, and for them the crossing is more inconvenience than deterrent. For both individuals and businesses, the border creates opportunity.

Soto Logistics only exists because there's a border, and Soto makes his money because his company knows how to deal with the complicated rules of shipping from Mexico to El Paso. Marta wouldn't at all be surprised if he pays bribes in Mexico, or worse, so that he makes as much money as he can. Soto can afford to hire the best attorney in El Paso, get her case dismissed with a flick of his wrist. This is what money and influence buys, the ability to evade justice.

If Marta had access to the pure power that Nena claims the nuns had, she would use it to get at Soto. She'd cast a spell to make Soto liquidate his companies, divide the money among the women he's hurt.

"Are there spells that can make someone do something?" Marta asks.

"I know what you're asking, mija."

"You do?" Marta asks, surprised.

"You could leave him," Nena says.

"Leave who?"

"Alejandro."

"Nena, why would you say a thing like that?" The last thing Marta wants to do is leave Alejandro, and she doesn't need to cast a love spell on him.

"For too much of life we're asleep. Don't you give me that look. I'm not criticizing. You do good work, helping people. You have a beautiful house. You have two handsome and smart boys. But being comfortable isn't the same as being happy."

"I don't disagree with you there."

"The problem is that no matter what you do, magic always complicates. You try to make one thing go in a certain direction, but the energy goes where it wants. It's like when Señor León went to Señora Beatriz to try to get Daisy to fall in love with him. Señor León ended up dead, with his pants down and his thing out, sprawled out on the floor of his store."

"Where to even start with that!"

"You must understand, Marta. La Vista isn't a tool, it's a force. An energy that enters you and uses you, not the other way around. If you're an artist or a musician, and you accept the energy of La Vista, you can end up with a painting or piece of music. But if you fight the energy, try to push it in another direction, then bad things happen. You start drinking too much, or you hurt yourself in other ways, and all of a sudden, La Vista stops visiting you, poof! You're left with nothing. La Vista is pure energy, not good or bad, not love or hate. It's creation and destruction in both, half-and-halfsy. If you're a volcano in the ocean, then La Vista might make you erupt, throwing lava and ash everywhere, killing people and fish. But even as you're causing destruction, you're also giving birth to a new island. This kind of energy is too wild to be used to control anyone or to change their mind. That I learned the hard way."

"Nena, just to be clear, I wasn't asking about love spells. There's no one I'm interested in. It's Alejandro or nothing for me, and we're good. Better than good. Sorry I asked."

"I'm glad you understand," Nena says, leaning forward, looking out the windshield and narrowing her eyes, scanning the street.

"What are you looking for?" Marta asks.

"The old El Paso del Norte. There are still a few buildings standing from that time."

"What was it like?" Marta asks, curious, even if she still doesn't fully believe Nena traveled in time. A coyote is one thing. There are lots of coyotes in the hills. And La Vista in Nena's definition sounds like nature. Marta believes in the power of nature. Time travel is something else entirely. Marta knows what impossible means, even if Nena doesn't.

"The acequias, you know, irrigation ditches, brought water from the Rio Bravo into town. Trees grew in the courtyards and streets, making the pueblo shady and cool, an oasis in the desert. The de Galvez family had brass candlesticks, a dozen iron pots, platters from China, steel knives from Spain. You probably learned this in school, but there was a law that kept iron things from being made in Mexico or the other Spanish colonies. All iron goods had to be imported directly from Spain."

"I didn't learn anything like that in school. We hardly learned about Mexico, even though California used to be part of Mexico, same as Texas. The victors really do write the history books, don't they?"

"When I came home, I spent time in the library trying to learn and understand where I had been. Families had one pot, maybe a lock for a single chest if they were lucky. Furniture was built without nails. Cloth and thread and needles were hard to find, too. I didn't realize any of that when I was in the convent. It wasn't until I was outside that I learned that some people were so poor that at remote estancias, they would run away when visitors came, embarrassed because they were naked, their only set of clothes worn to dust. When I lived in the convent and in the de Galvez house, I was the richest I've ever been in my entire life, and when I'm back in Ciudad Juárez, I remember all of that. I would have loved to live here for the rest of my life. With Rosa. With her father. That was the life I wanted."

"Oh, Nena. I don't know what to say. That breaks my heart."

"I'm just telling you the truth."

"In the mental hospital, you said your clothes fell apart. You were naked."

"That's right. What are you asking?"

"Nothing," Marta says. But she's disturbed. Here's another story that could be interpreted in more than one way, the rational explanation jerking Marta back to the path of reason. The problem is that path now seems too narrow. "Where should I park?"

"By the cathedral. Let's get something to eat. It helps to have a full stomach when La Vista comes. We'll have burritos upstairs at the Cuauhtémoc Market."

The mere mention of burritos makes Marta's stomach grumble. She skipped breakfast after her sleepless night, and now it's coming on lunchtime. In Juárez, the burritos aren't the massive, overstuffed logs like the ones in San Francisco, they're made with small, soft white tortillas, and the perfect amount of filling, just a few spoonfuls of beans and beef and cheese. She could eat one, wash it down with fizzy water in a glass bottle.

"There. Pull in there," Nena says. "I don't mind walking a few blocks. It's good for me to move my legs."

Marta turns off the car and steps outside. Her skin, chilled from the AC, prickles in the heat. It's like she's being defrosted, warmed to the center of her body. The California of Marta's youth was cold, with cloudy skies, gusts of sea-chilled air. Every time she got off the plane in El Paso, walking onto the jetway, the air-conditioning too weak to combat the heat seeping in through the cracks, Marta felt like she could relax, finally as hot as she longed to be. She has a similar feeling when she crosses to Juárez, the air distinct in a deeply comforting way, the buildings, the colors, the light all Mexican. It's miraculous how total the change is across a border that, like all borders, is an imaginary line.

Nena walks slowly but steadily, Marta at her side, past the Calle Mariscal, where the brothels were in the olden days, and maybe still are—Marta won't be asking anyone—and into the square, crossing behind the cathedral, past the Palacio Municipal.

Marta has already sweated through her clothes when they reach the market. It's a handsome building, if worn, with white stucco walls, arched windows, and a tile roof. Marta and Nena enter through the wide doors, past the stalls. Heaped piles of green medicinal herbs lie on tables, making the narrow passages feel like a hedge maze. The ladies at the stalls sell a variety of products, including aerosol spray cans with baffling names, like "Double Fast Luck" and "Scent of the Black Chicken." A red can features a drawing of a snarling dog, with the words "Arrasa Con Todo" circling the top. "Get Rid of Everything." *How's that supposed to work?* Marta wonders. *Do you spray yourself? Or the things you want to get rid of?*

At the end of the passage, a big stall features Santa Muerte–related items. Saint Death. Not Marta's favorite. The Santa Muerte skeletons hold scythes, shawls draped over their skulls and cascading to their ankle bones, like spooky Virgen de Guadalupes. Many of Marta's clients keep little altars in their houses, and some pray to Santa Muerte. She tries to wrap her head around the impulse to worship death. She thinks about the Santa Muerte prayer card that fell out of Sofia's purse. She pictures Sofia in front of an altar in the yard, sacrificing a chicken to Santa Muerte, sending a curse to punish Marta for supposedly ruining her life.

"Why are you wasting time looking at those?" Nena asks, tugging at Marta's sleeve. "C'mon."

Marta and Nena pass tables piled with marigolds, boxes of loose roots and seed pods, potted plants with delicate green leaves and tiny yellow flowers, candles for love and remembrance, teas, vegetable compounds for the "nervous system," cheap guitars hanging from pegs. Shoved underneath a folding table, Marta spots a cardboard box overflowing with hairy roots, the word "peyote" scrawled in marker on the side. Some stalls sell the piedra blanca that Nena kept piled in the brass bowl in her dining room.

Rarámuri women from the Sierra Madre Occidental sit on stools, dressed in bright skirts and headdresses, as they sell really witchy things: dried skate wings and—Marta notes with alarm—skunk skeletons, their black-and-white tails still attached.

Eye of newt, Marta thinks, gawking at these fantastical items for sale in modern Mexico. A whole market devoted to the occult! In El Paso there are little botánicos in strip malls, but no equivalent of this sprawling and macabre market exists on the American side of the border. That this place is here because the convent occupied the same corner can't be a coincidence. Is that how Nena came up with her story?

Nena has stopped and is in conversation with one of the vendors, a woman with white hair and shockingly blue eyes. Nena holds two bundles of herbs in her hand. She shakes the one in her right hand, and then holds it up to her ear. She does the same thing with the herbs in her left hand. Nena digs out a dollar bill to give to the stall-keeper, and then she hands the herbs to Marta, saying, "It's hard to find these. Let's go upstairs."

Marta stuffs the bundles of creosote and sage in her bag, their leafy scent catching at the back of her throat. As she shifts things around, she glimpses the tooth in its plastic bag. Like it's a magnet, Marta's finger shoots out, touching the tooth through the plastic, stroking it. *Weird, Marta, weird.* She snaps her bag shut.

On the second floor, she follows Nena to a restaurant stall overlooking the square. After they sit down on plastic chairs, the waiter approaches, setting two menus down on the plastic table.

"Dos. Con carne y queso. Y dos Cocas," Nena says.

The food arrives impossibly fast, the waiter already back to the table, holding two plates in one hand, two Coke bottles between the fingers of the other.

"Eat," Nena says, attacking her burrito with neat little bites, and before Marta's had the chance to swallow a single mouthful, Nena has finished with hers, licking the juice from her fingers. Marta's hunger from earlier is gone, replaced with a suspicion that if she tried to eat, she'd immediately hurl. What's going on?

Marta looks down at her plate, where the grease from the beef and the cheese has started to congeal. The burrito quivers, and the meat makes a noise, not mooing exactly, but giving her the picture of a cow in her mind's eye. The humming image spreads, and Marta feels something—La Vista?—gently touching every part of her body from the inside, pulling her senses out the window and on down to the street. She hears the vendors calling out, she hears the honking of horns, she smells elote cooking on charcoal. She's pulled thin, a taffy of sensation, stretched so tight that she feels she might snap. She hears the whinny of a horse, she smells raw sewage and burning mesquite, she shivers in the crisp air of winter. How is it possible that she's cold? Marta sees buildings of raw adobe, yellow-brown, not plastered or painted, a city of mud bricks. She hears a man laughing, a baby crying.

Marta watches as Nena tips her bottle into her mouth, swallowing the rest of her Coke, then claps the bottle down on the table. She burps. Or rather, the ninety-something-year-old Nena burps. At the same time, Marta is peering at a young woman with black hair and dark eyes, her skin unlined, her lips full. Her nose is too big, her cheekbones prominent, and her face has an asymmetry distinct from the soft prettiness of Olga's or the sophisticated sharpness of Luna's. She looks dangerous in the way that only the very young can, unaware of what they can do to themselves and to others.

Marta holds on to the arms of her chair.

"I'm feeling funny, Nena. Worse than funny. I'm seeing old adobe buildings."

Nena leans in. "You are? What else?"

"Am I going to faint?"

"Not if you eat the burrito."

"I can't."

"You have to."

Marta forces herself to take a bite, and she comes back into her body, slopping into it, aware that it's a bag of flesh and bones. She takes another bite of her burrito, trying not to choke. When she swallows, her vision clears. Her butt is on the plastic chair, her feet on the ground. She's herself again, but barely.

"What the hell was that?"

"Vibrations."

"Of what?"

"Different times. I wish there was a different word. Vibrations sounds so woo-woo, so New Age, como I'm a woman who wears crystals."

"I thought you liked crystals?"

"Yes, but only because they're pretty. I don't use them in my work. The better word is singing. Everything sings. The water in that cup, the ring on your hand, the paving stones in the square. Rocks have a very slow heartbeat, so it's a lot harder to hear their songs. The singing has gone on forever and will never end, and if La Vista lets you, you can hear the echoes of the vibrations from the past and the future, though they can't tell you everything," Nena says.

Either Marta's gone insane, or what's happened is as Nena said—La Vista has allowed her to hear the vibrations of other times. Marta longed for something like this as a child, and then she forgot that longing, buried it under the day-to-day of work and family. Marta may not have been asleep, but she wasn't fully awake either. "Is this what you expected would happen by coming here?"

"I have something to confess to you."

"Go ahead."

"I want to see my daughter again."

"Yes, Nena, I know that."

"I mean that I would do anything to see her."

"Of course you would."

"I'm sorry I brought you. I don't want to hurt you. You're as important as Rosa is."

"I'm confused, what's changed? I really do want to help however I can," Marta says, which is true, and true in a new way. Nena has been proven right, and Marta wants to see what else La Vista can show her. It was an odd feeling to be outside of her body like that, but strange as it was, she wouldn't mind doing it again. Maybe more than that. She needs to do that again.

"If you saw the real power of La Vista, the millions of eyes and the feathers and fur and teeth of it, you'd be very afraid. You'd understand what I'm saying. I want you to listen to me very carefully."

"I'm listening. I've been listening."

"I would sell you to the devil to see Rosa again."

"Nena!"

"I'm being very serious. I don't like it. I've been too hasty again. I wanted to fix something that can't be fixed, and now I'm afraid that I've made things worse for you. I should have been happy with what's here and what's to come."

"To me it seems like we've crossed more than one bridge today. If La Vista is so dangerous that it should be avoided, well, it's too late. La Vista has found me, and now there's no hiding."

"Yes," Nena says, shaking her head. "Yes, I saw La Vista on your face. You're right. I wanted to give you a chance to back out, but I waited too long. God help us and protect us. I need to be there for you and your family."

"You know I like to make plans, but I'm working in the dark here. I need you to tell me what happens next."

"Let me think," Nena says, reaching for Marta's Coke. She takes a generous swig, then thunks the bottle back down on the table. "Get the tooth out of your purse."

Marta digs into her bag and finds the Ziploc.

"Hold it in your hand."

Marta doesn't like to touch the thing, light and smooth, with a line of yellow plaque along the top edges.

"Tell me if you see anything."

"I see a tooth," Marta says.

"Don't be smart. What else do you see?"

"Nothing, Nena, I really—"

And then Marta's snatched away again. She's in the desert under dark skies, rain clouds above, a strong wind moving across the mesa, making the bushes shiver. Lightning flashes down in yellow zigzags, like in a child's drawing. Rain falls in sheets. There's grit in Marta's eyes, sand and salt on her tongue. The rain falls harder, pushing her out of the desert, and back to the market.

When Marta looks down at her hand, the tooth is gone.

"Where did it go, Nena?" she says, bending down to look under the table.

"La Vista came to me again, and strong," Nena says in an excited voice. "What did you see?"

"The desert."

"And rain?"

"Yes, it looked funny. Cartoony. Flat."

"That was Tlaloc. The rain god. One of the pictographs at the Hueco Tanks. We'll go there."

"And?" Marta asks. "What'll happen there?"

"Rosa will come to us."

"You want to go now?"

"Right now."

Marta's phone pings. She takes it out of her pocket to see a message from the science camp. Today was only a half-day session, and Marta's late to pick up the boys.

14

Sister Manuela, the nun who claimed that her tongue had turned to silver, was now in the infirmary. Nena arranged on a tray a small tureen of broth and a basket of bolillos, the little rolls that the nuns ate mountains of every day. Sister Benedicta had assigned Nena this job, forbidding her from ever bringing Madre Inocenta's afternoon chocolate to her. Nena had been relieved to receive this alternate assignment, not wanting to be forced to sing the encanto again or to see Madre Inocenta's eyes turn cold and greedy.

Nena set down the tray on the little table next to Sister Manuela's narrow bed. Sister Manuela struggled to sit up. She coughed, grabbing on to Nena's arm to brace herself as the coughs racked her body. Spittle landed onto Nena's cheek. She wiped it off with the napkin.

"I have some nice soup for you, Sister," Nena said, trying to disguise the revulsion in her voice. She wanted to flee the room, but she couldn't leave until Sister Manuela ate something. Nena picked up a spoon, dipping it into the broth. "Open up."

Sister Manuela pulled her hand out from under her blanket, extending her pointer finger at Nena, the tip wobbling.

"The day of the Lord will come like a thief in the night," Sister Manuela said.

"Yes, Sister," Nena said. She was pretty sure this came from the Bible, though from which part, she couldn't guess.

"While people are saying peace and safety, destruction will come on them suddenly as labor pains on a pregnant woman and they will not escape," Sister Manuela shouted.

She reminded Nena of the man with the dirty beard who stood in front of the train station and preached about the end of the world. Manuela's stories about the silver tongue and peeing string made a lot more sense now that Nena understood that she was a loca.

"Maybe you could try a few spoonfuls?" Nena asked. "You have to keep your strength up so that you can get better."

"I'm not hungry."

"I have to stay here until you've had your supper," Nena said. Her impatience was growing.

"Do you know why I don't have an appetite?"

"No," Nena said.

"I'm afflicted with the pox."

"How do you know?"

"If you're not hungry, you have la viruela. Everyone knows that," Sister Manuela said. But in the next moment, she relented, allowing Nena to feed her a bit of broth, and she ate a whole roll on her own. When she was done eating, Manuela slid down in the bed, resting her sweaty head on her small pillow and closing her eyes.

Nena pressed her palm to Sister Manuela's forehead. The nun burned. Could it be smallpox that she was sick with? There were people in Nena's own time who had the scars, a testament to the ravages of the disease. It might be that Sister Manuela was caught up in another of her deranged stories. But if she was telling the truth, it would be better to let someone know, just in case. Having learned her lesson, Nena went in search of Sister Benedicta instead of Madre Inocenta, Sister Benedicta now seeming to be the lesser of two evils.

Sister Benedicta wasn't in her office, and she wasn't in the kitchen or the storeroom, the portería, the chapel, or the dining room. Nena searched the courtyard and the servants' quarters, but she couldn't find her there either. She went to Sister Benedicta's cell and tapped on the door. Nena heard faint voices, and thinking she heard someone say "come in," she opened the door.

Sister Benedicta and Madre Inocenta sat close to each other on the narrow bed, their veils off. Madre Inocenta's head was covered in fuzzy short hair, like her scalp had recently been shaved. Sister Benedicta's black hair flowed down to her waist. The jar of brebaje nestled in her lap, she was wiping Madre Inocenta's lips with a cloth. Madre Inocenta turned her watery blue eyes on Nena, not looking at her, but through her, and Nena felt the cold indifference of the other side. Nena sucked in her breath, frozen in place by fear.

Sister Benedicta glared at Nena with a gaze of pure hatred. "Leave," she said, pushing Nena out of her cell with her hot breath.

Nena ran out of the room, back to the kitchen. She found Eugenia humming as she polished a copper pot with a paste of cream of tartar and vinegar, which surprised Nena. She'd never seen Eugenia enjoy herself while working.

"When I'm married, I'll never again step foot in a kitchen," Eugenia said, inspecting her reflection in the big kettle, the copper now brilliant. And then she coughed, covering her mouth with a handkerchief edged in lace. Cough, cough. Not one to get colds, Nena felt smugly superior to Eugenia, too delicate.

As she worked, Nena turned over in her mind what she had walked in on, what Madre Inocenta and Sister Benedicta had been doing. Is this what Eugenia had hinted at before? So what if the women had a special friendship? Nena couldn't care less. What worried her was that Madre Inocenta was eating the brebaje outside the protection of the aquelarre, and she seemed serious about finding a way to live in La Vista all the time, willing to use anybody to make that happen. Nena couldn't imagine living in the place that the brebaje had taken her, the way she'd jumped from one creature to another, her selfhood snatched away. But for whatever reason, Madre Inocenta liked it, or worse, needed it. Nena fretted. She'd brought the brebaje into the world and was certain that Sister Benedicta would make her pay a price for Madre Inocenta's desire.

The first pocks appeared on Sister Manuela's face the next day, raised bumps covering her right side, erupting all over her eyelids, her cheeks, and down her neck. The morning after, the niña Leonor fell sick, and by the afternoon, Sister Carlota nursed a cough. The next morning, Eugenia couldn't get out of bed.

The news raced around the convent that Father Iturbe had been the first to catch the sickness. No one blamed him out loud. But he was the only outsider allowed past the turnstiles of the portería. He sat across from the sisters in the confessional. He'd taken the confession of Sister Manuela, the first resident of the convent to catch the disease.

On Friday, Nena helped Carmela sew up Sister Manuela in a shroud. The man who brought the convent firewood carried her body out, and she was buried outside of town in a grave full of lye, along with all the pox-filled corpses from the city.

Three days later, Eugenia somehow was still alive, but so ill that she didn't recognize Nena when she tried to feed her. Eugenia had a rash all over her face, big pustules, so fat they looked to be on the verge of exploding. If Eugenia were to recover, she'd be scarred for the rest of her life. If this was some sort of punishment for Eugenia's vanity, Nena considered it overly cruel. Sister Benedicta's brother probably wouldn't marry a disfigured woman. Nena felt sorry for Eugenia, for her plans to have gone so wrong. Father Iturbe would no longer be able to depose Sister Benedicta, as he was now dead along with all the others.

Every night Nena went to sleep worrying that she would wake in the morning with a cough. If she lost her life in this time, she'd be covered in lye and buried in a grave, and her sisters would never know.

The next day, a maid summoned Nena to Sister Benedicta's office, a small closet off the chapel stacked with the red leather-bound ledgers she used to keep track of the convent's accounts. Nena was puzzled why she claimed such a room for herself, its dusty closeness at odds with Madre Inocenta's spacious and cool room. When Nena came in, she found Sister Benedicta making notations in the ledger. She scattered sand over the page to dry the ink, and then she looked up at Nena.

"I need you to do something for me," Sister Benedicta said.

"Yes," Nena said, though she was apprehensive about what this thing might be. She had yet to be disciplined for walking in on Sister Benedicta and Madre Inocenta.

"My brother is gravely ill. You will travel to my father's house and take care of him."

"Outside of the convent?" Nena asked.

"You will give him the brebaje."

"What? Why?"

"You haven't noticed? None of us who've eaten it have fallen ill. The aquelarre has been untouched."

"Yes, but how do you know that it's the brebaje that protected us? Maybe we've been spared so far because we're brujas."

"I've warned you not to say that word," Sister Benedicta hissed. "And I understand these matters better than you. I can see what gives strength to the brebaje, the life inside of it. Give my brother a taste. He's the last of the de Galvez line, and I won't let our name die out. After he eats it, sing your flying song over him."

"If the brebaje can heal the sick, then why haven't we fed it to Eugenia or Leonor? Why did you let Sister Manuela die?"

"We can't have miracles in the convent. They would bring us more unwanted attention from the bishop."

"More?"

"Father Iturbe managed to take his complaints to the bishop before he died. I didn't believe he would be so bold or so stupid."

Nena was afraid to ask the question, but she couldn't help herself. "Is that why the pox has spread through the convent? Did you bring it upon us so that Father Iturbe couldn't get rid of you?"

Sister Benedicta stared at Nena for a long time without uttering a word. Nena dug her fingernail into her thumb to keep from filling the silence.

"That would be a very evil thing, child. Do you think me capable of that?"

"No, I don't," Nena said, somewhat reassured.

"That's right. But you must know something. If I could have committed such an act, I would have. Other than my brother, there is nothing more important to me on this earthly plane than this convent. Nothing more important than protecting people like us. Your presence here threatens us all. That is why once you've completed your task and healed my brother, you shall stay in the house of my father until he finds you a husband."

"A husband?" Nena exclaimed.

"It is for the best, for all of our safety, that you leave the aquelarre."

"What do you mean?" Nena asked, panicking at the thought of being thrown out.

"If you hadn't sung that encanto into being, my brother would be as good as dead. But at what cost? As long as you're within these walls,

Madre Inocenta will use you to make more of the brebaje. Madre Inocenta has eaten enough. We all have had our fill."

"Please don't send me away," Nena begged.

"You're leaving us for the good of Madre Inocenta and for the good of the convent. For our souls," Sister Benedicta said, and Nena was surprised to see that for the first time Sister Benedicta looked scared.

"What about what's good for me?"

"You'll depart tomorrow at dawn. María will accompany you," Sister Benedicta said, pressing a small jar into Nena's trembling hands.

15

I'm barfy," Pablo says.

"I'm hungry," Rafa says.

They're crammed into the little car, Marta, the boys, Nena, driving to the Hueco Tanks. Marta would have preferred to go alone with Nena, but Jane couldn't babysit and Alejandro said he was doing rounds at the hospital. Marta scooped up the boys, turned off her phone so no one at work could reach her, and now she's driving fast, pushing the car hard.

"We'll have a snack as soon as we get there," Marta says.

"How long will that be?"

"About another half an hour."

"That's forever!"

Marta has some sympathy for him. She remembers how vast El Paso seemed when she was young, every drive a journey of months. Marta's parents' cars never had air-conditioning, never had windows that opened with a button, and they mostly visited in the summers, which were vile with heat, the smokestacks of the ASARCO copper smelter towering over the highway, the flames of the refining plant flares constantly burning, licking the sky.

The sky is very blue, the earth yellow, the hills studded with dark patches of creosote bushes and mesquite. Along the highway, tumbleweeds grow, but there's a different quality to the familiar plants, to the blue of the sky, and the circle of the sun, its edges liquid, sky melting into land.

Not wanting Nena to worry, Marta hasn't told her that since that morning's vision in Juárez, the hum she's been hearing has intensified, its vibrations running along her jaw, buzzing in her back teeth. It's distracting, but so far manageable, except that it's making her irritable. The road shimmers, a long, thin snake slithering away. Marta really needs to eat something.

"Nena, can you get the oranges out of the bag and peel one for us?" Marta asks. She needs to eat, that's what Nena had said in Juárez, that food helps with La Vista.

"I want an Oreo," Rafa says.

"We didn't bring any."

"Or chips."

Marta recognizes Rafa's tone, stubborn, and what it means, that he's willing to ruin the day just because he can. Marta's only hope is to distract him. Otherwise, he'll have a meltdown, and Marta and Nena won't be able to step away alone.

"Do you boys know the story of how the Kiowa ended up trapped at the Hueco Tanks?" Marta asks.

"It sounds boring," Rafa says.

"I don't have to tell it."

Nena hands Marta a section of orange. It's the most delicious thing Marta has ever tasted.

"Don't listen to him. I want you to tell the story," Pablo says.

"One day, a band of Kiowa came down from the north to raid El Paso, but before they could reach the town, they were ambushed by the Tigua," Marta says.

"What's a Tigua?" Pablo asks.

"Pueblo Indians. Do you remember when we went to the museum on the reservation?"

"There was a casino, too."

"That's right," Marta says, not pleased that this is what Pablo recalls. "At the Hueco Tanks there are drawings that commemorate what happened, and we can see them when we get there. Old pictographs from way back then. Do you know what a pictograph is?"

"Were people killed?" Rafa asks.

"Some."

"But how many people exactly?"

"So you do want to hear the story? I don't have to tell it if you think it's going to be too boring."

"No, no, no. How many people died?"

"When the Tigua scouts saw the Kiowa raiding band coming, they sent runners back to the pueblo. The women and children and old people in the pueblo got ready for the attack, stocking up on food and water, pulling the ladders to the entrances up on the sides of the buildings. Then the Tigua warriors loaded their rifles and rode out through the desert. They circled around behind the Kiowa, and then they attacked, yelling war cries and shooting. The Kiowa galloped away, racing to the north, and the Tigua chased them through the desert. But before the Tigua could catch them on the open plain, the Kiowa found a cave to hide in at the Hueco Tanks."

Nena hands Marta another orange section. She passes the rest of the orange to the back seat, and then she starts peeling another. The car is thick with the smell of orange zest.

"Why is the place called the Hueco Tanks?" Pablo asks.

"Hueco means hollow. The stone formations have lots of holes in them so that they look like giant sponges underground. Freshwater springs feed into these holes, so that there's water when the rest of the desert all around is dry."

"You mean it's an oasis," Pablo says.

"That's the exact right word. All sorts of animals come through, and over the last thousands of years, lots of people have stopped by, too."

"Why aren't you telling the story about the Indians?" Rafa asks. "What weapons did they have?"

"When the Kiowa were running away from the Tigua, they would have known that the Hueco Tanks were a place they could hide, where there would be water to drink and animals to hunt or trap. Theirs was a good plan, except that the Tigua knew where they were going, and they surrounded the cave. The only way into the cave was down a very steep shaft. The Tigua couldn't go down, and the Kiowa couldn't come up."

"OK, but if the Kiowa were down in a cave, they wouldn't have anything to eat or drink, they could be killed that way, too, of starvation or thirst," Rafa says.

"You're right, that was the problem. They didn't have any food except what they brought with them."

"So what happened?"

"The Tigua shouted down the shaft, saying they wanted to help the Kiowa, and that they were going to throw down food for them. They told them to come close so that they could catch the bag."

"What kind of food did they throw down?"

"Not food. Rattlesnakes. Live ones."

"Did the Kiowa get bit?" Pablo says.

"I don't know about that, but the Tigua had another idea to make the Kiowa leave the cave. They set fire to bundles of chiles and threw the burning peppers down into the cave to smoke them out. Can you imagine how that chile smoke would hurt your eyes and your skin?"

"Did they die?"

"Under the cover of the smoke, one of the Kiowa was able to sneak out, and he headed north for help."

"And what happened to the ones in the cave?"

Marta looks in the rearview mirror, seeing that both boys are worried. From what she remembers of the story, terrible injuries and grisly deaths befell most of the Kiowa. "The rest of the Kiowa found another way out, and they got home just fine," Marta says quickly, still looking at the rearview mirror.

"We're going to see the place where this happened?"

"Yes. And we'll see the pictograph, the painting on rock that someone did to keep the story alive," Marta says. "I brought paper and colored pencils so you can draw your own pictographs."

"Why did the Kiowa want to attack El Paso?" Pablo asks, sounding worried.

"The Tigua were farmers. Other tribes, like the Apaches and Kiowa, were hunters and warriors. I guess for them, they thought it was easier to steal horses than to hunt."

"But who were the good guys and who were the bad guys?"

"I think in this case it depends on which tribe you were born into. But I've always identified with the fighters," Marta says.

"I would have thought you'd be on the side of the underdogs," Nena says. "Papá told me another version of the story. He said that it was the Mexican militia, not the Tigua, who ambushed the Kiowa. One of our relatives could have been there, chicos."

"Maybe, Nena, but here's the funny thing. This story was passed down through both the tribes. The Kiowa had their version, and the Tigua had theirs. The Kiowa thought it was the Mexican militia they were fighting, and it wasn't until they met with the Tigua kind of recently and compared notes that they realized they'd both been telling the same story."

"Papá's grandpa could have been there. It didn't happen all that long ago if you think about it," Nena says. Marta has always thought of the story as being from the far distant past, untouchable, but Nena's right. The past lingers, woodsmoke and the whinny of horses, the vibrations of centuries of life humming through Marta's body and Nena's. The closer they get to the Hueco Tanks, the louder the hum seems to grow. Marta blinks. She hopes she's OK to keep on driving. She focuses her attention on the road, gripping the steering wheel.

A roadrunner stands on the white line separating the lanes, just like in the cartoon.

"Look, boys," Marta says, pointing as the bird takes off at a sprint, long-legging it down the shoulder of the road.

"Where's the coyote?" Pablo asks.

Good question, Marta thinks.

"The only other time I've been to the Hueco Tanks was when Olga kissed Beto," Nena says.

"Olga kissed who?" Pablo asks.

"Beto. When he was still Luna's boyfriend," Nena says.

"Nana Olga did that?" Rafa asks.

"Is that even allowed?" Pablo asks.

"That doesn't seem like her," Marta says.

"People do unexpected things when they're young," Nena says. "And everyone seems young to somebody my age."

Marta pulls into the parking lot by the old ranch house, the wheels of the car crunching in the pebbly dirt. The boys leap out of the car and start running up the path that leads to the head of the trail to the pictographs. They can't really get lost, but Marta frets, thinking about rattlesnakes, the kind of cactuses with barbed spines.

"Wait for me!" she yells, opening the trunk to pull out the backpack she loaded up with snacks and drinks, big camping bottles of water.

The monsoon rains of the summer have made the desert plants go bonkers. The nopales and saguaros, and even the little cactuses that look like giant pincushions seem plump, bristling with healthy needles. The bunchgrass, creosote, yucca, and lechuguilla are lush, too, tinged with green growth, and the air is thick with the herby smell of the plants, so thick that Marta suspects La Vista has enhanced her sense of smell, making it sensitive enough that she can smell the water of the pools.

At the end of the path, the boys are standing very still, close to each other, staring at something.

"What's up, boys?" Marta asks.

"I want to do that," Rafa says. He points at a group of teenagers climbing up a rock face. Big black oversized mattress-type cushions are arranged below. Marta speculates that the pads are there so that if someone falls, they have something soft to land on. But as thick as they are, the pads seem inadequate, too easy to miss. Marta pictures snapped ankles, broken backs, trips to the emergency room, the images oily in her mind, like she's seeing something that's already happened.

"Can we have our snack now?" Pablo asks.

"That's a good idea," Nena says. "The sun isn't in the right position to see Tlaloc. We can eat while we wait."

Out of the backpack, Marta pulls out a bag of pretzels, pickles in a jar, M&Ms, and little hard plums, whatever she could find when she ransacked the kitchen on the way out the door. She sets everything out on top of one of the picnic tables by the campsites.

Rafa begins a conversation with Nena about basketball players, and she actually seems to know what he's talking about, while Pablo takes miniscule bites out of a plum until long after Marta has cleaned up the rest of the food.

"When are you going to finish?" Rafa whines. "You're always so slow."

Marta hunts around for something to distract Rafa. "You want to see some shrimp?"

"What shrimp?" Pablo asks.

"The ones in the pools over there."

"Shrimp live in the ocean," Rafa says.

"Are you sure? Come with me."

Marta leads the boys up a path cut into a huge rock. At the top is a black pool partly covered by the overhang of another giant boulder so that half of the pool reflects the sky, and the other side is inky dark. Marta kneels down, pointing. The boys mimic her, and Nena bends at the waist. Marta stares into the water. Nothing, nothing, and then little silvery flashes, there, and there.

"I can't see anything," Pablo says, panic in his voice.

"I see millions of them," Rafa says, but Marta can tell he's only saying this to annoy his brother.

"Oh, they're tiny!" Pablo says, delighted by what he can finally make out.

Rafa kicks a rock into the pool. "Are we going to look at the drawing of the Kiowa?"

"Yes. And then you and Pablo are going to come back to the picnic table and draw."

"What are you going to do?"

"Nena and I are going to—" Marta reaches for something especially dull. "We're going to pray the rosary for Nana Olga."

"What's that? What's a rosary?" Rafa asks.

"Ay, Marta," Nena says. "How could these boys not know what a rosary is?"

"It's not far to the pictographs," Marta says. They walk up the path. Nena walks slowly, looking where she puts her feet. They stop under an outcropping, where Marta points out the signatures from 1849, of people heading out to California. Farther up the hill, they look at a pictograph of a stylized sun, inside of which is a rectangle with an arrow pointing north to where the Tigua were originally from, near Albuquerque. This one Pablo stares at, while Nena gazes at Pablo, the sharp look in her eye.

"If we keep going around that corner, we'll see the big pictograph of the battle between the Kiowa and the Tigua," Marta says, looking at the map on her phone.

The boys spend a long time inspecting the drawing, which has a few parts. There's a warrior, and a snake, and a man with a skinny waist.

Nena pulls at Marta's elbow. "The sun should be in the right position now for the Tlaloc."

"The drawing supplies are in here. Sit at a picnic table and wait for us," Marta says to Rafa, handing him her backpack. He slings it over his shoulders, tightening one strap and then the other, his care and precision reminding her of Alejandro.

"C'mon," Nena says to Marta.

"You're going to stay at the picnic table, right?" Marta asks Rafa.

"Don't worry, I won't let him go anywhere," Rafa says, taking Pablo by the hand. Marta watches them until they go around the bend of the path.

"We're going up there," Nena says, pointing at a path.

"How do you know where to go?"

Nena frowns at her. "I don't have to remember. You can hear it, can't you?"

Marta listens. "That hum?"

"That. Yes. The louder it gets, the closer we are to where we need to go."

Nena's right. The hum does grow louder. "I smell La Vista, too. Ozone. Fresh rain, like in the vision at the market," Marta says.

At the top of the trail, they turn down into a little ravine, moving out of the sun, a relief.

"Here, this is Tlaloc," Nena says, patting the pictograph, like she's introducing Marta to a friend. Marta sees why Nena wanted to wait. In the sun, the drawing would have been almost invisible, too faint to see, but in the shade, it glows.

"Touch it," Nena says.

It seems wrong to put her hand on the thing, potentially harming a historical artifact that's thousands of years old, but Marta rests her palm on the drawing, yellow pigment on gray rock still warm from the sun.

"Now sing."

"Sing what?"

"Didn't you say you can hear the hum?"

"Yes, but it's not a song."

"Not until you sing it."

Marta makes awkward and ugly humming noises, trying to match the drone she's been hearing. Nena joins in, and Marta's surprised when the drone starts to separate itself out into a kind of melody. The song is made up of vowels, long notes that jump up and down the scale, ah, ooh, oh, ha, hum hum hum. Marta and Nena's voices meld into each other, clicking in sync, their voices bouncing off the rocks, the song changing the texture of the air, and Marta feels her mind starting to touch Nena's. She senses Nena's fierce determination, a focus like Marta has never before experienced. Marta is not a noun but a verb, bubbling with creative force.

"That's my girl," Nena says, when they stop singing.

"What did I do?"

"You've brought the song of the aquelarre back to me."

"What does that mean?"

"In the convent we sang the song twice, the first time to open the meeting of the aquelarre, and the second to close it. In between, we were allowed to use the encantos in the room. But we don't have those rules here. We can leave the door open, and we will receive the encanto for the brebaje when La Vista is ready. That's how you catch an encanto, you open up the door and then you wait for it to come to you."

"Wait." Marta turns to Nena. "How long?"

"Soon."

"But I thought we were going to see Rosa here."

"I've told you, La Vista takes its own time."

"Will I keep on hearing the hum?"

"Maybe. La Vista is in you now," Nena says, a strange, pained look on her face that Marta can't place.

"Until when?" Marta asks.

"Until it releases you," Nena says simply, and Marta can tell that Nena really doesn't know, that she's not just hiding something from Marta. She felt so close to Nena when they were singing, intimate in a way that brought Marta closer to herself, the part that lies underneath everything she's layered on top. That part of her still hums; the door inside Marta is opened to La Vista, she knows this now for sure. Nena said that La Vista was power, the raw stuff, relentless nature, and that's what Marta senses. If what Nena says is true, then the closing song of the aquelarre can't be sung until the encanto appears. Until that happens, Marta's going to be in La Vista the way she is now, alert and jangly, almost too alive. No, not that. Extra alive, and Marta doesn't want to lose that. Marta's no longer doing this for Nena, but for herself.

Walking back up the trail, Marta notices that Nena's walking with a new assurance, steady and so fast that Marta has to pick up her pace. When Marta and Nena get back to the picnic area, the backpack is on top of the table, but the boys aren't there.

Marta scans the area, panicked, then relieved when she spots Pablo standing with a group of climbers crowded around one of the black mats resting on the ground. The boys are looking up at the cliff above them. Marta shades her eyes with her hand. She spots Rafa halfway up the cliff face, dozens of feet above the ground.

Marta takes off at a run toward the knot of boys, stopping when she gets to the black mat. She'd yell at Rafa to come down, but she doesn't want him to lose his concentration. She paces back and forth, her neck craned, watching Rafa's steady movements as he crawls up the face of the cliff. What was she thinking leaving the boys alone? As skinny as he is, Rafa looks strong, his movements steady. How high is he going to go? Higher. He puts his right foot up, his right leg stretched very far away from his torso. He starts to shift his left foot up the rock. Once he steadies himself, he reaches up with his left hand. He braces himself. He repeats the movements, inching up. Just as Marta begins to relax, Rafa loses his grip, falling, and landing with a nasty thud on the mat.

Marta runs to him, dropping down to her knees. He's clutching his belly, the whites of his eyes showing in panic. She wishes Alejandro were here. The bouldering boys have crowded too close, smelling of sweat and body spray and marijuana. One boy, with his long hair in a messy bun, puts out his hand, and Rafa takes it, standing up on the squishy surface of the mat.

"Nice, little dude! Good fall."

Rafa attempts a smile. If he and Marta were alone, he'd be crying.

"Are you hurt?" Marta asks, adrenaline racing through her veins.

"I'm fine. All OK," he says, gasping, the wind knocked out of him. He limps off the mat, but at the edge, he jumps to the ground and heads toward Nena, who takes a piece of candy out of her pocket and hands it to him. Marta chases after Rafa, pulling him toward her so that she can take a closer look at him. He's slowly unwrapping the piece of hard candy Nena gave him, and this worries Marta. It's when the kids are quiet that something is really wrong.

"We're going to the hospital so your dad can check you out," Marta says.

Rafa shakes his head no, but he doesn't say anything.

Marta feels foolish. All thoughts of helping Nena find Rosa are swept from her mind as she looks at the child right in front of her. She went to Juárez because she had a fear that something bad was going to happen. And then she left the boys so she could go off with Nena to practice magic, to make herself feel powerful, even though she knew what could happen.

On the drive home, the boys sleep, their heads thrown back, mouths open.

Please, she prays, *please let Rafa be OK. I promise I won't put him in danger again.*

The song of the aquelarre gave Marta a taste of something strong, but now it's gone. Has it been scared out of her? She wants to taste it again so badly she almost wishes she'd never sung the song, never felt its power.

Nena says they have to wait, that the encanto will come, but Marta doesn't want to wait. She hates waiting. Maybe there's a way to speed things up.

16

Nena had wanted to leave the convent, and yet now that she was walking out its gates with María, she already wished she could go back. The town seemed just as dirty as the first time Nena saw it, but it showed none of its former bustle. About every tenth house, red paint marked the door in an X. Nena and María made their way through the square, past the church. The bells of the church clanged, a lonely sound that echoed in the quiet square. The doors of the church were closed tight.

"You know, that dress you're wearing was Sister Benedicta's before she went into the convent in Mexico City," María said. "I saved it for her, thinking that she might decide to not become a nun. When I came to the convent to be her servant, I brought a trunk with all her things."

It wasn't a surprise to learn that the dress was old. It smelled awfully musty, and it was far too large for Nena. María had had to turn the ends of the sleeves and the bottom of the dress up, making a few quick stitches to create a hem, as there wasn't enough time to do the job properly.

"You've worked for Sister Benedicta since before she was a nun?" Nena asked, surprised.

"I was taken in by the de Galvez family when I was eleven. When Sister Benedicta was a girl, I was her maid, and then when she left for the convent, I became Emiliano's wet nurse."

"Wet nurse? You have a child?"

"My son died in the outbreak of 1780, as did Emiliano's mother. I don't want him to die, Señorita Elena. He's the closest thing I have to a son."

Nena wasn't sure what to say to that. She didn't think she could promise that the brebaje would do anything, despite what Sister Benedicta believed. Nena was the one who'd brought the stuff into the world, and it was a mystery even to her. She wasn't sure she could sing the flying encanto again.

Nena and María crossed to the other side of the square and headed down a narrow lane crowded on both sides by high mud-brick walls.

"Here we are," María said. Nena couldn't believe how close the de Galvez home was to the convent, just a short walk separating them. The gate swung open. A barefoot young man in a simple homespun shirt and pants bowed to Nena. Nena and María walked into the yard of packed dirt. To the right were stables, and to the left a small building with smoke coming out of a chimney. In the wall across was a door, through which Nena followed María, passing through a pretty courtyard where a fountain bubbled and citrus trees grew. Seeing Sister Benedicta's family home, Nena felt worlds away from the aquelarre.

They walked through a room with a huge, blackened table, carved chairs, and oil paintings of men with high collars and mean, piggy eyes, past a sala with rugs and wooden chests, and then through an inner courtyard into a little hallway. At the end of the passage, they walked into a dark room, shutters closed, a candle burning on a table next to the bed, on which a man lay. Nena yanked her hand up to her nose, her eyes watering at the smell of sickness and rot. María knelt next to the bed, taking Emiliano's hand in hers, praying in a quick mumble.

When Nena had cared for her niece and nephew, Chuy and Valentina, she'd had to deal with all sorts of strong smells, but compared to the odor coming off Emiliano, those smells were natural, healthy-smelling even. Nena looked down at Emiliano. His face was gaunt, the rash of pocks swollen to the edge of bursting.

Nena opened her bag and took out a spoon and the tiny jar that Sister Benedicta had given her. Nena scraped off the fat used to seal in the brebaje. She gave the brebaje a sniff. It smelled earthy, just this side of turned. Nena dipped the spoon into the stuff.

"Let me," María said, taking the jar and spoon from Nena's hand, putting the spoon in Emiliano's mouth. He clamped his mouth around the spoon, and Nena saw his Adam's apple roll as he swallowed. María fed Emiliano small spoonful by small spoonful until it was gone.

Nena braced herself, wondering what was going to happen. When Nena and the nuns had eaten the brebaje, they'd been hit with its magic right away, taken away into the sun and back while their bodies dropped to the ground. Nena watched Emiliano's face for any changes, not sure what she was looking for. It could be that Emiliano was going on his trip to the sun, but Nena didn't think so. His body remained too still, his breathing unchanged. Sister Benedicta had told Nena to sing the flying song to heal Emiliano, but Nena couldn't do it if María was there.

"I need to do something," Nena said.

"What can I do to help?"

"Alone."

"Let me stay. I've seen many things that I would tell no one about. I know who Sister Benedicta is, what she does," María said, looking down at Emiliano.

Nena had a flash of María's life, the life of a servant, always there, watching everything, hearing everything, and yet invisible to Sister Benedicta. But Nena didn't want to sing the encanto in front of María.

"Please leave, señora," Nena said.

María looked startled. Probably hardly anyone gave her the respect of calling her "señora." She gave Nena a quick nod. "There's a bell on the table there. I'll be here right away if you ring."

When María was gone, Nena picked up the jar, turning it sideways to find what she was looking for, the tiny bits of brebaje left in the corners. She used the tip of her pinkie to carefully gather up the sauce.

Nena put her finger in her mouth. She instantly felt different, her hair buzzing. She was wide awake, seeing the electrical currents in the room. She saw how the candle burned, the heat radiating off the wick in a circle. She turned her gaze on Emiliano, able to see the different layers of his body, investigating the small parts of him her eyes couldn't. She spotted the virus, singing its own encanto, replicating itself in his body.

Emiliano smelled worse than ever now that Nena's nose was as alive as her eyes and ears. She had to be brave. She wasn't with the aquelarre, and this made her afraid that if she sang the flying encanto, she wouldn't be able to control it. But what choice did she have? She sat on the edge of the bed, opening herself up so that the encanto could enter into her.

Nena sensed a movement on the bed, and looking down, she watched in surprise as Emiliano grabbed her arm. He opened his eyes, looking up at her with the lost, drunk expression that had come over the nuns when they'd eaten the brebaje.

"Who are you? Tell me your name."

"It doesn't matter what my name is," she said, frightened.

"You're an angel."

"No."

"You've come from heaven to save me," Emiliano said.

"You're confused," Nena said.

"Come closer, let me see you," Emiliano said. Emiliano reached his hand up to Nena's face, putting his palm on her cheek, moving his hand to her ear, pulling her down, and guiding Nena's mouth to his. She felt his tongue try to slip in, and she was horrified at how her cheek had touched his pocks, feeling their meaty bumpiness. She pushed herself up.

"Why won't you kiss me? You're very pretty."

"No, please, señor," she said.

"Come here," he said, grabbing Nena with both arms, and with more force than she thought he had in his weak state he brought her down next to him on the bed.

"No," she said, pushing his head away with a strong shove. Nena rolled out of the bed, landing on her knees, and hitting the table, knocking the bell off it.

She had no time to waste. Nena threw open her mind to La Vista, and just like that, she felt the encanto wriggling in her mouth. She sang out the vowels, deep and low in her chest, concentrating on Emiliano, asking God to put him back together again. As she sang, Nena smelled the perfume of desert plants growing toward the sky, fat with water from a thunderstorm, hungry for the sun. Emiliano lifted up off the bed a few inches, hovering. The pustules melted off his face like they'd been made of wax.

Nena heard María come into the room. If María was shocked to see Emiliano in the air, she didn't betray any emotion. She bowed her head to Nena.

Nena didn't know what else to do but to sing Emiliano down.

"I knew Sister Benedicta would do whatever she could to save him," María said, looking down at Emiliano, now sleeping. "But I've never seen her do anything like this. This is not her magic, but yours. Bless you, Elena. God has sent you to save him."

Nena looked around the room. Across from the bed stood a big dark armoire, its door open. Emiliano's boots were lined up inside, polished in a way that her papá would have approved of. A map of New Mexico hung on the wall. A penknife sat on a table, alongside a pot of ink and a leather folder full of paper.

Everyone in this place talked about God. But like at home, they all had their own ideas about who God was. In her papá's stories, God was always on the side of the settlers of New Mexico. The God her papá believed in wasn't magical or womanly. He was a man. God was the King, and the King was the empire. God had always been with the Montoyas, whatever empire they lived in, the empire of the United States included, so when her papá went to war in Europe, God came with him. Her papá had been wounded, but he could have died, which for him was proof that his God, the god of patriarchs, was always there.

Nena's mamá believed in the God of Jesus, who took care of the poor.

Sister Benedicta's God controlled chaos.

He was nothing like María's God, who performed miracles.

Emiliano blinked his eyes open, struggling to sit up. The drunk look he'd had was gone, his eyes clear.

"Who's she?" Emiliano asked María, looking at Nena like he'd never seen her before.

Only part of Nena was glad that she'd saved him. She was also afraid, sorry that she'd done what Sister Benedicta had asked her to do.

Because Nena's God never let an act of magic go unpunished.

17

The next day at the office, Marta arrives to the news that Soto is suing the women for a million dollars each. This number is purely about intimidation, another version of sending armed men to birthday parties and churches to harass Marta's clients.

Marta and Linda are on the phone with Belén Florez, whose voice is quivering. It's scary to be handed papers by a process server, to see your name and next to it, a number with a lot of zeros, like you're being handed a bill.

"You promised that he'd settle in six months," Belén says. "It doesn't seem like he's ready to settle."

"Have faith in God," Marta says. Linda raises an eyebrow.

"Dios es grande," Belén sighs.

Belén attends services at an evangelical church almost daily, and Marta's not happy that she's using Belén's religion in such a cynical way. From what Marta's seen, God doesn't reward the faith of the oppressed, whatever it says in the Bible about that topic. What she wishes she could say is that Belén should have faith in Marta. She feels the hum of La Vista droning in her teeth, vibrating along the outside edge of her right hand, thumping through her body with each beat of her heart. La Vista is talking to her, whispering to her through her skin. When Marta mentioned Silvia Soto's name to Soto at the fundraiser, she hit a nerve. The defamation lawsuit is because of her, and La Vista is telling her to hit Soto again.

"You OK?" Linda asks.

"Too much coffee," Marta says, though she hasn't had any. "You know what's weird about the defamation suit? Sofia isn't named as a defendant."

"But doesn't that make sense? She told you she was going to change her testimony, didn't she?"

"I want to talk to her. If she hasn't contacted the investigators yet, then it's not too late to keep her from hurting herself and the case. The other women are extra vulnerable now. I don't want her convincing them to withdraw."

Linda leafs through her notebook, pausing on a page of schedules. "She's working today at the packing shed, if you want to go see her there."

❋

At the Soto truck depot and packing shed, heavy-duty cyclone fence topped with loops of razor wire runs around the compound. Most of the space is taken up by warehouses with concrete loading docks sticking out from the mouths of the bays. It's a busy place, eighteen-wheelers rumbling in and out of the gates. The only reminder that this used to be a pecan stand is the sign that used to sit on top of the old wooden building, now affixed to the side of one of the warehouses.

Inside, giant circular lamps beam greenish light down onto a large open space dominated by clattering machinery. The women in the facility wear boxy blue overalls and puffy white hairnets making them look very much alike, but even as Marta peers at the women more closely, she can't pick out Sofia on the line.

A woman who's been moving around the room, a supervisor, bustles over. "Can I help you with something?"

"We're looking for Sofia Hernandez."

"She doesn't work here anymore."

"Did she quit?"

"I don't know nothing about it," the woman says. Her eyes tilt up at a camera that's pointing at the packing shed floor.

Since Sofia isn't there anyway, Marta doesn't need to make things more difficult for this forewoman, who has, without knowing it, given her something of value. These days everything is recorded. As Marta walks toward the exit, she counts three more cameras. They've subpoenaed Soto for all of the footage from security cameras. They haven't found anything damning, but maybe there's footage that Soto has hidden.

Walking out, Marta waves up at a camera over the door.

"What are you doing?" Linda asks.

"Saying hi," Marta says. She wants Soto to know she was on his property, hunting him down. She wants him to make another move. La Vista is still pumping through Marta, and she knows what to do next.

Sofia's house is tiny, with a tidy front yard of yellow lawn, a border of thirsty-looking juniper bushes. A new car sits in the driveway, a small white Kia with the dealership stickers still on it.

"What are you doing here?" Sofia asks Marta when she opens the front door, standing behind the screen. Sofia's stone-faced, looking back and forth between Marta and Linda like she can't decide which one she hates more.

"I've come to apologize. I'm sorry for what I said the other day."

Sofia opens the screen door a crack, saying, "Pásele," without any warmth. It's clear she's been crying.

The house smells like cooking grease, fried onions, and ammonia. An older woman on oxygen sits in a recliner, the TV blaring, and Marta has the urge to stop, to talk to this woman, to ask her to tell Marta everything she knows. The woman looks up at her, bewildered.

"Buenas tardes," Marta says.

"Dios te bendiga," the woman says, looking more ill than she had before.

Marta and Linda follow Sofia into the kitchen. Sofia puts a kettle on the stove.

"Why did you quit?" Marta asks Sofia.

"I don't want to work there anymore. I need to take care of my mother," Sofia says. Marta hears a song of worry singing high-pitched in the air. *How? How will I ever pay these bills for her prescriptions, the hospital, for the electricity and water, and, dios me salve, the rent?* The imprint of these thoughts hover in the air, repetition making them part of the kitchen's atmosphere. Marta has always known intellectually what her clients face. Now, La Vista appears to be giving her information that's more personal and private, the kind that she's always shied away from. But acknowledging this pain gives Marta more power.

"Did Soto make you quit?" Marta asks.

"No."

"Whose car is in the driveway?"

A flicker passes across Sofia's face. "Mine."

"It's a nice car," Linda says. It doesn't take La Vista to connect these dots.

"Sofia? Mija?" the woman calls from the other room in a weak voice. Voices whisper at Marta: *diabetes, a foot that may have to be amputated, a childhood in Villa Ahumada, mother a seamstress.*

"I'm coming, Mamá," Sofia calls. "I need to take her to her appointment at the clinic."

"I know why you wanted to change your testimony. You needed money right away."

Sofia's eyes dart back and forth between Marta's and Linda's faces. "I understand why you'd take things from Soto. But he owes you much more than that."

"I don't know what you're talking about."

"What else has he asked you to do? Other than change your testimony? What deal have you made with Benjamin Soto?"

"Nobody asked me to do anything."

"If someone threatened you, that could make our case stronger. There are rules against retaliation, and Señora Torres can help you," Linda says in Spanish. The word is represalias, reprisals.

"Leave," Sofia says, and there is grief in her voice.

"I don't want you talking to the other women," Marta says. She needs to minimize the damage Sofia can do.

"I'll do what I have to, we all have to eat," Sofia says, her voice shaking but her gaze defiant.

"I'm warning you, don't screw up this case," Marta says, meeting eyes with Sofia. La Vista surges in her. Sofia's face becomes disfigured with fear.

"Let's go," Linda says, touching Marta's shoulder gently.

Driving back to the office from San Elizario, Marta follows the course of the Rio Grande, passing cotton fields that turn into housing developments stretching for many miles, passing one of the entrances to Fort Bliss. The fort is the size of Rhode Island, stretching up to New Mexico, where it runs into the White Sands Missile Range, the size of two Rhode Islands. During the wars in the Middle East, soldiers poured into Fort Bliss, the ideal place to train for battle in the desert of Iraq, the craggy hills of Afghanistan. When the soldiers came back from war, they were hurt in mind and body, and the violence of the war had to go somewhere. They turned that violence against themselves and against the ones closest to them. This is the nature of abuse, that it comes from somewhere.

Marta's in battle mode now, and she's grateful for the familiar feeling of controlled professional rage. The aquelarre is open, and La Vista runs through her. She doesn't care if Rosa ever comes. She hopes she stays away, because Marta doesn't want the aquelarre to ever close.

18

Nena was invited to dine with the de Galvez men to celebrate Emiliano's recovery and the end of the family's quarantine.

During dinner, Emiliano and Don Javier talked about the acequias, about wine barrels, and about the price of horses. They didn't include Nena in the conversation, but she didn't mind, glad to be with other people at mealtime after so many days of eating alone. Emiliano wore a white shirt and black pants, a red sash. He looked like a completely different person than the rotting corpse she'd found in his bed two weeks before.

Nena watched Don Javier throw albóndigas down his throat, chewing while he talked. Not wanting to ruin her appetite, Nena looked down, concentrating on her own food. The little meatballs were delicious, served in a light tomato sauce. Next came lomo with carrots and potatoes, and then after that, coffee, with figs. This was the first grown-up dinner Nena had ever attended.

When Don Javier was done with the last fig, he patted the sides of his mouth daintily with his napkin. He took out a pipe and put tobacco in it, lighting it with a tinderbox, the dank smell of the tobacco filling the room.

For the first time that night, Don Javier turned his attention to Nena.

"I've been given the job of finding you a husband," he said.

"Well," Nena said, an objection ready to fly from her mouth.

"It's not going to be easy. You don't have a dowry. You're an orphan. You're small, but not in a pretty way, and your hair isn't really done like a lady's." Don Javier looked at her appraisingly, as though examining livestock. "Couldn't say what's wrong exactly."

"No, señor," Nena said. It was true her hair was taking a long time to grow out from when she'd cut it to look like Ingrid Bergman.

"My daughter tells me you're a hard worker."

"Yes."

"You know how to run a kitchen, tell the servants what to cook?"

"Yes."

"Convent trained. So you could teach the catechism to children?"

"Yes, I guess so."

"Men have lost their wives in this outbreak. You could marry a widower. One who doesn't need a dowry. We will attend the concert at the Palacio Municipal. Urrea will be there."

Emiliano laughed.

"What's funny?" Don Javier asked.

"Urrea's not a bad man, but he's the ugliest backside of a hog I've ever seen."

"What does that matter?"

"How about Fonseca instead? At least he's tall. And he's already outlived three wives, so why not a fourth?" Emiliano winked at Nena.

"Do you need to make light of everything?" Don Javier asked. "You've been saved from death, and you still won't act like a man."

Emiliano laughed at this, too.

"Maybe marriage will make you grow up!" Don Javier shouted. He turned to Nena. "You know Emiliano's novia from the convent?"

"Yes. Eugenia."

"She's coming with ten thousand."

Nena guessed that the number referred to pesos, and ten thousand sounded like a lot. Did Don Javier and Emiliano not know that Eugenia had fallen ill? Nena wondered what Don Javier would say if he knew the state of Eugenia's face. Would the money make up for the scars? It sounded like it might. Not that Eugenia was Nena's main concern. The two weeks she'd spent alone were dull, but they'd also been peaceful, the first time in her life she hadn't had to do any sort of work, and she'd daydreamed about the kind of life that she might find for herself in El Paso del Norte. But now she understood she was in a worse predicament at the de Galvez house than she'd been in at the convent.

She didn't want to marry anyone. She couldn't marry anyone. She had to get home. Without the magic of the aquelarre, leaving El Paso del Norte would now be even more difficult, if not impossible. The little bit of the brebaje that she'd had left was gone, used up to cure Emiliano, and since that day Nena hadn't felt any vibrations of La Vista. The two weeks she'd spent alone, she'd opened her mind often, inviting any sort of encanto to her, but none came.

On the night of the concert, María helped Nena out of the wool dress, sliding her into one made of a beautiful pink ivory silk that reflected the light and that sounded rich when it swished. This dress fit Nena much better than the one she'd been wearing, and she wondered where it came from. It was hard to imagine Sister Benedicta wearing such a dress. Nena couldn't picture her in anything that wasn't black. María sat Nena on a little stool, taking a silver brush off the dressing table. With long, even strokes, she gathered Nena's hair into what felt like a complicated braid at the back of her head, letting a few pieces fall around her face.

María picked up the silver mirror, holding it up in front of Nena.

Carmela's cross hung from a ribbon around Nena's neck. The corset had pushed up her breasts, so that it made her appear to have a bosom. Nena looked like a real woman, grown up. Olga and Luna would hardly recognize her if she were to show up at the front door. Nena quickly put this thought away. It made her feel lost, which she couldn't be right now. She had to be smart and calm, able to make the right choices.

When they got to the Palacio Municipal, Don Javier guided Nena through the rooms. The men bowed to them, and the women smiled tight, false smiles. Don Javier led Nena forward through the big sala, into another room with a low ceiling and a wooden chandelier, lit with dozens of flickering candles. Rough chairs, set up in rows, curved around a small spinet. Don Javier brought Nena to the middle row of seats, and they sat down.

Nena heard fans snapping open and closed. She smelled perfume, and the odor she was starting to understand was the smell that was always there in this time, of unwashed bodies and stale clothes.

The other guests began to find their seats. In front of Nena, two women sat down, their tall peinetas and scarves blocking Nena's view of the stage. Nena sat up, leaning to one side so that she could look in between their heads.

"Perdón," Emiliano said, sliding onto the chair next to her, his legs so long that he had to stretch them out underneath the chair in front. Nena flitted her gaze at him, taking in his long lashes, his big, proud nose. Nena fixed her eyes toward the front of the room.

A woman stomped out onto the space in front of the chairs. She wore a tall wig, lots of white powder, rouge on her cheeks, and blood-red lipstick. She was very unattractive under all the makeup. Nena felt sorry for her. Then she sang, sending her voice to the back of the room. People stopped talking. Nena leaned forward. All of the emotions Nena felt that she couldn't express seemed to be held by the voice of this singer, rage and fear and hope tied together. Through each song, Nena listened, feeling the notes touch the parts of her that ached. The last song took the hairs off the top of Nena's head. The song made Nena feel like if it was possible to make music like that, anything could be done.

Nena clapped and clapped when the singer was finished. She heard herself saying, "Oh, oh, oh."

"Haven't you ever heard opera before?" Emiliano asked.

Nena turned to look at him, taking in his waxed mustache, his big dark eyes.

"That was magnífico," Nena said. "I've never heard anything like it."

He stood up and bowed to Nena, as though he were just meeting her. He put out his hand. She put her hand in his, and he kissed it. "Encantado."

He was very handsome, but she'd seen him at his worst, dying and covered in pustules. And what kind of man kissed a girl's hand like that? It was so silly, she laughed.

Emiliano stepped back. He looked at Nena's breasts, pushed up. She wanted to tell him that what he saw was a lot of trouble over nothing.

"You're from the Santa Fe branch of the family, Papá tells us. Why haven't I ever heard about you?"

"Wasn't the singer divine?" Nena asked, thinking that divine was the right kind of word to describe her.

"You know, you aren't supposed to like music at things like this too much. You aren't even supposed to listen to it. You should be like those other women and talk during the performance."

"That would be very rude."

"I didn't say it wasn't. Would you like a bebida?" he asked. Nena looked at Don Javier for permission.

"Bring her back soon, there are a few people I want to introduce her to," Don Javier said.

They moved to the hallway. Emiliano took a couple of glasses from a servant holding a tray.

He looked at Nena's chest again as he spoke to her. "This champagne is from France, but it's been ruined by the ocean trip. They should be serving our wine. It's the finest in the New World."

"When will I get to taste the finest wine in the New World?" Nena asked.

"When? Every day you make it to the dining table."

Nena laughed again, though she wasn't quite sure why. Two sips of champagne had made her feel silly and warm.

"You find me amusing, but I find you something else," he said, leaning in, so close to Nena's face that she could feel his long eyelashes touching her cheek, his breath in her ear. He put his hand on her waist. His hand was big enough that it felt like it covered her whole side.

"Can I tell you a secret?" he asked Nena.

"Yes," she said, touching his forearm.

"I like listening to music, too."

"Can you hear the—the other music?" Nena asked, not sure how to ask if he had visions, or if he could hear encantos like she could. He was related to Sister Benedicta, and maybe eating the brebaje had awoken something in him.

"You mean like the quadrille? Very much so. I love to dance," he said.

"Oh, me too," Nena said, though she was a bad dancer. Maybe Emiliano could teach her.

Nena looked up at him. She wanted him to brush her cheek with his eyelashes again. She never wanted him to take his hand off her waist. He looked down at her and smiled.

"You were laughing before," he said. "Why are you so serious now?"

"Because I am serious," she said.

"There you are." Don Javier appeared next to them. "The singer is starting up again. We should take our seats."

The next day Nena walked with María to noon mass at the cathedral. Dark vigas stretched across the ceiling, black planks of wood lying on top of the beams, making the ceiling seem even higher up than it was. The place smelled like a barn, with bird poop in the font, and pigeons roosting in the vigas, flapping their wings and cooing. Instead of pews, rough benches sat in rows, also dirty with the mess of birds. The area behind the altar seemed to be used for storage, crates and barrels stacked up high. Nena had never seen a building, let alone a church, this badly taken care of. Nena wondered what her sisters would think of the cathedral.

Nena and María kneeled. Nena closed her eyes, thinking rather than praying. She couldn't marry anyone here, not even Emiliano. Not that he was an option for her. She didn't have one peso, let alone thousands. Not that she wanted to marry him. But if he were in her time, she would allow him to take her to the movies. Thinking about the movies made Nena sick with longing, wishing she could sit on a velvet chair in the dark, listening to the overture, excited to enter a new world for a few precious hours.

Nena felt something crawling on her shoe, and she opened her eyes. A mouse. She kept her mouth closed, stifling her scream as she kicked at it.

"Shh," María said, her eyes still closed.

When mass ended, María and Nena walked out through the square toward the outdoor market. Pieces of colorful cloth hung over the crude tables to make some shade, giving the market the look of a festival.

Walking closer to the market, Nena smelled food frying in oil, the smoke from the mesquite fire under the cauldron of pozole, sold by a small woman who reminded Nena of her mamá. A seller called out, "Masa! Masa!" At one stall, a man sold bags of wheat, at another, coffee. On the butchers' tables sat liver and pieces of beef and whole legs of goats. The meat let off a strong rotten odor, and flies covered every part of the goat legs, turning them black. When the butcher waved his hand, the flies jumped up all at once, and then they settled down again, crawling on top of each other.

Nena heard a noise, loud laughing, breaking glass, and next to the market, on the plaza, she saw Emiliano sitting at a table outside a rough adobe building, drinking with friends. The young men shouted when they talked, leaning back in their chairs. The waiter bent over, picking up the pieces of the broken glasses.

"It's not ladylike to stare," María said, pulling at Nena's arm.

"He was very kind to me last night," Nena said, instantly angry with herself for saying anything.

"He flirts with all the pretty girls," María said.

"You think I'm pretty?" Nena asked. This was a pitiful thing to ask, but Nena couldn't help herself.

"Oh, Elena," María said, which was not answering the question. She meant no. María shook her head. "You be careful."

She really tried her best most of the time. It was true that she sometimes made bad choices, but that was only because she was trying to help other people.

"Señorita Elena," Nena heard. Emiliano was calling to her from his table. Nena walked closer to him. Emiliano tried to bow to her, stumbling, knocking his chair over. He smelled of drink. He threw his arm around the shoulders of a man with red hair.

"Joaquín, this is our ward, Señorita Elena," Emiliano said. "She loves opera."

"Me too," Joaquín said, bowing to Nena.

"But she doesn't know much about going to recitals. She doesn't know you're not supposed to listen. Real ladies talk and fan themselves," Emiliano said.

"My sister could give you lessons on how to do that," Joaquín said.

"She knows your sister. They were in the convent together."

"Then you know that Eugenia's so sophisticated she never closes her mouth," Joaquín said, laughing.

"Don't talk about her that way," Emiliano said, a darkness flooding his face.

"I'll talk about Eugenia however I want," Joaquín replied. Nena saw that though he was steady on his feet, Joaquín was drunk, too.

"I'm warning you." Emiliano stepped closer to his friend.

Joaquín put his hand on Emiliano's shoulder, squeezing it.

Emiliano shoved Joaquín, who fell backward onto the dusty stones. Joaquín got up, his face now the same color as his hair. He punched Emiliano in the eye. Emiliano punched him back, and then they were on the ground, wrestling.

The other three friends shouted "pégale!" laughing, but the fight seemed serious to Nena, a dark shadow racing under the feet of the boys. She started to feel hot, and dizzy. A buzzing in her ears grew louder. She touched Carmela's cross. She made herself think about the solid riverbank as she was pulled into the waters of La Vista. She saw flashes of men on horses. Men in buckskins, with lances, making an unholy sound at the back of their throats, high-pitched and meant to scare. A musket shot. A knife flashing in the sun. Nena felt the knife in her belly, and she choked, coughing up blood on the road outside of El Paso del Norte.

Nena was back in her body, lying on the ground, and María was loosening the back of her dress. The boys looked down at her.

Nena stood up, too quickly, the blood pounding in her head, ashamed of herself. She'd thought La Vista no longer made her faint.

Emiliano was laughing, holding his eye. "We thought we'd lost you!"

She hated for Emiliano to see her like that, helpless and gone, lying in the dust. María was already pulling Nena away in the direction of the de Galvez house, and Nena was glad to go with her. She had let her guard slip.

"I told you to be careful," María said. "If you faint like that in public, you're going to get a reputation for yourself, and then where will you be? No one will want to marry you. Why do you think Sister Benedicta had to go to the convent?"

Nena wouldn't be allowed back at the convent, so where would she be sent? She was afraid to ask.

❋

At supper that evening, a dull headache throbbed behind Nena's eyes, but Emiliano appeared fresher and more alert than seemed possible after being so drunk earlier in the day. His hair was neatly combed, and he'd changed clothes. He had a black eye, but it didn't do anything to hurt his healthy color.

"You're too hotheaded," Don Javier said, eating his pigeon pie in giant bites. "You need to learn some discipline."

"The boys and I were just having fun."

"You should be spending your time working."

"Elena told me she wanted to see the vineyard," Emiliano said, winking at Nena with his good eye.

"The vineyard? Women don't belong there," Don Javier said.

"She says she doesn't believe we grow the best grapes in the New World," Emiliano said.

"I didn't say that," Nena said.

"You don't think our wine is the best?" Don Javier asked.

"That's not—"

"We can't have her spreading rumors like that, right?" Emiliano asked.

"I don't know anything about wine. I've never seen how vines grow," Nena said, mad at Emiliano for teasing her.

Don Javier stopped eating. He wiped his mouth with his napkin, but he missed a spot of grease on his chin. He looked directly at Elena. "How vines grow. You think you can see it happening? The stupidity of women never ceases to amaze me."

"Don't you think we should make her less ignorant?" Emiliano asked, smiling.

"We can do better than that. When we take you to the vineyard, we'll invite Señor Urrea to come. He wrote to tell me that he saw you at the concert, and he wants to meet you," Don Javier said.

"I don't want to go to the vineyard," Nena said.

"I have the perfect horse for you to ride," Emiliano said.

Nena kept quiet, furious. Emiliano, she now understood, was the kind of person who liked to toy with people. But Nena wasn't a toy, she was a witch.

A lot of good that did.

It was true that the brebaje had protected her from smallpox, but making that brebaje had also gotten her banished from the convent.

Her visions had never brought anything but grief.

Foretelling how and when Señor Echeverria would die hadn't stopped him from evicting the Montoyas. He was very much alive when he stood outside their house, his car running, watching the family move. The tíos had sent over a truck and some workers to help cart the furniture. The new house had two rooms: a bedroom for Nena's parents, and the other room for everything else—living, eating, and the place the girls would sleep. The paint on the walls peeled. There was one toilet in a room off the kitchen, but no proper bathroom.

After the trip to the Jockey Club and the move, Nena's papá never went outdoors, and he hardly ever left his bedroom, but he still loved to tell stories. When Nena came home from school, she'd put down her books, pour two glasses of water, make a plate of food for her papá, and bring it to him, sitting on the edge of his bed, listening as he wheezed out his narratives, usually needing to stop to catch his breath right at the point where the soldiers faced Apaches bristling with weapons on the other side of the river.

"Now, listen. You wouldn't think that a woman named Eduviges would be beautiful, but she was," her papá would say, telling the story of two ancestors, Eduviges, the daughter of the owner of a silver mine in Zacatecas, and Dionicio, a railroad engineer from New Mexico. After a secret courtship, Eduviges rode her horse, chasing after Dionicio's slow-moving train, leaping out of her saddle and into Dionicio's waiting arms, leaving behind a fortune for love. What names people had in the old days! Nena loved hearing about family silver mines, even if they were long gone.

Nena didn't like it when her papá told stories about witches, like the one about the bruja who taught a woman how to peer into a washbasin to check on her shepherd son. These stories gave Nena jabs of embarrassment and shame, afraid she was going to be found out for what she was. She didn't want to end up like Doña Hilaria in her dirty house with all those dogs, yelling curses at little girls. Nena wanted to be brave and smart like her sisters were, each in their own way.

When Olga was a senior in high school, she started a Spanish Speaking Club, a protest against the prohibition of speaking Spanish at school. The club met for the first time at lunch in the cafeteria, a small group sitting at one table, Olga at the head. Everyone waited to see what the principal was going to do, but the lunch hour passed, and nothing happened. The next day, the members of the club again spoke only Spanish at lunch, and still the principal didn't say anything. On the third day, Luna started the Speak English Only Club, sitting her group down at the table next to Olga's club.

Luna and Olga started arguing at school, and they were still fighting when they picked Nena up from her school. Nena liked it when they fought, because then they forgot to nag her about doing her homework, to order her to wash her hands. In Spanish, Olga told Luna to make dinner, which Luna pretended not to understand. Olga, who was just as stubborn as Luna in her own way, refused to speak English, and they went back and forth, Olga telling Luna what to do in Spanish, and Luna telling Olga to "Please use the language of the United States." It got bad enough that Nena started to worry. She said that they didn't have to fight, she would fix dinner instead.

They both told her to shut up, Olga in Spanish and Luna in English. Nena started to cry, and then they heard their papá shouting at them from his room. He had a hard time even whispering, so they knew it was serious.

Luna and Olga told Papá their versions of what had happened. After listening, Papá told Luna that she had to disband her club, reminding her that theirs had been one of the founding families in Albuquerque and that the Montoyas had been speaking Spanish in their part of the world since 1584, almost two hundred years before the United States was a country. He was disappointed in Luna, and so were their ancestors.

Even though Nena usually loved it when Papá talked about the ancestors, she felt sorry for Luna. As Luna changed into her waitress uniform, getting ready to go in for the evening shift, Nena tried to help her. She found Luna's waistband bunched up on the floor of the closet, and she crawled under the bed to drag out Luna's work shoes. Nena watched Luna take her lipstick out of its hiding place in the hollow post of the bed and put it in her pocketbook. This frightened Nena. It meant that Luna was planning to go somewhere after work.

When Luna finally came home, it was late. Mamá, Olga, and Nena were waiting for her, sitting together on the sofa. Luna smelled like cigarettes, and she was wearing someone else's dress, lipstick bright on her face. She was beautiful and very alive, and Nena was sorry she was so wicked.

"Where were you?" their mamá asked her in Spanish.

"Nowhere."

"Who were you with?"

"A couple of the chicas from the restaurant. We went dancing," Luna said. And then she admitted that they'd been out with a man, too, one of the waiters. There was a huge escándalo, lots of tears and slammed doors, and their papá said he would not have his daughter shame the family, but at the end of all of the arguing, it was decided that Luna could be out in public with Beto—that was the name of the waiter—if Olga went with them to chaperone.

Beto was twenty-four, which seemed ancient to Nena. He slicked his hair back with pomade and he had huge brown eyes. His face looked kind of flattened out, like someone had smashed it with a cast-iron pan. He had big hands and forearms, and he was the kind of handsome that makes you think that nobody else notices how good-looking he is but you.

The first time Olga chaperoned Beto and Luna, she wore a dress with a high collar, her hair pinned tight to her skull. She brought her math textbook for the streetcar ride, so that she wouldn't waste any time. But as the months passed, Nena watched Olga transform. She started to curl her hair. She fixed some of her dresses in the new style, shorter. And before she went out with Luna and Beto she put on her own secret lipstick, applying it and then blotting all but a tiny bit off with her handkerchief. As they walked down the street, Beto put his arms around both girls, and when he said goodbye, he didn't kiss either of them, he performed a little bow, like a real caballero.

One week, Beto told the girls he'd borrowed a car and he was going to take all of them to the Hueco Tanks for a picnic. It wasn't really a park then, but Beto was somehow related to the Escontrias, the family that owned the land. Luna bought Cokes and store-bought rolls, and Olga made tiny little albóndigas in a red chile sauce. But the Saturday they were supposed to go, one of the busboys came by the house to tell Luna that she was needed to cover the lunch shift at the restaurant. "Go without me," she ordered her sisters.

During the car ride, Olga's voice got very high-pitched, and she giggled at everything Beto said, even dumb things like "Look, a roadrunner." Once they got to the Hueco Tanks, they passed the Escontrias' adobe ranch house, following a path through a thicket of mesquite, walking out toward the red rocks. A family of javelinas ran across the path, disappearing into the sage and the sotol. At the tanks they walked around looking at the paintings on the rocks, made by many different bands of Indios over many centuries.

Beto pointed out the Apache paintings of men on horses, of running deer. Underneath an overhang, like it was meant to be hidden, he showed the girls a yellow painting of triangles arranged in a grid, four across and five down. Even then Nena knew it was something powerful, without understanding that it was a prayer for rain, or maybe more like a map, offered to the god Tlaloc so that he could find his way from Central Mexico to this dry part of the world. Looking at the triangles, Olga made a joke about geometry, something about the hypotenuse that Nena didn't understand and that Beto didn't seem to get either, but he laughed and moved close to her, putting his finger out to trace the same triangles Olga had just touched. Under another overhang, they all three touched the signatures of the passengers of the Butterfield Express, written in axel grease on top of the older paintings made by the Indios. At noon, they ate, sitting on a big rock next to a dark pool of water, cool under the overhang. Beto's contribution to the lunch was a box of chocolate-covered cherries. They were the most delicious thing Nena had ever tasted, and she had five before Olga made her stop.

Nena had to go to the bathroom. She walked around the hill and behind a bush, where she squatted. When she was done, she wandered around by herself. She touched one of the pictographs, a thunderbird, putting her whole palm on it. She got down on her stomach and looked into one of the pools, trying to see the freshwater shrimp that were supposed to live there, and then she saw them, tiny little ghost bodies, floating in the water. She heard a rattle—it had to be a snake—and she ran back to where Olga and Beto were sitting. They were kissing, and when they saw her, they were so shameless they kept holding on to each other.

When they got home, Luna was waiting for them. She'd shaved ice off the block in the icebox with a butter knife and was rubbing it into her face, her feet in a basin of water. She smelled like tortillas and grease, and she looked tired. She knew. Olga knew that she knew. The two sisters didn't talk to each other for a week, but as terrible as that week was, Nena had loved Olga more for doing what she did, for not being perfect.

Remembering this gave Nena some comfort. It wasn't just the fact that Olga made mistakes like everyone else. It was what happened afterward. Beto gave Luna a ring, and they set a date to be married. When Beto came by the house the first time after that, Olga asked him if he wanted coffee, and she went into the kitchen to make it. Nena found her standing in front of the percolator, tears flowing silently down her cheeks. Nena had hugged her, but Olga's arms hung limply by her sides, and her tears wouldn't stop. Nena finished making the coffee, putting cups on a tray to take out to Beto and Luna, who she interrupted kissing on the couch. Nena thought it very cruel of Luna to shove it in Olga's face like this.

Nena watched over the months as Olga slowly healed herself. She finally started going to the movies with a boy who had sometimes taken her to high school dances, a boy Olga and Luna had made fun of for his thick glasses, the grease under his fingernails from working on the weekends at his father's garage. He was nowhere near as good-looking as Beto, but he had something that Beto didn't have. He read books, and Olga loved nothing more than reading.

Nena wasn't a reader. She wasn't the kind of person to attract a beautiful man. She was herself. Her sisters had their talents, and she had hers. It was time that she admitted to herself what she was.

She was no longer the girl who was afflicted by visions, the girl who had tried to keep herself from seeing what La Vista brought to her. Nena was a grown-up now, and she had brought into the world a very powerful encanto. She had done it, Elena Eduviges Montoya, not Sister Benedicta, not Madre Inocenta.

Nena was a real bruja now, and when she went to the vineyard she was going to use her powers to put things right, to go home.

The next morning, Nena found herself sitting in her underclothes, María brushing her hair with many dozens of strokes, making it crackly and full of electricity instead of smoothing it out.

Nena could hear Emiliano singing in the stable yard, belting out something like a ranchero, a cowboy song, about a naughty maid. He had a bad voice, off-key, but loud. She wished she could pay him back for his teasing.

"Arms up," María said, pulling a petticoat over Nena's head, the first of many layers. When she was done, Nena wore a big fluffy white skirt, a tight jacket with loose sleeves, a hat with a veil, and tall riding boots.

Out in the stable yard, Emiliano's servant Antonio and the groom saddled up the horses. A tiny gray burro teetered under a huge pile of baskets loaded onto its back, so many that it seemed like they were going on a long trip, not simply a ride and a picnic. María held the bridle of the burro, stroking his nose. Emiliano wore a beautiful linen shirt with a brown suede jacket, tight pants with gold buttons. His hair was neatly combed, his neck was thick from exercise. The edges of his black eye were already turning yellow. He looked practically ugly, Nena told herself, wishing it were true.

Don Javier had also dressed up to go out riding, similarly to Emiliano, except that the gold buttons along the sides of his pants strained, right on the edge of popping off. But once he was on his horse, he sat tall in the saddle, elegant in a way he wasn't on the ground. He wore giant spurs, each with five big spikes an inch in length. Nena felt sorry for his horse.

Emiliano walked toward Nena, leading a very large gray horse. "May I present to you Palomita," he said, bowing.

The beast may have been called Palomita—Little Dove—but except for her color, she looked nothing like her name. She had huge nostrils, and big muscles in her pompies, muscles she could use to buck Nena off her. Nena's stomach felt weak when she thought about climbing up on the back of the creature. She told herself that she'd wanted to be like Pilar, fighting the fascists in Spain, as skillful at horseback riding as shooting rifles, and now here finally was her chance to learn how to ride. Nena touched the horse's side, patting it, feeling her warmth. Nena pulled her hand away, finding little hairs all over her palm. Disgusted, she rubbed them off on her riding outfit.

"She's a sweet mare, very gentle," Emiliano said.

Palomita showed Nena her big teeth. In her neighborhood at home, Nena saw plenty of working horses, pulling wagons for the milkman and the man who took away the rubbish, but Nena was a city girl, and the only horse she'd ever ridden was the broken-down nag named Margarita. People paid a nickel to have a picture taken, wearing the owner's sombrero and a bandolier to look like the Mexican revolutionaries who had lived in her neighborhood not that long before.

"Antonio," Emiliano yelled at the man who had opened the gate the first day Nena arrived at the de Galvez house. "Come and help Señorita Montoya up."

Antonio kneeled, offering his cupped palms. Nena felt everyone watching her. She stepped into Antonio's hands and then started to swing her leg over the horse.

María and Don Javier gasped. Emiliano laughed. "Ja, ja, ja!" He was laughing at her again.

"No, not like that," Antonio hissed up at Nena as María shook her head back and forth. "Don't you know how to sit sidesaddle?"

Nena tried again.

"No, no. Keep your right knee bent, there, now put your left leg in the stirrup. Lean back, pull in your stomach, now turn your body toward the horse's head."

Nena followed his instructions, wedging herself in. Palomita twisted her ears, rolling her eyes back at Nena while she danced, shivering her behind. Nena felt pinched and pulled, her feet, her chest, her legs twisted underneath her body. She pressed her knee more firmly into the front of the saddle. Pilar and Ingrid Bergman had not had to ride this way.

While Emiliano and Don Javier settled themselves onto their horses, Antonio added a few packages to the burro's load, then he jumped on top of his own horse. It didn't seem to bother him that he was barefoot and that the horse had no saddle, just a rope. María got to ride a fat pony, the horse Nena wished she could be on instead. The stable boy opened the gate, and they headed out of the courtyard and onto the street.

Nena stayed very still in the saddle as Palomita picked her way through the garbage on the street. Palomita fit herself behind Emiliano's horse, putting her nose right up against the other horse's tail, even though the horse kept farting awful clouds of gas. Nena breathed through her mouth, taking the smallest breaths possible of the foul air. When they arrived at Señor Urrea's house, a little boy ran out. "Papá can't come today, his piles are too bad, and he can't sit on a horse."

Emiliano laughed. Nena didn't think it was funny, but she was relieved that Señor Urrea wouldn't be joining them.

They rode toward the ferry crossing. The Rio Bravo still ran big and fast. On the other side, they rode northwest in the direction of Santa Fe. Nena had always imagined El Camino Real as a grand road, paved with cobblestones, instead of just a track of hard-packed dirt only occasionally rutted by wagon wheels, cutting across an open plain scattered with rocks, yucca, and sage. She was in the land of her father's stories, where people were always being killed by Apaches on the Jornada del Muerto, the dangerous stretch of El Camino Real in the wilds between El Paso and Santa Fe.

Emiliano drew his sword, slicing the air with it, and then he kicked his horse, heading off fast. Don Javier whipped his horse to follow Emiliano, and then without Nena doing anything, Palomita took off after the other horses, laying her ears back and stretching her nose forward. Nena hung on tight. They raced along the river, toward the east, finally coming to the edge of the vineyard, stopping next to the acequia.

The horses drank. Antonio helped Nena off Palomita. Her back had become one big knot from the twisting and bouncing, and she could barely walk. But it smelled nice out here away from the town, with the scent of the rich earth, of the river fat with melted snow. The very tips of the grapevines had fresh growth, giving a green haze to the rows of trellises intersecting with irrigation ditches.

Nena adjusted her veil, watching as Antonio and María quickly unloaded the baskets and undid a bundle of sticks, arranging them as kindling to make a fire.

Emiliano hurried toward Nena. He'd taken off his jacket, and his shirt was unbuttoned at the top. He swung out his elbow, leaning in toward her, like he was expecting her to slip her hand between his arm and his chest, which she did, dismayed how easily she gave in to him. Through the linen of his shirt, Nena felt his muscles. He led her down a row of vines, stopping in the middle, where they were out of sight of the others.

Birds swooped down in the vines, and it was warm, dry, and not at all unpleasant. Emiliano took out a knife and cut a tendril from one of the vines, handing it to Nena.

"We grew these vines from cuttings that were brought here from Spain."

"That's very far."

"Once the Apaches are subdued, I'm going to build a house right here, above the flood zone."

"Apaches?"

"I'll grow old and fat like Papá and I'll plant flower gardens for Eugenia. She loves flowers."

"I don't," Nena said. Emiliano smiled at her.

Nena let go of Emiliano's arm, walking away from him.

Emiliano walked fast to catch up to her. "You're a funny person. Is everyone from up north like you?"

"Yes, we're all bad horsewomen."

"Emiliano!" Don Javier called.

"Vengo!"

Back in front of the bunkhouse, María handed Nena a tablecloth to put over the rough table the vaqueros used outside the casita. Nena smoothed out the tablecloth, beautifully embroidered, white floss on white linen. It seemed far too nice to use outside, and Nena wondered who'd made it. Maybe Emiliano's mamá. Out of the burro's packs, Antonio unloaded china, silverware, and pewter cups packed in straw, setting the places at the table. He had water boiling in a copper pot hanging from an iron crossbar over the fire, and he'd set up a grill. On top of that he'd put a heavy iron pan. He poked the embers of the fire, feeding it more wood. Nena put the tendril Emiliano had given her into one of the pewter cups.

She looked out at the desert, at the tidy irrigation ditches cut from the river to the vines. It hit Nena for the thousandth time that she didn't belong in this place, that this was not her real life. She was on the north side of the river, east of where home was in her time, but close enough to walk if she could sing herself back. It made sense to sing the healing song here, putting things back into place, blinking Nena forward to her own time, traveling like a mariquita.

"Let's eat," Don Javier called out.

Nena and the others sat down, perching on camp stools. Don Javier looked ridiculous balancing on the stool, the three little legs sprouting out of his bottom. Nena was sorry to admit to herself that in the sun, Emiliano was even more handsome than indoors. He had very fine bones in his face, which made him look almost delicate. This made Nena mad. She didn't want to be thinking about Emiliano. Antonio passed around bolillos in a little basket, a bowl of beans, a platter of squash. He served the meat, spooning a cream sauce over the pieces of pork. Emiliano poured the wine. Nena drank a sip. She didn't like the flavor, and that single swallow made her feel too warm.

"Riding always gives me an appetite," Don Javier said.

"What doesn't make you hungry?" Emiliano asked, grinning.

"Who taught you to say things like that? I would never talk to my father that way." Don Javier jabbed a cutlet with his knife. "You'll have to calm down when you're married."

"I was already telling Cousin Elena that I'm planning on growing fat like you."

"You should follow my example in some way. If it weren't for your mamá's dowry, we'd only have half the vineyards. You could use Eugenia's dowry to plant another dozen hectares."

"Yes," Emiliano said, suddenly serious. "We could get the Chávez land for a good price. There's a house on the land that I could fix up for me and Eugenia."

"More foolishness. You can't live out here," Don Javier said.

"If the garrison isn't doing its job with the Apaches, then maybe we should do it ourselves."

"Don't talk nonsense."

"You don't think I know how to fight?" Emiliano asked.

"What do you think about that, Señorita Elena? Do you think this lazy son of mine would have the guts to ride out against Apaches?"

"No," Nena said, and Emiliano looked at her with surprise, anger twisting his face. Good.

Nena got up from the table, and walked off into the vineyard by herself, hoping that Emiliano and Don Javier would be too busy bickering to worry about her.

Once she was sure that she hadn't been followed, she took in a breath, and opening her mouth to breathe out, she began to sing the encanto of healing, surprised that it came to her so easily. Madre Inocenta had said that Nena would go home when the time was right. This had to be it, now. Nena felt certain that at any moment, the earth would twirl and her El Paso would spin back into view.

Nena sang louder. Her feet lifted off the ground. The song seemed to be working, but Nena stayed in El Paso del Norte.

"Señorita Elena," Nena heard. Emiliano was calling for her, very close. "Where are you?"

Nena stopped singing, falling to the ground and landing on her hands and knees.

"Señorita Elena? What were you doing?" Emiliano asked.

"I tripped," Nena said quickly, wondering what he'd seen.

Emiliano reached out his hand, helping her stand. Emiliano was frowning, thinking. "That song you were singing."

"Yes?"

"I've heard it before."

"I don't think so."

"Yes, I'm sure of it."

"I sang it to you the day I came to nurse you," Nena said, too frustrated to lie.

"I understand," he replied, and the way he looked at her, she felt like this was the very first time he had actually listened to her.

19

God," Alejandro says, staring down at Marta. Alejandro has skipped his run, and he and Marta have stayed in bed this morning. It's late. "God, you're beautiful. In San Diego, we may never leave the hotel room."

"Is that so bad?"

"I mean, we weren't even like this when we first got together."

"How about Chiapas?" Marta asks. Over Christmas vacation one year, they'd paid $10 a night to sleep in hostels, zipping their sleeping bags together, Alejandro's body electric and strange next to hers.

"Right. Chiapas. I was half the age I am now. I always thought middle-aged would mean gray hair, a beer belly, a Porsche, that sort of thing. That I'd be dissatisfied with life."

"And you're happy."

"I'm doing what I want to be doing. I'm busy. And so are you."

"Yes," Marta says carefully. "I was going through a rough patch for a while. I wasn't sure I was doing the right thing. Part of me wanted to burn everything down."

"Doesn't everyone think that sometimes? Maybe that's why I like running. Once you get in the rhythm, you can't worry about anything except staying upright and breathing. It's automatic, but it takes enough effort that the brain gives up on fixing anything else. During the long races, I always get to a point where I tell myself I'll never do it again—let's say about mile twenty—but then I pass through to the other side, and I start to feel like I could run forever. For the rest of the day, I feel completely free." Alejandro isn't usually this eloquent.

"And then?"

"And then what?"

"What happens after the feeling goes away?"

"And then I have to do it again."

"Your running has gotten extreme lately," Marta blurts out. That isn't what she had intended to say. But the more he runs, the less time he spends with her. The less time they spend together, the further apart they feel. She used to know him so well.

"I'm not sure what you're getting at, Marta."

"I'm wondering if you started to run more, longer, for any particular reason."

"Other than that I like to challenge myself?"

"Because you're the age that you are."

Alejandro turns so he's on his side, propping his head up with one hand. "Are you trying to pick a fight?"

"I just wanted to know if there are things you think you've missed out on."

"This is how you feel? What've you missed out on?"

"I don't know. Like the Supreme Court."

"Seriously? That's what you're thinking about? Among other things in the way, it's not like you've been trying to take that path."

"But still."

"Help me out here. What are we talking about?"

"Nothing. Everything is great," Marta says, and she's surprised to see that she's speaking the truth.

She has two hearings at the courthouse, and looking at the clock on the bedside table, she realizes she's behind schedule. An hour later, the boys are dawdling. Rafa is in the bathroom, slicking down his hair with gel, a first for him. Pablo and Nena are chatting in Nena's room. Marta pokes her head in and hears Pablo say, "At the end of camp next week, one of us gets to take the mouse home."

Nena's still in bed, wearing a nightgown.

"You feel OK?" Marta asks.

"Have you heard any encantos?" Nena asks.

Marta shakes her head firmly at Nena, like, *let's not talk about this in front of Pablo*, but she also means no, she hasn't heard anything.

"Where did you put my backpack?" Rafa whines from down the hallway, as though Marta's hidden it from him.

Marta hustles the boys into the hot garage, into the car. Next door, Mrs. Price nods hello from her front porch. She's pointing a hose at her potted plants.

Marta cranks up the air conditioner. The sun has risen over the mountain, shining down on the wide valley. Marta drives down the hill, through the neighborhood of long, low brick houses and adobes, neat lawns or cactus and rock gardens in the front yards, and then down a busy road, past strip malls, and up the street that leads to a school sitting on the edge of a dusty mesa. Pablo and Rafa run out of the car without looking at her, heading toward the front doors. Rafa drags his backpack on the ground. Pablo holds his above his head like he's trying to launch a kite. They hardly ever kiss her in public anymore, making every goodbye with them feel incomplete.

Marta turns on the radio to try to cover up the noise of the hum, flipping away from the murmurings of public radio to a Mexican station that plays violent narcocorridos. She turns the song up, "Never been afraid of death, tell Pac I'm coming soon," the man sings in Spanish. Her little car shakes. One of the speakers is blown out, some small component rattling around in the casing. She presses the accelerator, making the engine whine until it matches the sound of La Vista.

In the first hearing of the day, Marta succeeds in securing a restraining order in a domestic violence case. She retrieves the signed order from the clerk before hurrying down the hall to argue for the order to compel Soto to sit for his deposition. The courtroom is chilly. The carpet, the walls, and acoustic tiles on the ceiling swallow the sounds of speech, the buzzing of the recording devices, the clacking of the court reporter typing in the corner. Under all of this, Marta hears the hum.

The lawyer on the opposing side wears Tony Lama snakeskin cowboy boots and a bolo tie. He fumbles in his argument, getting the language of a statute wrong.

"Objection," Marta says.

"Sustained," Judge Sullivan says, nodding at Marta. "I know, I know, he misquoted." Marta feels the glee of winning a point. But then when Judge Sullivan asks Marta a question, the hum grows so loud that Marta can't understand what he's saying. She asks the judge to repeat himself.

A black patch of soot appears on the wall behind him, winking at Marta. The stain detaches itself, turning into a tiny cloud. Marta moves the cloud over the judge's head. A clap of thunder rumbles through the courtroom, and there's the smell of ozone, the dampness of rain, and wet creosote bush, like during a summer storm. Marta looks at the wall. The door to the judge's chambers is gone, replaced with the rock formations of the Hueco Tanks.

Judge Sullivan lifts his hand to touch the top of his head, inspecting it and narrowing his eyes at the water.

"You know what? Never mind, motion approved," he says.

Marta walks out of the courtroom, fast, her whole body now a tuning fork, even her eyeballs vibrating. A thousand bees buzz under Marta's scalp. She needs to eat. That's what Nena said about La Vista, it needs to be fed. Marta digs into her purse, retrieving a package of trail mix, gobbling it down—salty peanuts, bitter sunflower seeds, sweet raisins holding on to the droplets of sun that honeyed them. Marta swallows the last handful, and that settles the storm so that she can see the real world again.

Sofia's sitting on a bench in the hallway, very upright.

Marta eases herself down next to her.

"Your office said you'd be here," Sofia says.

"What can I do for you?"

Sofia takes Marta's hand and opens it so that her palm faces up. On it, Sofia places a tiny curl of metal.

"I scraped this off my tongue last night."

"What is it?"

"I woke up because I thought I heard Mamá calling for me. I went to check on her, but she was sleeping. My tongue felt funny. I went to look at it in the mirror in the bathroom. I stuck it out, and it was silver, a piece of silver shaped like a tongue, solid, but warm because it was in my mouth. I thought I was having a dream. I touched it. The silver was soft. I scraped off three strips with my fingernail. In the morning, when I went to the bathroom, I found the shavings on the sink. You put the mal de ojo on me," Sofia chokes out, and Marta can see the pit of fear behind her eyes.

"I didn't," Marta says, but did she? Now she doesn't know.

"I know what you are. Mamá told me. She said she could smell it on you. She warned me yesterday when you came to my house. That's when you must have done it. You threatened me."

"Did you talk to any of the other plaintiffs?"

"I called Belén. She's my friend. Why won't you leave me alone?

Haven't you done enough to me? I was just trying to take care of my family."

"Why are you here?"

"Take the curse off me, and I'll do anything you want."

"All I ever wanted was for you and the other plaintiffs to win the case against Soto," Marta says, but what if she has done this to Sofia? They'd met eyes, and Marta had sent her anger into her. If Marta could cause a small storm, why not a silver tongue?

"Please. I'll do anything you want, just make this stop," Sofia begs.

"Did you recant your testimony to the state investigators?"

"Yes. I did it right after I left your office the other day. I told you I would. I keep my word."

"Soto gave you that car."

"Yes."

"Has he given you anything else?"

"Money."

"How much?"

"Ten thousand dollars."

"That must help out at home."

"It's not enough."

"I'm not sure what to do with you. Your testimony for your deposition contradicts what you told the investigators. We could depose you again, but you're not a good witness anymore for anyone. You're not credible."

"Please, there must be something I could do."

Marta considers how far she is willing to go to win this case. It's for Sofia's own good that Marta needs to steer her in the right direction, keep her away from Soto. Sofia stands to make a lot more than ten thousand dollars if they settle the case.

Marta thinks about the packing shed. All those cameras.

"Do you know where he keeps his tapes?"

Sofia shakes her head. "But I made recordings."

"You have copies of the tapes at the packing shed?"

"No, no. Of conversations."

"With Soto?"

"He said if I told the investigators that I'd made up my story he would pay me. And give me the car."

Texas is a one-party consent state for voice recordings, which means that Sofia's recordings can be used against Soto. It's worth it to push Sofia to do what's right. Marta can't lose her nerve now that she has a real chance to help all of the clients.

"Send me the recordings, and I'll lift the curse."

20

Nena sat next to Emiliano in the courtyard of the de Galvez house, looking at a page of a prayer book, not really reading it. Other than the Bible, this was the only other book in the house. It had pretty pictures that Nena had spent many hours examining, but she wasn't interested in the pious verses that reminded her of the convent. Emiliano held a red ledger of accounts on his lap, making notations in the columns. Never having seen Emiliano do any work before, Nena was surprised that he had the ability to concentrate and do math.

María came into the courtyard, holding a folded letter that she handed to Emiliano. Emiliano slid his finger under the sealing wax, ripping the paper. Nena watched as his eyes darted across the paper. He threw the letter on the ground.

"What's happened?" Nena asked.

"She says she's going to profess."

"Who?" Nena asked.

"Eugenia."

"She wants to be a nun?" Nena asked. That couldn't be true. Emiliano must have misread the letter. "That's the last thing Eugenia would do."

"Here, read it yourself. She states her plans very clearly."

Nena took the letter from Emiliano and scanned it. Emiliano stood up, the ledger sliding off his lap to the ground.

"She can do as she wishes, but Papá is going to be very angry when he hears that we aren't going to get that dowry. It would have been very useful," Emiliano says. Nena didn't believe that Emiliano wasn't hurt, or at least embarrassed.

Joaquín came in through the arch from the stable yard, holding his hat in one hand and a bottle of brandy in the other.

"Thirsty?" Joaquín asked.

Emiliano grunted. Joaquín opened the bottle, pouring some of the liquor into the glasses Nena and Emiliano had been drinking water out of.

"I'm sorry about my sister," Joaquín said.

"What are you sorry for?"

"She's the last one I ever thought would become a nun."

"That's what everyone keeps saying," Emiliano said, glaring at Nena. He drank his brandy, slamming his glass on the table with a bang.

"You're probably better off without her."

"I've warned you that you shouldn't speak ill of your sister," Emiliano said. His tone was so cold, snow might as well have been falling from the blue sky. Nena felt ashamed for him.

"It was very nice of you to come," Nena said to Joaquín. Nena felt Emiliano's stare freezing the side of her face.

"I'm glad to know I have one friend here in the de Galvez house," Joaquín said.

"Friend?" Emiliano asked. "Who?"

"Maybe you'd like to take a walk around the plaza on Sunday?" Joaquín asked, bowing to Nena. "With the permission of Don Javier, of course."

"Yes, that would be nice," Nena said. She needed to go home, but if Joaquín were to court her, then maybe Don Javier wouldn't try to pawn her off onto some old man with fourteen children.

"Fuck him," Emiliano said when Joaquín left.

"Why were you so rude? He only came to apologize to you."

"He came to flirt with you," Emiliano muttered.

"Why does it matter to you so much?" Nena burst out. She hoped it wasn't because of her. He had no claim on her.

Emiliano stood up, walking toward her.

"What are you doing?" Nena asked, alarmed, as he put his arms around her and pulled her up off her chair. Oh. She tilted her face up. He leaned down to kiss her, and she kissed him back.

"There," he said. "I don't want to talk about Joaquín anymore."

The night of her first real kiss, Nena woke up in the dark, hearing with La Vista that Emiliano was awake. She pulled a thick rebozo around herself, moving through the dark house, following the sound of his breath. She found him standing in the courtyard.

"Elena, how did you know I wanted you to come?" Emiliano asked her.

She hadn't told him he could use her first name, but he'd taken it. And he'd said tú. Tú, closing the distance between them, even though he was a man, and she was a woman. He knew what he'd done speaking to her this way. He knew his power over her, that she wanted what he wanted.

But she was a good girl. She couldn't let herself do what she knew was wrong. She wasn't married to Emiliano.

"I'm not what you think I am," Nena said.

"I know exactly who you are." He touched Nena's cheek with the back of his hand.

"I'm not like you. I'm like your sister—" Nena couldn't say her name. She didn't want to bring Sister Benedicta into the courtyard with them.

"When I saw you in the vineyard singing, I remembered what you did to me, when I was sick. You kissed me and you made me better."

"No," Nena said. "You kissed me."

"Is there a difference?" Emiliano leaned down to kiss Nena. She extended up on her tiptoes and felt the kiss flow down her body. She wanted to stay there and keep kissing, but Emiliano pulled away. He put his finger to his lips, and then he took Nena's hand, leading her through the house and to his bedroom. He lifted the latch to his door, holding it open so Nena could pass through first. He was gentle as he took her nightgown off her, gentle as he kissed her neck, her breasts. He pulled his shirt over his head, wriggled out of his pants, and then he brought Nena to his bed.

After that first night, they couldn't keep their minds or their hands off each other. With that first kiss, the door to the hot center of the earth had swung open. Nena was sure that they were the only two people who had ever felt this way.

When they were together, they were animals in the barnyard. Nena liked it. She hadn't known women could crave sex like that. She was always told that men would take what they wanted, and women had to guard their honor. She'd been lied to, protected from something that was hers by right. Nena burned with a beautiful fever, unable to think about anything but her desire, the world on fire just for her.

Nena longed for Emiliano with every bit of her body. She'd been wrong about everything. La Vista had brought her to this place for a reason, and Emiliano was the only spell she wanted to have in her mouth. This was the only place she wanted to be.

She tried to be with him in every part of the house. She was glad that the good girl in her had died. Why not admit to herself how sex really was? There was sweat and the other smells of the body, and Nena made strange sounds. It wasn't a pretty thing. But it was beautiful in how maleducado it was.

Nena thought about Emiliano when she got up, when she washed her face, and when she rode Palomita with him through town. She thought about him when she said her prayers, and when she dreamed, Emiliano dreamed with her. Weeks passed, a month, and then another. When María tied Nena's corset and the cords pulled the breath out of her, it made her feel like Emiliano was on top of her, heavy on her chest.

"Tighter," Nena said to María.

When they were at breakfast, Emiliano found Nena's foot under the table. She slid her shoe to the inside of his leg, toward the heat of his lap.

One week, Emiliano had to return to Chihuahua to sell wine, and every day that he was gone, Nena grew hungrier. When María brought her breakfast, Nena wanted a hundred more rolls, a bucket of chocolate instead of the little cup that she drank in one gulp. It disgusted her that she'd become as obsessed with food as Don Javier.

"Chicken," Don Javier grunted in greeting when Nena came into the dining room near the end of the week.

"Chicken?" Nena asked.

Don Javier pointed at the man carrying in a platter of roasted hens. The cook had browned the skin perfectly. The meat smelled of oregano and chile. María placed a leg and thigh on Nena's plate. Nena cut off a piece and took a small bite, trying to keep the overwhelming hunger from gaining control of her. She took a second bite of the chicken. It was juicy, the skin salty and crisp.

Nena chewed every bit of meat off the chicken bones, cracking the little huesos between her teeth and sucking out the marrow. She ate a half dozen bolillos, cramming her mouth with the softness of the bread, and then when the rolls were gone, she scooped rice into her mouth, holding her head as close to the plate as she could, making it easier to get the food into her.

Nena looked up from her hunched position to see Don Javier staring at her, holding on to his knife. Their eyes met. Nena put her hands around her plate, like a dog protecting something she'd dragged out of the trash. Don Javier looked away from Nena, like he was afraid that she was going to eat him next, and if María hadn't brought out the beef in a wine sauce, Nena might have. Nena gobbled up the meat and the roasted zucchini, stuffing herself so full she thought she would snap the laces of her corset.

Nena only stopped eating when there was no more food on the table. While she waited for her cup of chocolate, she felt she could finally take a breath, a stomach breath, like her stomach had run out of air. She'd eaten more than seemed possible, but she was still very hungry, and not just for chicken and rice, beef and potatoes, the bowl of bread she'd eaten like a pig. This was a magical hunger that had taken control of her, caused by what she didn't know, sex, or her love for Emiliano, or a manifestation of La Vista.

"Tomorrow we'll slaughter an ox for you," Don Javier said, thinking he was making a joke. Nena didn't laugh. She worried about what had happened to her. She knew what it was like to not have enough to eat, going all day without during the very lean years, until she came home and had a dry tortilla and a few beans, but this was something else.

When Emiliano came back, sex took the place of her hunger for food.

Nena fed herself as much of Emiliano as she could get. They left each other notes under the statue of la Virgin in the courtyard with the lemons.

Meet me in the stables after la cena, Nena read one morning, and then she slipped the note into her pocket, beginning the countdown until they would be able to touch each other.

To go to him, she wore a petticoat but no underwear, walking through the house and out to the stables. She heard the horses in their stalls, snorting and stepping. Emiliano had arranged it so that Antonio was out with the groom. Nena smelled the odor of the barn, the manure and the horse pipí, and she didn't want to lie down on the dirt floor, so they stayed standing, kissing. Nena put her legs around him and he pulled up her skirts and slid himself inside of her. Nena had been trying to be quiet, but she screamed.

"Have I hurt you?" he asked, putting her down.

"Do it again," Nena told him.

"You are a diablita," he said, kissing her. "Tell me again where you came from."

"I came from the future," Nena said, and though she hadn't planned on telling him that, it felt good to tell the truth, even if Emiliano wouldn't believe her.

"That's how women behave in the future? Take me with you. What else happens in the future?"

"We don't have horses. We have cars and we fly in machines in the sky." Nena was exaggerating here. She'd never flown, not like that.

"You tell good stories. Tell me more."

"Yes," Nena said. He thought she was making up stories, so she could tell him anything. "We have palaces where you look at a wall and watch pictures move, and you can hear the people in the pictures talk."

"Now I don't know what you're talking about. Tell me more about what you want me to do to you."

"Like this?" Nena asked. She slipped her hand between his legs, feeling him, and a shiver ran through her. She laughed. He pulled her to him, and they kissed, long and hard, just kissing, holding each other. Nena buried her face into his chest, smelling his sweat. He kissed her again, and then she bit him hard on the shoulder.

"See, you are a diabla."

Nena traced the bite mark with her finger. The light came through the small window, picking up the dust suspended in the air. Nena kissed his shoulder, and he pulled her face to his, kissing her back, brushing the hair off her face with his thumbs. Nena wanted to tell him what she really was, that she could do magical things. She wanted to make him fly, not in an airplane but by lifting him up with her song.

"Do you know how you got better when you were so sick?"

"You kissed me."

"Yes, and I fed you something that made you better."

"Medicine?"

"A magical elixir. I'm a bruja," Nena said.

"I believe it. You've enchanted me," he said, the joke in his voice.

"No. Listen to me. I can do things no one else can."

"I know that already," he said, grinning. He reached into Nena's dress, holding on to her breast, running his thumb along the underside of her nipple, kissing her.

Nena heard the gate opening and the jingling of tack. She jumped back from Emiliano and adjusted her dress, pulled the veil over her face, and slipped out the back door, across the stable yard and into the kitchen, where the cook pulled out a stool for her.

"Siéntese, señorita," she said.

The room was too hot. An olla of beans bubbled over the ashy fire. The kitchen smelled like mesquite. The cook plucked pigeons, putting the feathers in a basket. Without thinking, Nena started to help, holding on to the body of a pigeon and ripping out the tiny breast feathers. She'd always hated plucking chickens at home, but the feathers of pigeons were a lot easier to remove. It was satisfying to rip the things off, getting down to the bare flesh. This was the first bit of decent work she'd done her whole time there.

"Señorita Elena, no!" the cook said, trying to take the bird away from her.

"No one's coming in here. The men won't," Nena said, but right as this came out of her mouth, Don Javier appeared in the kitchen.

"What are you doing here?" he asked.

"I miss the convent kitchen," Nena said.

"I came to tell Cook that I changed my mind about the soup, but I'm happy you're here," Don Javier said. He'd never used a word like "happy" before. He reached toward Nena and plucked a piece of straw off her shoulder. "Put on your nice dress for dinner. We have some good news to celebrate."

❋

In the dining room that evening, Don Javier opened a bottle of champagne, pouring the stuff into real glasses, crystal. Nena wondered what they were celebrating, but she took her glass, drinking, savoring the feel of the bubbles on her tongue, remembering the night of the concert, the first time Emiliano had kissed her hand. She finished her glass, feeling happy, amazed at how young she'd been at the concert. She hadn't known anything.

"Mi amor," Don Javier said, looking at Nena. She frowned, not sure why he was using that word with her. "I've found a man for you who doesn't need you to provide a dowry."

"Who?"

"Me."

Nena's body went cold, but she tried to school her face to stay neutral. "You?"

"Don't we get along well? I like a woman with an appetite, and you're much better at riding than when you first arrived."

"Yes," Nena said, remembering the day last week she'd gone out to ride with Emiliano. How they'd sent Antonio and María away while she and Emiliano had sex under the blanket they'd brought, how Emiliano had licked her breasts. They'd been on the north side of the river, but Nena hadn't wanted to sing herself home. She'd wanted to stay with Emiliano forever.

Emiliano stared down at his knife, and Nena couldn't catch his eye. Had he known this was coming?

What could Nena do? Don Javier hadn't asked her to marry him. He had simply made an announcement, like she didn't have a choice in the matter. If she said no, then what? She had nowhere to go. Don Javier knew this even better than she did. Nena had to accept his plan for her, even though he didn't love her. To him, she was nothing, just a woman, barely human. They'd hardly ever talked. Sometimes it seemed like he didn't even know she was in the room. Even now, he wasn't waiting for an answer from her, he was pouring himself another glass of champagne.

"I don't think long engagements are healthy. Right, Emiliano? Women become nuns if you're not careful."

"No, Papá," Emiliano said. Nena waited for Emiliano to say more, to tell Don Javier that he and Nena were—what? How could Emiliano tell his father what he and Nena had been doing? Under the table, Nena felt around with her foot, hunting for Emiliano's toes, but she couldn't find them. Even just one tap back from him would have given her some hope.

Don Javier finished the champagne, and then called for a jug of wine. Emiliano drank only water, but he made his way through all the food, a dove pie, trout in a cream sauce. Nena took small portions of everything, no longer hungry, a hole in the center of her being aching for Emiliano's touch. She felt sick, like she could throw up. When the cognac was brought out, Emiliano poured himself a big glass. Nena could barely drink her chocolate, and she waved away the plate of pastries.

"What happened to your appetite today?" Don Javier asked Nena.

"Tonight, I'm too happy to eat, señor," Nena said, smiling weakly.

"Well don't starve yourself. I like a woman who has some substance to her. We'll marry at the end of the month."

In her room that night, Nena sat on the edge of her bed, her back straight, her hands in fists, madder than she'd ever been. Mad at Emiliano for being cowardly. Mad at Sister Benedicta and Madre Inocenta for taking Nena from her real home. Mad at herself for being curious that night. Mad at Luna and Olga for making her take care of the babies all the time. If she hadn't been so tired and mistreated, she wouldn't have left. Mad at the sick-hungry feeling eating her away from the inside.

It grew dark. The adobe walls kept out the sound from the street, and eventually the noises of the house died down as the servants finished their work for the day, the house as quiet as the convent after the completas had been sung. Even though Nena still felt queasy, there was a gnawing in her stomach that she had to do something about. Maybe she could manage a dry tortilla.

She walked out of her room and down the hallway, holding her candle in front of her, heading toward the kitchen, walking through the courtyard. An owl hooted. Nena smelled the blossoms of the lemons and the limes that had started to bear fruit. She stopped and picked an orange, peeled it, then ate the segments one by one, savoring the juice. Nena smelled the smoky wood fire from the kitchen house. She pictured the food of the kitchen, the beans and the tortillas, the stewed green chiles, the spicy pozole. The cook slept in a cot in the kitchen. Nena didn't want to wake her up, but the orange wasn't quite enough to satisfy her hunger.

Nena felt hands on her arms, strong. She was dragged into the dining room, her candle going out in the struggle.

"I don't want you to marry my father," Emiliano whispered. "You believe that, don't you?"

"I have to do what he tells me. I have nowhere to go."

"I'm my own man," Emiliano said, squeezing Nena's arms. He was being too rough, and Nena pushed him away. She wasn't sure what she wanted to do. Slap him? Run from the room? She wasn't going to cry.

Emiliano kept holding Nena tight as he slipped down her body, squeezing her chest, her belly, her waist, until he was down on his knees, his arms wrapped around her thighs. "I'm your servant. Tell me what you want me to do."

Nena touched the top of his head. She knew what she wanted. She wanted to go home, to start over again. But she also wanted Emiliano, every piece of him in every way possible, forever. She wished she could take him back to her own time, away from this El Paso where she had even less control over her life. Nena pictured Emiliano in an army uniform, more handsome than Beto.

But Nena was here, in this El Paso. Nena had always known that Emiliano was bad, knew he was going to get her in trouble. None of that had mattered to her. Nena pulled Emiliano up, and then they kissed. He picked Nena up and carried her over to the big, blackened table, laying her down in front of the paintings, the ancestors looking down through the dark. Nena felt the vibrations from them, and this excited her, too.

She pulled up her dress. He put his hand on her mouth.

"No grites," he said, but Nena couldn't help herself. She made a lot of noise against his hand, keeping it just for the two of them. The nature of desire is that it never ends. But that night, in that moment, Nena felt like she was getting everything she wanted.

When they were done, Emiliano kissed Nena on her cheek, the side of her nose, her forehead. He squeezed her closer to him. She heard the beating of his heart, happy to feel his strong arm around her. But as they lay there, the table grew uncomfortable, hard on her back. She shifted, propping herself up.

"Papá—" Emiliano started to say, but Nena stopped his talking with a kiss. She didn't want to think about what would happen next.

"You have to listen to me," Emiliano said, getting up off the table, pulling on his clothes. It was so dark, Nena couldn't see his face, but he'd moved so close to her that his whisper touched her skin. "You're not going to marry him. I won't allow it. I want to marry you."

Nena smelled wine on his breath, and her stomach did a turn. The sick feeling came back, bringing the salty taste to her mouth.

Nena jumped up off the table and ran out to the courtyard. The owl hooted again. She threw up in the pot holding the lemon tree, heaving, even though there was nothing in her stomach.

And then Nena knew what was happening to her.

21

A flash of lightning brightens the kitchen, a clap of thunder following right after, making Marta jump. Through the glass doors at the back of the house, she watches giant raindrops strafe the surface of the pool. That's a relief anyway. Marta hadn't realized that she'd been waiting for the storm to start.

This storm is vastly larger than the one she saw in the courtroom earlier in the day. When Marta moved the little cloud and it rained on Judge Sullivan, he ruled in her favor. At Sofia's house, she made a threat, vague, but very much intended, and Sofia's tongue turned into a hunk of silver. Now Sofia has promised to give Marta evidence that could make Soto settle. If La Vista has given Marta these powers, she's curious what else she can do. She'll get on the phone to donors to the law firm, sure, but there are quite a few other things Marta would like to fix in the world, bigger things than funding for her nonprofit.

"Can I have a snack?" Pablo asks from the big table, where he's drawing with Rafa and Nena.

"I'll help you make quesadillas," Marta says. Her children don't care that she's a powerful lawyer witch. That's OK. Everything's OK right now, except for how buzzy she feels, electricity running between her skin and her muscles.

Pablo scoots a stool up to the counter, banging the old box grater down on the cutting board. He pushes the whole giant block of Monterey Jack against the side.

Rafa comes into the kitchen and sits on a stool next to his brother. He starts kicking the cabinet, hard, thump, thump, thump. Marta always hates it when he does that, but with La Vista's currents running through her, the thumping makes her heart jump in time.

"If you don't stop doing that, you won't be allowed to watch a TV program after dinner," Marta says.

Rafa stares at her, considering. Thump.

"I'm going to make a flan for dessert," Nena says, getting up from the table.

"Do I like flan?" Rafa asks.

"It has a caramel sauce."

"I'll help you," he says, sliding off his stool. Marta won't tell him that flan is slithery, a texture he hates.

Pablo lines up the tortillas, carefully mounding cheese in the center of each. Nena moves around the kitchen, assembling the ingredients for the flan.

Marta oils the comal, putting it on the stove to heat up. When Marta cooks the quesadillas, she takes care to make some of the tortillas crispy around the edges the way Pablo likes them, while keeping others soft, the way Rafa prefers his.

"Dedos," Pablo commands as Marta takes the first batch off the comal. Marta cuts the quesadillas into strips. "Dedos" is the word that her mom used, fingers. Olga, too. Marta slides the dedos onto a blue platter, then takes one for herself.

Pablo licks the grease off his own fingers. "Tell the joke about the ear."

"Again?" Marta asks.

"Tell the joke. And I want some milk," Pablo says.

"Say please."

"Please. Tell the joke."

Marta pours milk into plastic cups, setting one in front of each boy.

"There was once a lawyer who was defending a man accused of biting off another man's ear in a bar fight," Marta says.

"What's a bar fight?" Rafa asks.

"A fight."

"But it was in a bar? Were people drinking beer?"

"The important thing," Marta says, "is that the lawyer was a very young man, very inexperienced. He's sure he's going to win, and he starts cross-examining the witness for the prosecution.

"'Did you see my client fight the alleged victim?' he asks.

"'No.'

"'Did you see my client bite the victim?'

"'No.'

"And then, sure that he's cornered the witness, he asks, 'Then how do you know he bit his ear off?'

"'I saw him spit it out.'"

Milk shoots out of Pablo's nose. Marta mops the milk up with a dishrag. The corners of Rafa's mouth twitch up before he pulls them back down again; he's not going to give Marta the satisfaction of a smile.

"That's funny," Nena says. "I've never heard that one before."

"The lesson here is that in court, you don't ask questions you don't know the answer to," Marta says. This is something most lawyers have learned the hard way, Marta included. Information is power, and the way to get information is to do your homework. This is how Marta has organized her work life, to be super prepared. Or it has been up until now. Now with La Vista, it seems all Marta has to do is think about what she wants, and then the world shifts to meet her needs. She could worry that it's been too easy, but maybe what's been happening is water flowing down a hill, nature following its path.

Quesadillas and cut-up carrots and celery are dinner, easy, quick. Marta retreats into her office while Nena and the boys slurp flan and watch TV together. It's nice that Nena's there to keep an eye on the boys. She even puts them to bed.

Alejandro arrives late, takes a shower, and when Marta goes into their bedroom to check on him, he's in bed, glasses on, eyes closed, a book about sailing facedown across his chest. Marta removes his glasses, slides an envelope in the book to mark his place, and turns out his light. She looks at his small, dark mouth, his bushy eyebrows. She wants to put her hand on his cheek, run her fingers through his hair, down his neck, and then— Marta shakes her head. She can wait until the morning.

Marta changes into her bathing suit. The water of the pool glows green, and it's quiet out, the air freshened by the rain, velvety with its retained heat. Marta swims a handful of laps, slow and easy.

When Marta swam on teams in childhood and all through high school, her hair was always brownish-green and hay-like, the pool a second home. In college, she wasn't good enough to compete, but most mornings, she woke in the dark and hurried to the gym under the low skies of winters in western Massachusetts, past naked trees, through the snow and cold, to open the door to the pool and be hit with the smell of chlorine, the warmth of the humid air. After her swim and shower, Marta would race back to the dorm, the strands of wet hair falling out of her wool cap, freezing as she ran to her breakfast of oatmeal and burnt coffee. It was on those cold mornings that Marta longed for El Paso the most, dreaming of heat and blue sky and sun, remembering what Nena had told her when she was eight, that she would end up living in El Paso in a house with a pool, with kids, a husband. And now here she is, in that pool.

El Paso has always been magical for Marta, even without La Vista. In El Paso, Marta was allowed to play with water guns. In El Paso, she went on black widow spider hunts, Marta and Juan stealing matches and napkins from Olga's kitchen, smuggling them out to the horse shed at the back of the lot, trapping the spiders under glass jars, burning them alive. The taste for smoke still hovered inside her now; there were so many spiders in her life that she wished to trap.

They had picked burrs off tumbleweeds and cracked them open like oysters, eating the tiny seeds. At Chico's Tacos, the tacos came three to an order, crispy tortillas rolled around mashed up beef, placed on top of a puddle of a spicy red tomato sauce, covered with little squiggles of grated orange cheese. After mass, they'd go to Luby's, a cafeteria very different from anything called that name in California. Marta loved moving through the food line, picking up the flatware that came rolled in a smooth cloth napkin, watching the man in a tall paper chef's hat cut thick slices of prime rib sitting under an orange heat lamp. Marta always had fried chicken, mashed potatoes, and green beans, even though she hated having to choke down the slimy things before being allowed to eat dessert, selected from the tiers at the end of the food line, the bottom level of the rack featuring puddings and bowls of red Jell-O cubes topped with whipped cream, the top, slices of cherry, apple, and pecan pie. In El Paso it snowed in the winter, and in the summer, it burned.

El Paso was magical because it was where Marta's mother was from, and where she and her cousins had fled, like characters in a fairy tale leaving to seek their fortunes. They went to the best schools they could get into, becoming doctors and lawyers and teachers and social workers. In the El Paso they grew up in, there were signs in store windows that read "No Dogs or Mexicans." Once in the first grade, when Chuy spoke Spanish in class, his teacher taped his mouth shut. Anglos held all of the elected positions until not that long ago. That was the word used, Anglos, meaning not Hispanos, an old word that used to have meaning. Since then, things have changed in El Paso, and the old prejudices, though still there, are only part of the mix of cultures. Everyone speaks a little Spanish, and there are lots of completely bilingual people, nobody is just one thing, and this mix is why Marta lives here. Marta is a mix herself, the witchy bit of her only just now stirred in, the thing she's been missing. She's in love with Nena and Alejandro and the boys and El Paso, the place that has brought her to La Vista.

Rafa and Pablo open the sliding glass door from the living room, dressed in their bathing suits.

"What are you doing out of bed? Get back to your room right now, you two."

"We heard you swimming. We wanted to get in the pool with you," Rafa says, and before she can tell him no, he jumps in, swimming toward her. He doesn't have a bad stroke, but his arms are too cramped, his movements jerky. He needs to learn how to open up, stretch out. When Marta was on the swim team, she never imagined, couldn't have imagined, that she'd be where she is now and that she'd have a son like Rafa. Pablo enters the water more gingerly, walking down the stairs, paddling over to her.

When Pablo reaches her, he winds his arms around her neck.

"Mamá, I need to tell you something."

"Yes?" Marta asks, guessing he has some small sin to confess.

"I saw the old lady in black."

"What old lady?"

"She said she was Nena's sister."

"Where did you see this person?"

"In our room. She said she had a message for you."

"Tell me," Marta says, putting her arms around Pablo, squeezing him, moving her legs to keep them both afloat.

"She said it in Spanish. 'Ven aquí.' That means come here," Pablo says.

Imperative. Informal you. Come here. A command, not a request.

"Did she say anything else?"

"She sang a song," Pablo says.

"He's making it up," Rafa says, swimming next to Marta. "The other day we heard you and Nena talking about nuns. He's so dumb that he doesn't even know that sister means nun," Rafa says. His face is twisted in anger.

"Out of the pool," Marta says, taking an arm of each boy, practically dragging them out. She wraps a beach towel around them both, rubbing the towel up and down their arms.

"Ow," Rafa says.

Nena warned Marta that La Vista was dangerous. Marta didn't think to be afraid of this, that Sister Benedicta would come for Pablo. Marta will kill Sister Benedicta if she comes anywhere near her son again. How dare she use Pablo as a messenger.

Come here.

Marta could ignore Sister Benedicta's call. Marta doesn't have to tell Nena any of this. Marta could stay right where she is, happier than she's ever been.

A ladybug lands on Pablo's shoulder.

"If a bug walks on you, it's peeing on your skin," Rafa says.

"Get it off me!" Pablo yelps.

As Marta reaches up to brush it off, it disappears into thin air.

"Sing it to me," Marta says to Pablo, and he brings his mouth to her ear.

22

Nena opened the shutters of her room, letting in fresh air, feeling the breeze on her face. She was a disgraced woman, with no family, no money, no place to go. What was she going to do with herself?

One day when she was a girl playing in the front yard, Nena had heard loud whining and terrible gritos. Out on the sidewalk, a dog pumping away on top of another. The lady dog looked very upset, but when Luna ran outside and sprayed the pair with a hose, they ran off together, nipping at each other, ready to go again.

That had been Nena for two months—not thinking, not caring, her hunger endless. And now she was going to end up like one of the neighborhood dogs with their heavy bellies and swollen nipples, having nothing but her teeth for protection. How could Nena have been so stupid? She knew that sex caused pregnancy; she just hadn't thought it would happen to her. She was too young, she wasn't married, she wasn't ready. She thought that what she did here couldn't have real consequences.

Nena hadn't been able to sleep that night, and twice in the morning she'd thrown up in the chamber pot. When María came to dress her, Nena told her that she was sick, which was nothing less than the truth.

María nodded curtly, but soon enough she was back, bringing with her a tisana that she put in Nena's hands.

"Maybe I can help you."

"With what?"

"Oh, señorita. It won't help to ignore the problem. What are you going to do?"

"I have a cold. I'll get over it soon."

"You don't have to tell stories to me. I know what's going on. There are herbs to make it go away. I owe you. I could help you in that way."

"No. I don't want to do that."

"Then he needs to take care of you."

"How?" Nena asked.

"Emiliano's a good boy."

"Is he?"

"I'm going to tell him what's happened to you."

"Please don't." Along with everything else, Nena was embarrassed. Emiliano wouldn't understand. A man's thing got big and then it got small again, but that was all that happened to his body. The baby was growing in her, and soon everyone would see what she had just discovered for herself. María left the room, leaving Nena lying on top of the covers. She drank the tea, forced down a few bites of bolillo. An hour later, Nena heard the latch lift.

Emiliano stood at the doorway, grinning, which seemed wrong. "María said I needed to come talk to you."

"We can't be here alone," Nena said. He was going to make things worse than they already were. Nena would be the one to pay the price, not Emiliano, if they were discovered alone together.

Emiliano closed the space between them, standing right next to her bed. He put his hands on Nena's stomach, spreading them wide.

"Stop," Nena said.

"Good thing we're getting married."

"No, we're not. We can't."

"Is there something you aren't telling me? Is there another man? Joaquín?" Emiliano asked, laughing.

"Never. Don't say that."

"Then what?"

"I'm not someone you can marry. Your father will never allow it."

"We can do whatever we want."

"I don't have a family here, no one to look out for me. Your father has already made plans—"

"Yes, he has."

"So, you see what I mean," Nena said, her heart breaking at his cowardice.

"I won't let him marry you. You're mine. But you're right, we can't marry here. We'll have to go somewhere else. Together." Emiliano sat down on the edge of the bed.

Nena looked up at him. She needed to know if he could leave behind everything he had in the world. She stared hard into his eyes, seeing only his dark irises, the little veins in the glossy whites. His eyes told her nothing. What had she been expecting to see? What else did she need to know except for the testimony of his presence? He knew that she was pregnant. He wanted to take care of her.

"If we go, we have to go right away," Nena said.

"Tomorrow morning then."

"How do we do it?" Nena asked.

"They'll be suspicious if we go out riding together, so we'll leave separately."

"Yes."

"I'll ride to the vineyard early in the morning, and I'll bring Palomita with me. You and María will say you're going to mass, but you'll take the ferry to the north, and we'll meet at the crossroads."

"And then what?"

"We'll ride to the mission at San Elizario, where we'll be married. By tomorrow night you'll be Señora de Galvez. Yes?"

"Yes. And where will we live?"

"Where do you want to go?"

"To the north, to the United States," Nena said. "St. Louis."

"Isn't that French territory?"

Nena wasn't sure about that, hazy on her history. She just wanted to get far enough away from Don Javier, out of Mexico and New Spain. "How about New Orleans?"

"I didn't know you liked the French so much! We could sail from Veracruz, but it would be a very long journey. Let's go to Santa Fe instead. Don't you have family there?"

"Yes," Nena said, even though she knew no one. The important thing was to get away, and now. Nena knew how to ride. "What do we do about money?"

"I'll take care of that. No te preocupes," Emiliano said, touching Nena's lips with his.

The next morning, Nena and María left the house as though they were going to early mass. Nena's excitement was a trembling ache running through her body. She and María walked quickly through town, across the plaza and past the church, north to the ferry, then they crossed to the other side of the Rio Bravo.

The insects of the desert droned, and the wind swept across the sand, rustling the sage and creosote bushes. The sun rose higher. Sweat made Nena's mantilla stick to her forehead, and her wrist felt funny, itchy. She pushed back her sleeve, not seeing a rash. She scratched at it, hard.

"You're going to make it itch worse," María said to her.

The two of them walked out on the road away from town. With each step, the desert grew bigger, the mountains higher. The difficulty of the plan she'd made with Emiliano became clearer the longer she and María walked. Even if Nena and Emiliano made it to San Elizario and were married, then what? They'd still have to find their way up through the pass. On the other side, they'd have to ride hundreds, if not thousands, of miles, most of that distance through wilderness, prey for animals and Apaches. What would they eat? Where would they find water to drink? How would they feed the horses? Nena had nothing with her but the leftover breakfast rolls. She should have taken the silver candlesticks, a cold pigeon from the kitchen, anything she could lay her hands on.

Nena told herself she shouldn't think that way. She should trust that Emiliano would come prepared, with horses and water and wine and gold. Nena looked up at the sun. He was supposed to have been here before she arrived. What would she say if someone asked why she and María were waiting at the crossroads, unaccompanied women without the protection of a man? Whoever saw her might make Nena and María go back to town. But there were worse things that could happen. There were Apaches around here, too. If they were attacked, what could she do? Fly away? She'd never actually flown, only hovered, useless magic.

The wind picked up, blowing in gusts, covering Nena in a layer of yellow dust. She felt it on her lips, in the creases of her eyelids. Already her tongue was like the tongue of a lizard, scaly and rough. She felt ill, dizzy with thirst.

"Something must have happened," María said. "We'll go back home."

"No, let's stay here just a bit longer," Nena said.

María nodded, slipping her rosary out of her pocket to click the beads between her fingers. Nena didn't want to pray with her. Nena needed to have faith that Emiliano would come.

The wind died down and the skies cleared. It was a beautiful afternoon, the most beautiful afternoon of Nena's life. They waited until the sun was at its highest point, and then longer, one hour, two. Nena watched the sun start to make its way down the sky. Then she saw a horse and rider coming their way, fast. No, not a horse, a burro, carrying Antonio. When he reached them, Antonio jumped down, his bare feet sending up puffs of dust. He took a letter from inside his shirt and handed it to Nena. Nena unfolded the piece of paper, recognizing Emiliano's handwriting: *Antonio will accompany you back to the house. Today is not a good day for a horseback ride north.*

Nena folded the letter back up, following the original creases. Why had Nena let herself get her hopes up? Why had she put her future in the hands of a man? She'd known that Emiliano was bad, that he drank too much, that he cared too much about himself. Her mistake had been in thinking that she could change him. He liked what he had, the promise of his future, and he liked having Nena in the house to use for his pleasure. Why would he want to give up his comfort?

Nena couldn't return to the de Galvez house. If she went back, she would have to accept Emiliano for what he was. If she went back, she'd have to marry Don Javier.

"We're going to the convent," Nena said to María.

"Yes," María said. "I've been praying for Sister Benedicta to show you mercy."

Nena sang the encanto to call the ladybugs to her, feeling the familiar tugging at her brain as she connected to the other side.

Three ladybugs blinked in, landing on Nena's hand. She opened up their little minds, inscribing the message that she was coming to the convent. Then Nena sang the ladybugs to Carmela, watching as they blinked out, one, two, three.

23

Before singing the encanto, Nena insisted that they turn off the air-conditioning and open the doors to the backyard, and all the windows. Now, it's at least a hundred degrees in Marta's kitchen.

Alejandro and the boys are at Carlsbad Caverns for the weekend. Alejandro had been confused about why he needed to take the boys, alone, why Marta couldn't go, and then Marta, frustrated, had conjured a little storm that rained on Alejandro's head. After that, he started packing bags for him and the boys, leaving within the hour.

"Last time, it wasn't just insects and slimy things that made their way into the pot. There were deer and birds and other animals. It was more like a stew instead of a powder, and it tasted delicious," Nena says.

Marta and Nena are staring down at an enameled Dutch oven that Kika gave Marta one Christmas. The pot is full of a fine dust that smells like sulfur. The butcher block on which the pot sits is charred from where Nena set down a bundle of burning creosote bush.

"What do we do with this stuff?" Marta asks.

"Eat it," Nena says.

"You really think that's a good idea?"

"You know the joke about the immigrants crossing the river?"

"Oh, no, Nena, please not a joke right now," Marta says.

"Why did the immigrants cross only in pairs?"

"Why?"

"Because they saw a sign that said no tres-passing."

"That's a very bad pun, Nena."

"At any crossing there are rules. You have to prove you're allowed to go to the other side. Now we have what we need, this is our ticket."

Marta can't quite believe that when she sang the encanto Pablo gave her from Sister Benedicta, the ants and scorpions and snails and worms appeared, covering every inch of the tiles, climbing up the sides of the island and fighting each other into the pot, where they cooked, shells clattering.

Nena wets her finger and dips it in the dust, popping it in her mouth.

"Te toca a ti," Nena says. Your turn.

Marta's gone too far down this path to hesitate any longer.

The dust doesn't taste as bad as she expected. More than anything, it's bland, like eating raw flour. Marta braces herself, expecting to be taken away to the sun like Nena had warned her, but all Marta feels is a snapping-to, an extra awareness, an extreme version of when she puts her glasses on first thing in the morning.

The furry soot that was on the wall at Nena's is in Marta's kitchen now, just as black, covering the wall next to the pantry. At Nena's, Marta had no idea what was going on, the pulsing soot too bizarre for her to pick out any details. But now, with the clarity of La Vista, she can see how the soot folds in on itself, with a darker black at the center. In the blackness, there's not so much a door, but a flap, like the entrance to a tent.

Marta takes Nena's hand, and they walk through to the other side.

They enter a place that's chilly with refrigerated air, the sounds muffled by a carpet of a familiar red and blue pattern, an intentionally busy design meant to hide crumbs and spilled drinks. The votives are lit on the tables of La Sirena, glowing red. Marta and Nena stand in the long hallway lined with pews at the entrance. Behind them are the bathrooms and the cigarette machine, in front, the big arched doorway that leads to the dining room, the sign with gold lettering on a black background, "Please Wait to be Seated."

Marta looks over at the bar, hoping to see Luna bent over her papers, a cup of coffee by her side. But La Sirena is empty of people, even if the tables are all set, the restaurant ready for guests to arrive. Marta doesn't think they've traveled in time, so then where are they?

"What are we waiting for, Nena?" Marta asks, but Nena isn't listening. She's staring at the carved door being pulled open from the street.

24

The convent looked and felt the same as when Nena had first arrived, saturated with the familiar smells of incense and mesquite smoke, echoing with the distant sound of chanting. Nena was grateful for the thick walls keeping out the sun and heat of the desert.

In Madre Inocenta's office, Sister Benedicta sat behind the desk, the convent's red ledgers in neat stacks around her. Sister Benedicta nodded at the backless chair in front of the desk, and Nena lowered herself into it, not sure how to start the conversation. There was no point in trying to hide the pregnancy from Sister Benedicta, but Nena couldn't find the words to talk about her condition.

Sister Benedicta poured wine from a decanter into two pewter cups instead of the rough clay tazas the nuns usually used. This seemed like a good sign. Sister Benedicta held out one of the cups, and Nena took it from her, so thirsty she took a big gulp, choking once she recognized the taste of the stuff, wine from the de Galvez vineyards, now vinegar in her mouth. Nena felt her hurt and anger at Emiliano burning in every cell of her body.

"I came back to the convent because I had nowhere else to go," Nena said, bowing her head, willing to grovel.

"You can't be a niña if you're expecting." Sister Benedicta's voice was strained, and Nena wondered who she thought the child's father was.

"No."

"But you may stay here as a servant."

"Yes, Sister Benedicta."

"Once you have the child, I'll find a family for it."

Nena stayed quiet, grateful that at least she wasn't going to be sent back to Don Javier. If Nena had to live as a servant, then she would. She knew how to do that kind of work. She was safe for now, and she had a little bit of time to figure out how to escape the convent with her baby, how to make it across the river and sing herself home. "Are you the abadesa now?" Nena asked.

"I'm in charge while Madre Inocenta is ill."

"She got smallpox?"

"No."

"What then?"

"She ate the brebaje until it was gone, and now she's trapped in La Vista. Her mind is away, living on the other side. It didn't do any good to send you away."

Nena heard the pain in Sister Benedicta's voice, and she was sure that Sister Benedicta still blamed Nena for what Madre Inocenta had done to herself, unfair though that was. Nena hadn't asked to be brought to this El Paso, hadn't asked to have the awful power of La Vista within her. But Nena knew saying this to Sister Benedicta would change nothing.

That same evening, wearing the homespun dress of a servant, Nena returned to the kitchen. She breathed in the welcome smells of roasting tomatoes, fried onion, and the earthy sweet scent of masa. Nena was glad Sister Benedicta hadn't assigned her to a worse job, like tending to the pigs.

Nena looked around the kitchen for Carmela. One servant peeled potatoes. A nun stood over a cauldron, cooking soup. At the back of the room, another nun in a white veil chopped carrots, a huge pile of diced onion already on the side of the chopping block. And then Nena saw Carmela, talking to a servant preparing the chocolate. Carmela wiped her hands on her apron, walking over fast.

"Come with me," Carmela said. She took Nena's arm, pulling her into the storeroom packed with bags of rice and beans, barrels of flour, dried chiles hanging in bunches from hooks. Carmela lunged forward, burying her head in Nena's chest, her body shaking. Was Carmela crying or laughing? Crying. Nena stroked the top of Carmela's head.

"Oh, Nena, how could you have let this happen?" Carmela asked, her voice muffled by Nena's body.

There wasn't anything Nena could say that would make Carmela understand why she and Emiliano had been so reckless, so full of love and lust. But Carmela was right to cry. Nena was ruined, no matter what she'd intended or how she felt about Emiliano.

"Sister Benedicta is going to take the baby away from me once I give birth."

"She can't do that," Carmela said, pulling away from the embrace and wiping the tears off her cheeks. "I don't know how I'll be of aid to you, but I'll do whatever you need. Let's ask Eugenia if she has any ideas."

"Eugenia?"

"You'll see," Carmela said, opening the door of the storeroom.

Back in the kitchen, Carmela following a short distance behind, Nena was shocked to realize that the woman she'd seen chopping vegetables was Eugenia. Her face was horribly scarred, her eyes open but not seeing. Eugenia had been blinded by the infection. How was she able to cut things and not hurt herself?

"Is that Elena?" Eugenia called out.

"Sister," Nena said, not sure what to call her.

"You're pregnant," Eugenia said, a statement not a question, so Nena was silent, and Eugenia continued. Her demeanor was different now, steady in a way only a great loss can make a person.

"What?" Nena asked. Did everyone know?

"I can see it with La Vista," Eugenia explained quietly, so only Nena could hear.

"What do you know about La Vista?"

"I wasn't getting better, so they gave me a bit of the brebaje. Carmela compelled Sister Benedicta to do it. Sick as I was, when I ate the stuff, I saw all the animals in the brebaje running into the room—awful—and I felt them clawing their way down my throat. Now I'm like you."

When Emiliano ate the brebaje, he'd been completely healed, but nothing had been added. He was still a normal person, with a normal person's ability to see the world. Nena didn't understand the randomness of La Vista, its cold cruelty and its rich gifts. This was how the world worked, gifts and punishments unevenly and unjustly distributed.

"La Vista saved my life, but now my visions keep me from leaving the convent," Eugenia said. "So, I professed. Not that anyone would marry me now. They won't even tell me what my face looks like."

"You're healthy and alive, and that's the important thing," Nena said quickly, shocked at how badly the dark scars had marred Eugenia's face. But once Nena took a moment to really examine Eugenia, she was surprised at how alive she looked. Yes, she had scars, but her skin was plump and rosy, her hair glossy.

"I can't forgive you for what you did with Emiliano," Eugenia said quietly.

"Why would you care? Weren't you carrying on with Father Iturbe?"

"I only did that because I needed to leave right away, and Father Iturbe promised he would help me."

"You couldn't wait until Emiliano married you?" Nena asked.

Eugenia shook her head, her face turned to the floor. "I'm not sorry Father Iturbe died. He was punished by God for what he did. And so was I." Her unseeing eyes turned on Nena. "Just like you have been punished for your sins."

Nena felt her pride rush up to meet Eugenia's judgment, and she spoke before she could think. "What about Emiliano? Do you think he'll be punished, too?"

Eugenia's laugh was cold. "Why should he? Soon enough he'll marry a woman of the right class. And when he marries her, he shouldn't be inexperienced as a man," Eugenia said. Nena felt the hurt radiating off Eugenia, her bitterness mingled with the amplifying power of La Vista, the grief at what she could have had, what could have been, racing just beneath her skin. Nena understood all too well what it was like to be changed by this world, to be disfigured, to be discarded. She and Eugenia were sisters now.

"I'm going to need your help getting myself back home," Nena said, taking Eugenia by the arm to draw her closer into a circle with Carmela.

"Home?" Eugenia's brow wrinkled in confusion.

"I need to get back to the time I belong in. Madre Inocenta said that a door would open when the moment was right, and now is that time," Nena said.

"I knew you weren't a Montoya from here or from Santa Fe," Eugenia murmured, gazing sightlessly over Nena's shoulder, deep in thought. Nena could not tell what Eugenia saw, but when she turned back to Nena, her expression was fierce. "What must we do?"

"I need to find the door and return home before I have this baby. If I don't, Sister Benedicta will take her from me and send her away, and who knows what she will do to me. She blames me for what's happened to Madre Inocenta, I'm sure of it. I fear she will do anything she can to hurt me." Turning to Carmela, Nena asked, "Is there any way Madre Inocenta could help?"

Carmela looked pained. "I think not. I'm afraid Madre Inocenta is not herself. She doesn't even talk anymore. None of the nuns will go into her room. Strange things happen there. Cups jump off the table. The chair walks across the tiles. Sometimes the sheets lift up off her body and float in the air."

"If La Vista is making itself known in those ways, then there's something there for me to work with," Nena said, hoping that this was true. "Do you think I could take over Madre Inocenta's nursing?"

"There is no way to make that happen without Sister Benedicta catching on," Carmela started, then turned to Eugenia, who nodded, "but we can get you in the room with Madre Inocenta for a few moments."

"That will have to be enough," Nena said.

❋

When Carmela smuggled Nena into Madre Inocenta's cell, she was shocked at how skinny the abbess had become. Madre Inocenta lay in bed, her skin bagging around her bones, her eyes sunken in so deep that her head looked like a skull. Her lips parted, a very thin rasp coming from her mouth. Nena leaned down, putting her ear close to Madre Inocenta's mouth, and what she heard surprised her, the encanto of flying and healing.

Nena spoke to Madre Inocenta, hoping that some part of her could hear what Nena had to say. "I gave you that encanto. You owe it to me to help me get home to my sisters. I don't belong here. Olga and Nena will take care of me. They won't care that I'm pregnant," Nena pled, though she knew they'd be furious at her, ashamed. "If you're in La Vista now, time and doors are nothing to you. Open up the way and help me go back home. I will do anything to go home. Please."

Nena wasn't expecting a response from Madre Inocenta, but she was still disappointed when none came. Madre Inocenta's body wouldn't maintain itself for much longer. Right now, she was in an in-between place, all the possibility and power of La Vista surrounding her, above and below, on her outside and on her inside. When she died, Nena was afraid Madre Inocenta would pull all the doors shut behind herself.

Over the next few months, the baby grew. Nena could feel its cells gathering in the clockwise motion of incarnation until one day, she felt a kick, the quickening. She knew she had only a handful of months left before she was to give birth.

Nena spent her days working in the kitchen. At night, she slept on a mat in a dirt-floored room with the rest of the servants. Once a week, on Sunday, she went to mass.

When she made her confession to the new priest, she admitted to missing her family. She confessed to having impure thoughts. She said nothing about her impure actions. To confess was to be absolved of your sins, but Nena didn't want to be absolved for what she'd done with Emiliano. Emiliano had given her this baby. The baby was all Nena had left of him, and was all Nena had in the world.

Every time she had a chance, Carmela snuck Nena into Madre Inocenta's cell. Madre Inocenta and the baby communicated with each other, buzzes of electricity passing between them. Nena hoped they were hatching a plan, but she didn't know what they were saying, the buzzing happening on a frequency she had no access to.

As Nena grew bigger, Madre Inocenta grew weaker. One day, Madre Inocenta stopped singing, and Nena despaired. Carmela told Nena that she shouldn't worry, that even if Madre Inocenta died, they would still find a way to get Nena home. Eugenia assured Nena that she knew a lot about knives now, and that if Sister Benedicta tried to take the baby, she would get a nasty surprise.

Nena became so big that everyone in the convent could see that she was going to give birth any day. Within a couple of weeks of each other, Luna and Olga had delivered their babies in the hospital, in the hygienic and modern way. Nena worried about going into labor in the convent, about what would happen if something went wrong. When Luna and Olga were pregnant, Nena remembered the feeling of excitement she'd had about the babies before they came. She'd been thrilled she was going to be an aunt twice over. When they came home, Chuy and Valentina were tiny, so clearly in need of protection. At first, all Nena had to do was to hold the babies when she felt like it, comforting them with a jiggling walk, a pat on the back. It wasn't until later, when Luna and Olga went back to work, that the burden of caring for them fell on her. But for her own baby, Nena told herself, she would do everything without resentment. She wouldn't get tired. She wouldn't complain, she wouldn't pray for supernatural help, or for a different life. She would stay.

Nena knew now that she could not depend on Madre Inocenta to take her home. She had packed a bag. She'd saved food. As much as Nena feared being out in El Paso del Norte without the protection of the convent or the de Galvezes, she would be brave. If Madre Inocenta died, Nena would go to the ferry crossing herself, take her baby to the north of the river and sing the encanto, make her own door, praying that it would return her to where she belonged.

On the day of the birth, Nena squatted in her cell, pushing. Eugenia and Carmela put cold cloths on her forehead and sang over her. Nena stood, she walked, she squatted again, pushing, bellowing, loud enough for everyone in the convent to hear, even through the thick walls of adobe and stucco, but Nena didn't care. She had a job to do. She felt like she was made only of muscle. She pushed and pushed again, pushed forever, long hours, riding waves of pain and then its aftermath, not quite relief, but the exhilaration of being able to do this, feeling strong. The infirmary was dark, hardly any light coming from the small windows high up on the wall.

When the baby was born, Carmela wrapped her in a blanket, handing Nena the wriggling, tiny girl with skinny little frog legs, a lot of hair, a wrinkled face, a stork's mark on her right shoulder. This baby's mouth was a tiny little folded rosebud. She'd named herself, and Nena was in love, cooing *Rosa*. Nena held her, amazed that this tiny person had grown inside of her. The baby had Emiliano's eyes. Nena kissed her forehead. Rosa cried with her strong lungs. She put her mouth to Nena's breast, nuzzling around until she figured out how to make Nena's body do its job.

Nena was tired, but she was young and strong and very happy. Nena held Rosa's body to her chest, stroking down her forehead to between her eyes. She would have to get up soon, find her bag, and leave through the portería, but for at least a few minutes, Nena could rest.

She didn't know when she had dozed off, but Nena woke to a light shining in her face. She looked up, blinded by a light brighter than anything she had ever seen, brighter even than the sun that she'd flown into. She raised her hand, shading Rosa's face. Nena squinted her eyes, surprised to see Madre Inocenta holding open a door, a portal through the walls of the convent and into the sky.

"Come with me," Madre Inocenta said.

"Gracias a dios," Nena said, hugging Rosa closer to her.

Nena walked toward Madre Inocenta, stepping on air to reach the rectangle of light. But then everything went wrong. Time warped and Rosa was slipping from her grasp, no longer in her arms. Turning around, Nena saw that Sister Benedicta was holding her baby, Carmela next to her, shading her eyes with her hand.

"Elena!" Carmela cried, like she couldn't see that Nena was right there, grasping for Rosa.

"Give her back to me," Nena yelled at Sister Benedicta.

"Come with me now," Madre Inocenta said, holding out her hand as the light got, impossibly, brighter.

Time ripped, a low song singing across the desert, bringing with it the sounds of home, of the babies crying and her sisters talking, the sound of water rushing away from the river, draining itself and her away from that time and back into hers. It didn't matter that Nena refused Madre Inocenta's hand, it didn't matter that Nena threw herself on the ground and that she screamed and clawed at the earth, trying to stay with her baby.

Madre Inocenta folded time up like a fan, touching one moment to another, collapsing time and space, and then Nena was lying on East Paisano Drive in El Paso, in the state of Texas, in the United States of America.

25

The door opens, bright sun penetrating the restaurant, two women silhouetted against the light. One of the women is wearing a nun's habit, the other a long dress with a high collar. They are both old.

The woman in the dress runs toward Nena, throwing her arms around her in a rough embrace. Nena hugs this woman back just as fiercely.

"Mamá," the woman says.

Marta watches this, humbled and amazed at this reunion. Looking at this very old mother and her slightly less old daughter, Marta feels La Vista all around her, soupy, moving in eddies and swirls, smelling of cinnamon and cumin, mesquite fires burnt ashy, the west winds, heavy with rain.

Nena and Rosa keep their arms around each other, their heads close, talking quietly, their voices buzzing, too quiet for Marta to make out the words.

Marta can't imagine what this must be like for Nena, what she must feel. Happiness. Pain at the loss of the years she and her daughter have spent apart, separated by a thousand borders. Rosa's thoughts must be just as mixed, love for this mother she never knew, the object of longing, blame, and hurt. But what does Marta know? They're both smiling, big face-stretching grins, and Marta holds the knot of their relationship in her throat.

Marta shivers, suddenly cold to the bone, and she turns to see Sister Benedicta, who is giving her the kind of look Marta hates, a sweeping up-and-down rake that takes in and dismisses everything it sees. Marta may not like being given the once-over, but it's been a long time since she has been intimidated by a look like that. She puts her shoulders back.

"Don't ever go near Pablo again," Marta says.

"I only came to him because I couldn't get through to you. You were using La Vista for your own purposes, blocking us out. Rosa insisted we do something to hurry you and Elena up. She's a very willful child."

"Child?" Marta asks, peering back at Nena and Rosa.

"Don't pay attention to how she appears to you for now. She's only twelve years old."

"I don't understand."

"Even if it looks like we're here in the bodies and minds we had when we died, it's Rosa at age twelve who brought us here. Carmela has been telling her stories about Elena since she was born. This was contrary to my wishes, you understand. I didn't think there was any reason to tell Rosa about a mother she could never know, a mother who brought so much pain to the convent and the aquelarre. I prayed that Rosa wouldn't be cursed with La Vista, but God didn't hear my prayers.

"One day a few months ago, all on her own, Rosa found an encanto in the kitchen. Before that, no one told her about encantos, no one told her she shouldn't sing a wild one. I blame myself. Rabbits were being prepared for dinner that night. The carcasses lay on the worktable, cleaned and dressed, ready to be put on the spits. When Rosa sang the encanto, the rabbits stood up on their hind legs and performed a dance. The servants were so terrified they sent a representative to tell me what they'd witnessed. To keep worse things from happening, I decided to have Rosa enter the aquelarre. Once she joined, all she wanted was to find her mamá, and she was the one who found the encanto I sent to you."

Rosa and Nena are sitting next to each other on the pew closest to the cigarette vending machine. They've shed decades, Rosa now a tween, Nena a very young woman. Rosa is curled up against Nena. Nena strokes her hair with hands that are no longer knobby with arthritis.

"Why couldn't Nena stay with Rosa? Why did you send her away?"

"I don't know what Elena told you, but that had nothing to do with me. They can't exist in the same time. Rosa is your grandmother's mother's mother's mother, all the way back. Look closer," Sister Benedicta says.

The edges of Marta's brain and body go fuzzy, and before she can be truly alarmed, La Vista is showing her everything. Now she's the one hugging Nena, smelling Nena's baby powder scent and the slight sourness of her breath. She feels safe in Nena's arms.

She's Rosa, and she's telling Nena about her childhood, passing on these memories in a wordless way, a seamless flow of images and sensations. She's sitting in the kitchen with Carmela, eating lágrimas de obispo, bishop's tears, pine nut candy that she shoves in her mouth before they're cooled, burning her tongue.

Paloma and Francisca teach her how to read Spanish, and Latin, Greek, and French and English. She opens the page of a book, the Greek letters legible, familiar.

Often when she's growing up, she wakes in the middle of the night, hearing the nuns of the aquelarre creeping along passages, and she imagines her mother doing the same.

She pricks her finger when she's being taught by Eugenia how to embroider, quickly wiping away the blood so that it doesn't stain the fabric. Eugenia is the vicaria, in charge of discipline, and not known for her patience.

"But she's not cruel to you, mija, is she?" Nena asks out loud.

"She never hits me."

"She'd better not," Nena says. "Tell me more. Tell me what happens to you."

Rosa is herself, the twelve-year-old, but she can remember the rest of her long life, since this is before and after it happens. She's a young mother, married with three children, receiving the news of the revolution. They hear of the Grito de Dolores, celebrating the freedom of Mexico from Spanish rule. Guns are fired in the air, a goat roasted in the courtyard. In her middle age, Rosa gives her granddaughter and her husband a blessing, making the sign of the cross on their foreheads before they leave for the Doña Ana Bend grant colony in the wilds of New Mexico up the Mesilla Valley. This granddaughter becomes a citizen of the United States after the Gadsden Purchase. *She was an estadounidense like you*, Rosa says to Nena in her mind. *Now it's your turn: Tell me what happened to you when you left El Paso del Norte.*

And now Marta is Nena, her hair grown out, running down her back.

When she's returned to her El Paso, the streets are full of convoys going to and from Fort Bliss. An army truck full of men passes her, the soldiers whistling and hooting. She walks faster, hunching her shoulders to try to make herself invisible.

A civilian car, a Ford, stops right next to her. Señor Obregon from the corner store honks, reaching across the passenger seat to throw open the door. He tells her to get in before anyone sees her, and when they get to the house, he walks her up to the front door, where Luna is standing. She's wearing a smart navy suit, a hat with a black mesh veil, and white gloves, a little pocketbook tucked under her arm. When she sees Nena, she looks incensed. "Where have you been? Where did you go this morning?" Then she looks down at Nena's clothes, her crude homespun dress, her bare feet. "What happened to you?"

Luna draws a bath, helping Nena take her clothes off, easing her into the tub. The water turns pink. Luna washes her hair, and when she gets out of the bath, Luna applies Mercurochrome to the scratches on her feet. Luna puts her to bed, pulls a cool sheet over her, turning on the fan and pointing it at her.

Her breasts leak milk.

"Es una loca," Luna says when Olga comes home from the hotel that night, but Luna doesn't say it like she usually does. She says it like she's worried Nena is crazy for real. The babies lie on the bed next to Nena, tucked into either side of her, Chuy sleeping, and Valentina gnawing her fist.

Marta remembers who she is. The baby Valentina is her own mother. Marta tries to point her thoughts into this baby's head. What was her mother thinking then? But Marta has no access to the baby's brain, and Marta returns to Nena's exhausted body, her battered mind. The comfort of this real mattress taunts Nena. She'd much rather be lying on the unforgiving planks of the narrow convent beds, holding Rosa.

"Tell us what happened," Olga says to Nena. Luna stands in the corner of the room, smoking a cigarette.

Nena tells her sisters about the convent, about Emiliano, about becoming pregnant and having Rosa. When she's done talking, she closes her eyes, tired beyond tired, the insides of her eyelids gritty with lack of sleep.

She hears Olga and Luna whispering about her. They argue for what seems like hours.

That night, they take her to the El Paso Home for the Insane. She begs them not to leave her, holding their hands, squeezing tight. The orderlies grab her, put a shot in her arm, drag her away. In the hospital, she wishes bad things would happen to her sisters, punishment for their betrayal. If they suffered like she has, then maybe they'd understand, maybe they'd believe her, they'd decide she'd been there long enough, they'd tell her they were sorry and bring her home.

When she's finally allowed out of the hospital, she's been scraped clean. Everything she thought was hers is gone. There's no one she can talk to about El Paso del Norte. If she says anything, she'll have to go back to the hospital. It'd be easier if she could convince herself that she dreamed being in that other time. Or if she could accept that she is crazy like everyone says. But she has stretch marks to prove what happened, her breasts heavy and aching, her history written on her body. She remembers everything.

That's enough, Marta says to La Vista. *I don't want to see any more of this. Let me come back to myself.*

But where is that?

Where's her body?

In her kitchen, passed out on the floor? Marta doesn't want to be stuck in this place where time and energy have collapsed in on themselves. Marta's edges are fuzzy in this in-between place, so fuzzy that they don't really exist. How much time has passed in this place? Hundreds of years? She can't control anything here because there's no her to do it. Maybe there's never been a her, the borders she thought defined her only imagined, a story meant to create and protect the self that doesn't really exist.

Back at the house on Overland Street, after being freed from the home, she takes care of the babies. She hides indoors, not wanting to see anyone from the neighborhood. One day, she hears a knock on the door. She sits afraid, unable to answer, waiting for Luna to come from her room and open the door.

A man in uniform stands on the porch, and Nena's first thought is that Beto has come home from the war. She blinks, and Beto's gone, replaced by a Western Union deliveryman, thin and mustachioed. Luna receives the telegram from the man with a trembling hand.

When Olga's husband comes back from the war, he returns to his job as a mechanic at Montoya Brothers. Olga quits her job, staying at home to tend to the babies, and Olga arranges for Nena to work at the hotel. Everyone smokes in the hotel offices, even in the morning, thick clouds of smoke filling the rooms, ashtrays overflowing with butts. She hates everything about the office, the smell, the way that the secretaries look at her, with pity or something worse, judging her because of her hair, because of her ill-fitting clothes, because she finds it difficult to walk in heels. But she doesn't want to disappoint Luna or Olga, and to keep from being sent back to the home, she knows she must keep her grief as buried as Luna keeps hers. Any reckoning with God and fate and La Vista has to happen in private.

She doesn't even make it through a whole week at the hotel. It's the presence of the spirits there that does it. The bald man in the corner of the ballroom who laughs into his cupped hands. The woman dressed like one of the ladies from the Mansion House. She faces the wall, never turning around, never moving, the back of her skull missing.

Not sure what else to do, Nena goes to see Doña Hilaria, hoping she can receive some sort of advice about how to live her life. But when Nena arrives at the correct address, the tangled mesquite bushes are gone, the house razed, the lot bare, and she understands that there is no help for her anywhere.

She starts going to bars, crossing the bridge into Juárez, to meet men. One time, she catches sight of herself in the mirror behind a bar on Avenida Benito Juárez. She's sturdy, boyish almost, dark-eyed and quick. She's able to drink a lot, and she likes a joke. She's willing to go home with almost anyone—skinny men, fat men, tall men, bookies, cabdrivers, doctors, men who have wives. She doesn't do it for the money, but if someone gives her cash, she doesn't give it back. She would keep the baby if she got pregnant again. She's offered marriage more than once, mostly in jest, one time seriously. She refuses every time.

She hates to sleep because when she sleeps, she dreams. She dreams about a baby she's forgotten to feed. She dreams about a girl with an extra nose. She dreams of a child who whispers curses at her, *Damn you to hell, you witch.*

Not that she needs a dream to tell her she's damned.

The years pass, and there comes a time when Nena starts to think that maybe she's been lost long enough that she can start to find her way back home.

There has always been one thing she's known about herself.

She's not like everyone else. She's like a bird in the air, untroubled by rivers or fences, able to fly to the other side and come back. She'll become a nun in an aquelarre of one, helping people in the only way she knows how. If someone comes to her with questions for the other side, she'll tell them what they may not want to hear. La Vista never lies. Comfort is not its aim. Security and safety have nothing to do with La Vista. La Vista is life itself, and to engage with it is to be awake.

Marta pulls herself back to her being. She understands a bit more how this fiction of La Sirena works. The walls aren't solid, and neither is anything else. She is a bubble in a bubble, floating in nothingness, moving in the sine wave of story, a rotary motion that comes back around to itself. This is how time travel worked for Nena, she jumped from one iteration of the story to the other. For her it was like a kid doing a cartwheel, a task best done without thinking, since thinking makes actions like that impossible.

It's too bad that all Marta does is think. She's never been able to do a cartwheel.

How are they going to get home?

"Am I going to be here forever?" Marta asks Sister Benedicta.

"No. When it is time, we will sing you home. But before you go, I want you to listen to me very carefully," Sister Benedicta says, clamping her hand on Marta's arm. "Pablo was never in danger from me, but you were right to be afraid."

Marta is surprised by her sudden urgency, by how tightly she grips her arm.

"I have seen what La Vista can do to a person. Madre Inocenta lost herself to her greed, to her desire to control things, to live in that power forever," Sister Benedicta says, her eyes searching Marta's. "But La Vista does not bend to our desires. Do you understand what I'm telling you?" Marta's suddenly a schoolgirl again. She can see how Sister Benedicta inspired such fear in Nena. Marta nods yes, so that Sister Benedicta will stop looking at her with such focus, but she doesn't really understand what Sister Benedicta is warning her about. Marta's not Madre Inocenta. Her use of La Vista has been for a greater good, not for her own benefit.

Sister Benedicta turns briskly as Nena and Rosa get up off the pew and walk over to where Marta and Sister Benedicta stand.

Nena has a fierce look, mirrored by Rosa's. "We've decided that I'll go back with you to the convent."

"You know you can't do that," Sister Benedicta says.

"Then we'll stay here."

"Here is nowhere. It will be gone in the next breath. Rosa has her whole life in front of her. You don't exist if she doesn't live to give birth to the rest of the line. The baby won't be born if you stay here. You know that. There are rules that must be followed."

"Why? Why are there rules that only apply to me?" Nena asks.

"You never understood that all I've ever wanted is to protect my girls."

"Not me. You didn't want to protect me."

"I didn't know you were mine until it was too late," Sister Benedicta says.

Rosa is looking down at her hands, young hands. She's a twelve-year-old, upset, overwhelmed. Nena reaches over and tucks a stray piece of hair behind Rosa's ear.

"I'll take good care of your mother," Marta says to Rosa, deciding that Nena is not going to Los Piñones or anywhere else unless there's no other choice.

Sister Benedicta puts her arm around Rosa, and she starts singing the song of the aquelarre. First Rosa and then Nena joins in. Marta sings, too, and when they come to the end, Sister Benedicta and Rosa are gone, Nena and Marta left alone in the darkness. They crawl next to each other, pushing forward through mud.

26

When they come to, the first thing Marta notices is the gap in her mouth.

"What happened to your tooth?" Nena asks.

Marta walks to the mirror in the front hallway. Pulling up her lip, she sees a scabby hole where her right canine should be. She must have lost the tooth on the journey home. Marta pictures the coyote holding the sock in its mouth the night of the fundraiser. The tooth traveled from one time to another, but Marta doesn't care to spend any time thinking more about this mystery. It's not just her tooth that's missing. La Vista is gone, no longer in her or around her.

Back in the kitchen, Nena's spooning the burnt insect stew into a plastic container, snapping the lid in place.

"What are you going to do with that?" Marta asks.

"I'll keep it with my things, so nobody accidentally eats it."

"Is somebody going to intentionally eat it?" Marta asks, though she knows the answer. If eating it would bring back La Vista, Marta would down the whole container.

"This kitchen is very dirty," Nena says, but she sounds cheerful, annoyingly so. Marta thought she'd be more broken up about leaving Rosa for a second time.

"The first time you made the brebaje, didn't you have a song to put things back in place? The song that made you fly? Why can't we do that?" Marta asks.

"You must feel it, the aquelarre is closed now," Nena says, and of course Marta feels it. That's the problem. Nena used Marta, just like she said she would. Nena must have known that once they made their journey to see Rosa, La Vista would be taken from Marta. Sister Benedicta had warned Marta not to think she could control La Vista. The cruel joke is that there's no longer anything for Marta to try to control.

"Alejandro and the boys will be home soon, and we've got to get this place cleaned up," Marta says, her skin prickling with anxiety and anger. She pulls cleaning supplies from the pantry. The cabinets, walls, and floor are covered in insect gunk, and it smells like rotten eggs in the kitchen. The big cutting board is so charred it's completely ruined. Marta picks it up, anger helping her heave the thing close to her body. She carries it out to the garbage bin on the side of the house, where it lands at the bottom with a dull clunk.

"Good morning, dear," Marta hears. Mrs. Price from next door is in her side yard, smoking, one hand encased in a yellow dishwashing glove, the other holding a teacup that she drops ashes in. "You were having a choir practice last night?"

"Excuse me?"

"I heard the singing. What would you call that kind of music?"

"A waste of time."

"Oh my," Mrs. Price says, stubbing out her cigarette. "Somebody woke up on the wrong side of the bed."

Marta doesn't care if Mrs. Price thinks her rude for walking away without responding. When Marta comes back inside, she closes the doors and windows to the outside, turns on the air-conditioning.

"Children who are adopted think that they've been abandoned. They think they're unwanted," Nena says, answering a question Marta hasn't asked. "I had to see Rosa to tell her I loved her. To tell her that I didn't leave her on purpose. And Sister Benedicta was right, I couldn't stay there, I belong here with you. I need to—"

"You did everything you could to get to her," Marta says, not wanting to hear Nena's justifications.

Nena opens her eyes wide, the bitterness of Marta's tone hanging in the air between them. In a strained silence, Marta and Nena scrub the insect tracks from the floors and the fronts of cabinets. All the surfaces in the kitchen are covered in a layer of ooze, and it's satisfying to get down to clean wood, tile, stone, even as the kitchen reeks of ammonia, so heavy in the air that Marta's eyes burn.

"I'm glad of one thing," Nena says, breaking the silence. "Sister Benedicta wasn't out to hurt Pablo. All that worry for nothing."

But it wasn't for nothing. If Marta hadn't been so worried about Pablo, she wouldn't have sent Alejandro and the boys away, she wouldn't have sung the encanto, Nena would never have seen Rosa again, but Marta would still be in La Vista. The midday sun spills in through the windows, the summer heat beating its fist on the glass.

"I don't think Sister Benedicta's the monster you made her out to be," Marta says, wanting to provoke Nena.

"She's not. She spoke the truth when she said I had to come back here. And I know she did what she had to, to keep us all safe. She never wanted me there, and for good reason. When I was a girl, I prayed for something to take me away from the pains of my life, and Madre Inocenta heard me. She sent Sister Benedicta to bring me to El Paso del Norte so I would make the brebaje. Once Madre Inocenta had it, she didn't care what happened to me. I paid the price for her greed and mine. I thought I could mold the power of La Vista to my will. I was a fool then."

"But isn't that how you had Rosa? By using your magic?"

"And I am glad for it." Nena smiles. "But I know now that La Vista was guiding me all along, not the other way around. I'm not saying you should close yourself off to La Vista, Marta. You know as well as I do that it will find you. I'm saying the opposite.

"When I got back from the convent, I grieved the life I had lost, I grieved Emiliano and Rosa, I grieved Carmela, I even grieved Eugenia and Sister Benedicta. I vowed to close myself off from La Vista forever. I tried to shut my mind to it with drink and men. But this was an illusion, too. I had to learn to live in the wilderness of La Vista."

"But aren't you curious how it works? Like how La Vista was passed down through the generations? Why it came to you when it did?" What Marta really wants to ask about is herself. How things turn out the way they do. Why she lives in El Paso, why Alejandro. Why not New York, some other man, some other life? How did she receive this inheritance of La Vista and why, and where has it gone? She longs to know if it will ever come back. For a little while, everything felt possible.

"That's what I want to talk to you about. About how La Vista is passed down. I need to apologize to you, mija," Nena says. "When I told you I'd do anything to see Rosa again, I wasn't lying. I saw at the Cuauhtémoc Market what was happening to you, but I still made you go to the Hueco Tanks, and once we had the song of the aquelarre, I didn't say a word even then. I made you sing the encanto for the brebaje, and I made you eat it."

"You knew La Vista would leave me."

"No, I'm telling you, it hasn't. It's always there, whether you feel it or not. You had a few days where you were in it completely. But everything ends, and everything begins, over and over forever," Nena says.

But Marta isn't interested in platitudes. She wants La Vista back. She's grateful when she hears the whirr of the garage door, the slamming of car doors, the door into the front hallway being flung open.

"We saw a snake," Rafa shouts as he runs in. He slips his backpack off his shoulders, letting it drop to the floor.

"A real rattlesnake, with a rattle," Pablo says, following Rafa into the kitchen. A rubber bat falls out of his pocket.

"It stinks in here. Nena, come look at the things we got from the gift shop at Carlsbad Caverns. We bought you a sweatshirt. It has a drawing of stalagmites on it," Rafa says.

Marta picks up the bat, setting it on the counter. The boys fly out of the kitchen, and Nena follows them at her own pace. The door to the boys' room slams shut. Alejandro comes in, a duffel bag hoisted over his shoulder.

"What the—" Alejandro says, his eyes widening as he drops the duffel on the floor. "What happened to your mouth?"

"I lost a tooth," Marta says.

"Where is it? We should push it back in."

"It's too late for that, and anyway, I don't have it," Marta says.

Alejandro moves across the kitchen quickly. He grasps her face with his hands, firmly, easing open her jaw to peer into her mouth. He walks his hands down her arms, her torso, like he's checking for broken bones. He fishes a penlight out from the junk drawer and looks into Marta's eyes. She likes how Alejandro touches her, with skill and care, the certainty of his training in the quality of his touch. She wishes he could lend her some of that professional certainty. Marta doesn't think she can win the Soto case without the help of La Vista.

"There's nothing wrong with me other than the missing tooth," Marta says.

"I know you better than that," Alejandro says, holding her arms and searching her eyes.

"The best I can calculate, I lost the tooth when we were coming back."

"From where?"

Marta doesn't know how to say she's afraid that with La Vista gone, she and Alejandro will go back to the way they were, too busy, not connected. She wishes that she'd told him about La Vista earlier. Now there's no way for Marta to explain anything to him. She can't sing him any encantos, not even the song of the aquelarre. That's left her, too.

"What I mean is I slipped while getting out of the pool. I landed on my mouth and knocked the tooth out. I didn't think to push the thing back in. I just threw it away."

"Oh," Alejandro says, shaking his head, like he's as dazed as Marta feels, like he's also trying to shake off the hangover of La Vista. "Beth took over my rounds yesterday, but I have to run to the hospital tonight. I'd say you should come with me, but the ER will just tell you to go to a dentist. I'll probably be home late. No need to wait for me for dinner."

At dinner, the boys notice the missing tooth. Marta explains that it fell out, which they accept. They've lost many teeth.

"I think you should probably keep your mouth closed until it grows back," Pablo suggests.

The first thing the next day, Marta swings by her dentist's office right as it's opening. The dentist takes pity on her, fashioning a temporary flipper that attaches with metal clasps to the teeth on either side of it. In the hand mirror the dentist gives her, Marta's smile appears more or less normal.

Walking back to work, Marta's surprised to see Jacqui in front of the office building, sucking on a vape pen. She waves at Marta, exhaling a white plume that smells of toilet cleaner.

"I was hoping to find you here," Jacqui says. "I thought I'd thank you for changing your mind about Benjamin Soto."

"What are you talking about?"

"He's giving a big donation to the hospital. He says it's because of you. Six figures," Jacqui says. "A naming opportunity. Not enough money for a wing of the hospital, but we can make it work for the room where she received chemo. What do you think, the Silvia Soto Suite? Something like that. I'll buy you a drink in San Diego to celebrate."

Marta rides the elevator up to the office, seething as the floors flick by. She knows Soto is trying to get under her skin, the way she got under his. He's throwing his weight around in the way only a man sure of his position can.

"Nena called me and told me what happened," Cristina says, right when Marta gets off the elevator. "Same thing happened to Hugo's tooth. He was such a quejoso about it for so long that he had a choice, he could get it checked out, or I'd go stay with my sister, and good thing, because his molar was cracked, all the way down to the root! They yanked it out right then and there."

"Yes, same, cracked to the root," Marta says distractedly. "Where's Linda?"

Linda comes out of Jerome's office. When she sees Marta, she stops, motioning her in.

"I still haven't received a text of the recordings from Sofia. Did she send anything to you?" Marta asks Linda as she follows her into Jerome's office.

"We did receive one recording," Linda starts, her eyes darting to Jerome and then back to Marta.

"Oh, good," Marta says, but she is unsettled by the air in the room.

Jerome leans forward. "The recording is of you."

"Me?"

"Saying that you'll lift a curse. I don't understand, Marta, that doesn't sound like you. You can't threaten clients like that. Even if you're joking, it sounds bad."

Marta's scalp tingles, her face hot with shame. She's never been more embarrassed in her life.

"You're lucky Sofia didn't go to Soto or his lawyers. You'd be facing an ethics complaint with the bar now. She came to Linda instead, and from what Linda says, boy was she freaked out, even more afraid of you than Soto. Soto gave her money, but he's been threatening her and her family. Sofia's smart. She knows Soto won't stop. She said she'd rejoin the case as long as the silver tongue didn't come back, whatever that means."

The collar of Marta's shirt is tight around her neck. She'd thought she had La Vista's number, her string of victories at work proof that she had aligned herself in the correct way. She'd been drunk from the gifts that La Vista brought. This is what Sister Benedicta was warning her about. She had thought La Vista would keep on being her friend; she did not understand La Vista's uncaring nature, its endlessness. Marta hadn't understood her own capacity for cruelty.

"I wasn't myself when I threatened Sofia. I promise you, it won't ever happen again," she says.

"Good. Because I'm retiring at the end of the year, and you're my pick to take over the firm."

"I didn't think it was possible for you to retire."

"The boss told me I had to," Jerome says. "Patricia wants to move closer to the grandkids. And what can I say? I'm tired, Marta. I've had a good run, but now ay te wacho."

Jerome has been Marta's boss for eighteen years. She's been with him more waking hours than she has with Alejandro. This is everything she's wanted for the past few years, and yet she can't imagine the practice without Jerome, her friend. She thought she'd be happy when this day came.

27

"Nena?" Marta calls from the entryway, moving through the house. Nena doesn't answer. Looking in Nena's room, she finds the bed made, the coverlet stretched tight. Herbs hang from red string tied to the dresser drawer pulls. Piedra blanca and unlit candles perch on top of the dresser, fighting for room with framed snapshots of the family, black-and-white photos, Polaroids, pictures from her phone that Marta printed for Nena.

Marta walks out into the backyard, not sure where else Nena could be. She isn't under the awning, the only place with shade. Nena's Carlsbad Caverns sweatshirt is draped over the gate that leads to the path up into the state park. Marta walks around the pool and then through the gate. Footprints from Nena's shoes head up the path, crisp and new in the powdery dirt. Nena can't have been gone long, and she moves slowly, but still, Marta's concerned. Nena shouldn't be going up into the park by herself.

Marta finds a rubber band in her pocket. She pulls back her hair, walking up the path, kicking up dust as she walks, smelling the sage breathing out its herby breath. From the hill, she can see down over El

Paso, south to Mexico. The little birds of the desert skitter around in the bushes, cheeping and rustling.

"Nena?" Marta calls.

"Over here," Nena says. Marta walks up a steep little path around a giant outcropping of red granite.

She finds Nena sitting on a red rock. She's wearing her running shoes and her little jeans, and she's applied a sparkly pink lipstick, the color a ten-year-old might choose.

"Why did you come up here?" Marta asks, sitting down next to Nena.

"To pray."

"What for?"

"You."

"Why?"

Nena stares down at El Paso and Juárez. Marta follows her gaze. From their position, Marta takes in the rubble where the copper smelting chimneys used to be. Down the valley, there's El Chamisal, the island in the middle of the dry river. Right past that, on the Mexican side, is the massive red sculpture in the shape of an X that you can see from even the flat part of El Paso. Next to the X, a giant Mexican flag flaps in the wind, and it's so big that Marta's heard it takes dozens of people to hoist it up the flagpole. Three states can be seen, Texas, New Mexico, and Chihuahua, but everything in sight is the same color, with the same rocks, the same plants under the same blue sky and fiery sun.

Nena points at the cross at the top of Mount Cristo Rey.

"After Mamá died, we made a pilgrimage up the mountain. The monument had just been built. We'd only barely started, and Luna was already complaining, saying that it felt like her toes had fallen off, and Olga scolded her for wearing high heels."

"Yes," Marta says. She's heard this story many times.

Nena reaches over and takes Marta's right hand.

"Would you like to make the pilgrimage again?" Marta asks, wanting to apologize for being so nasty to Nena when they came back from the other side.

"I can't walk that far."

"We could put you in a wheelbarrow. The boys could each take a handle and push you up."

"Very undignified. And too dangerous now. You've heard about the bandits? They sneak over from the Mexican side. You can't build a fence up that mountain, too steep. The bandits follow you up the path. When they rob you, they steal your shoes so you can't chase them."

"I did something dumb at work because of La Vista, and I got caught. Now I'm thinking it's OK that I don't have La Vista anymore. It's probably for the best."

Nena shakes her head, smiling.

"Oh, but La Vista is just getting started with you. I'm sorry I didn't tell you before that she was coming. I could have given you the chance to decide about eating the brebaje and going to the other side. But I'm not sorry she's on her way. She's why you woke up, and I think she's why we were able to open the door. I hope the brebaje didn't hurt her. I don't think it did. I've wanted both things so much, to see Rosa again, and to meet her."

"Her who?"

"Your daughter. You're pregnant."

Marta laughs. "No, I'm not. I can't be. You know what all it took for me to have the boys. Anyway, I'm too old."

"You're a child."

"I'm forty-five," Marta says.

"That's right," Nena says, and Marta sees her morning sickness for what it is, an announcement, La Vista humming with power and life.

The dark-haired girl she's been imagining isn't Rosa, but her own baby. Marta pictures them now, Nena holding the baby, rocking her, Marta and Nena singing the song of the aquelarre to this girl, the one who comes next.

Acknowledgments

I wrote this book for my relatives who have lived in and around El Paso for many generations. I'm grateful for their guidance, from the living and from those on the other side.

I'd like to thank my editor Michelle Herrera Mulligan for her visionary ideas about publishing and for her care and attention with this book. Thank you to Erica Siudzinski for her brilliant edits, and to Norma Perez-Hernandez and the rest of the remarkable team at Atria and Primero Sueño. Thank you to the extraordinary Kent Wolf at Neon Literary for sharing his many talents.

Thank you to Gloria and Frank Rea, Irene Harkey, Albert Jaramillo, and Greg Hampshire, and the rest of the Jaramillo clan. Thank you to my brother Mateo, and to Virginia, Carolina, August, and Luis Oscar. Thank you to the Brookshires, Marsha Hirano-Nakanishi, and David Kirkpatrick and Pamela Prime.

I couldn't have written this book without help from Josie and Forrest Brostrom, and David and Sandy Rascon in El Paso. Thank you to the generous El Pasoans who shared their stories with me: Susana

Navarro and Arturo Pacheco; David Dorado Romo; Kathleen Staudt at UTEP; Kerry Doyle, director of the Rubin Center for the Arts in El Paso; and Melissa Lopez, director of Diocesan Migrant & Refugee Services. Thank you to Jud Burgess at Brave Books. Thank you to Estefania Sansores, Rocio Andazola Rayas, Antonio Ramos Solis, and Pablo Montalvo Barajas for showing me around Ciudad Juárez and sharing your vast knowledge with me.

Thank you to friends who've supported me along the way, including Sara Lamm and Matt, Juno, and Obi Aselton; Matthew Burgess; Annie Sullivan Cobb; Olly Cobb; Meaghan Looram; Conrad Mulcahy; Natasha Chefer; Joel Tompkins; Matthew Sandager; and Erich Nagler.

Thank you to Mira Jacob, Alexander Chee, Julia Phillips, Brittany Allen, Tennessee Jones, and Crystal Hana Kim. Thank you to Heather Abel and Alison Hart, and to Abigail Thomas, always. Thank you to Jane Ciabattari.

I want to thank my friends and comrades at The New School, including Executive Dean Mary Watson, John Reed, Robert Polito, Honor Moore, and Helen Schulman, along with all the other smart and creative people I've had the honor to work with over the years. Gracias a Valentina Sarmiento Cruz. A huge thank-you to Leah Iannone, Laura Cronk, and Lori Lynn Turner. And thank you to my students who have taught me so much.

When I'm not writing or teaching, I'm on the water. Thank you to Hudson River Community Sailing for changing my life.

Thank you to Isa Catto and Daniel Shaw for being such warm hosts in Woody Creek. Thank you Adrienne Brodeur, Caroline Tory, and Marie Chan at Aspen Words and the Aspen Institute. Thank you to the Sewanee Writers' Conference, especially Tony Earley and Alice McDermott, and the many incredible writers I met there. Thank you to Asari

Beale and the Teachers & Writers Collaborative community, and Eric Banks and the New York Institute for the Humanities. Thank you to Neta Katz for all kinds of alignment.

Thank you to my parents, Ann and Luis Jaramillo, for their support and love. And to Matthew, for everything.

About the Author

Luis Jaramillo is also the author of the award-winning short story collection *The Doctor's Wife*. His writing has appeared in *Literary Hub*, *BOMB Magazine*, the *Los Angeles Review of Books*, and other publications. He is an assistant professor of creative writing at The New School. He received an undergraduate degree from Stanford University and an MFA in creative writing from The New School.